1909

1909

1909

Martin Godleman

ZITEBOOKS
LONDON

Published by ZiteBooks 2015
www.zitebooks.com

ISBN 978-1-910697-19-1

A CIP catalogue record for this book is available from the British Library.

Typeset by flamin ape
Printed and bound in Great Britain by CPI Group (UK) Ltd, Croydon, CR0 4YY.

ZiteBooks has a band of writers from around the world to challenge
the imagination of readers.
We publish in ebook and hard copy format on Amazon.

To find out more visit: www.zitebooks.com

Acknowledgements

Thanks to Jon Thurley for faith, and Philippa Pearce for approval.
Thanks to Rosa for all the secondary typing.

For NS.

Contents

January

Groups of young men crowded excitedly round the streets, waiting. Several police officers were stationed around the house, guns trained at every possible exit. There was talk of a hostage, but there had been no activity since lunch-time and it had been dark for nearly three hours. A distant tram clattered across the High Street, its upper feeler shooting sparks across the raised pylon.

A face appeared at one of the upper windows, accompanied by a shout from the street. A policewoman moved the front row of the crowd back a few feet towards the other side of the road. A voice suddenly cut into the stillness of the winter evening.

"Fifteen minutes," it said. Another flutter of movement at the window and the spindly end of a gun came into view. Several shouts came from the back of the crowd and two shots were fired. In a synchronised movement, the officers around the house ran at the door, kicking it in. The growing crowd surged forward, but the police had moved quickly, and after a minute or so, two loudspeaker messages came from the police unit stationed by the front garden.

"Go home," one of them said. "It is an offence to obstruct the police in the execution of their duty..."

"...after Curfew," the other was saying. "Will you please return to your homes." Three officers emerged from the darkness of the inside, the third dragging a man behind him, who was clutching at his stomach. By the time the other two men were brought out, the crowd had dispersed.

This was as much as Morda could make out, as he stood by the police van. Several faceless officers stood in the garden and around the house.

"We ought to get home," Provlyn said. "It's quarter to ten and the last train back leaves Whitechapel at quarter past."

"Don't you want to find out what happened?"

"Not particularly."

They crossed the road, passing a police van with darkened

windows. Two policewomen were examining someone inside. Morda moved towards the opened rear doors.

"You're in the wrong place young man," one of them said. "You ought to be home." Morda moved towards the stretcher.

"He's still alive," the other said, reassuringly. "He'll be alright."

"Well enough to stand trial for this."

"He might as well have died," Morda said. He looked at the man's face. It shaped an expression of dull pain, a blow to the temple evident in a bruising around the side of the head. But the face. Morda knew it well, though he had not seen it for five years; it was Harvil. Not that he should have been surprised. One of the reasons they had parted had been Harvil's obsession with the *Republican* activists. They had been ready to sire, they had lived together for almost four and a half years. They had been teenage lovers, but had been changed by the war. Harvil had met many new friends and had found a new purpose in his life, as he had often said. And now...

"Morda?"

He crossed the road. He had met Provlyn a few months later at a Peacetime Ball. Provlyn's interest in politics was confined to being in service at the home of Serboth Challis, MP for Putney and Wimbledon, and current Home Secretary for the government.

"How was he?"

"Beaten up; shot, probably."

"He's an *activist*, Morda. Probably didn't go to war; busy organising the killing of innocent people. It's difficult to feel any sympathy for them."

They crossed the road to the station, passing underneath a huge poster declaring *'A paid Toll Tax return gives you your free democratic rights.'* Underneath this a sign flashed *Curfew*. Local curfew hours had just returned to ten o'clock, but it was generally accepted that you were safe until eleven, providing you had a good reason for being out.

Morda enjoyed the public houses in Whitechapel from the days when he had lived in Musbury Street with Harvil, but Provlyn did not mind the journey across London. He was still only twenty. He loved to hear Morda's stories about wartime and would tolerate any distance to please him and settle his mood.

They reached the station and boarded one of the waiting red trains, joining one of the preferred central carriages, with their low lighting and dark tables. They sat together, arm in arm.

"What do you really think of the activists?" Morda finally asked as the train pulled away.

"I've heard Challis say that they should all be strung up."

"Forty-three already have been, since the riots last July."

"Why does it matter what I think?"

Morda looked at him and smiled. When you committed yourself to such ideals, you could lose everything. Your sense of humour, your friends, your job. Underneath it all, it seemed that most working people outside of the Populite found the government contemptible. It was something at the centre of what it was to be part of the Populace. But contempt had become a reserved emotion, if it were an emotion at all. Since the war, people had lost their political acumen. We had won after all, we had beaten off the militant faction in the country. Now we were free, and someone had to run the country, didn't they? And nobody likes the boss, everybody knew that.

"I care about you," Morda said. "I worry about you. You're still very young."

"I have you," he said. "And I have a job."

Morda remembered the darkness of Harvil's back, and the hot summer when they had first met. He had been the young one then. Harvil spoke so well, had such far-reaching ideas; he was someone who knew what he wanted to do, he had plans, he would be a *successful man*. And tonight he was a bloody darkness on a stretcher, and Morda had left him there. He hadn't even tried to wake him - tell him that he had been. He had just walked away. And the other two Nark activists were both dead, probably close friends.

"This country fucks me off," he said, suddenly. An elderly man on the other side of the carriage looked up.

"Let's make love when we get back," Provlyn said. "I love you."

The elderly man looked away.

Morda awoke at half past eleven the following morning. It was a grey and cloudy day with a hint of rain in the air. He read Provlyn's note on the bed beside him.

> *I have to-morrow afternoon off. I meant to tell you. We could go somewhere. Hampstead?*
> *P. x*

He screwed the note up and threw it towards the bin. A few letters including a second red Toll Tax return lay on the mat downstairs. He raised himself up slowly and began his exercises, pushing himself up on stilt forearms. ...nineteen, twenty.

They had lived in the mews house in Hammersmith for nearly five years; Provlyn's father had been killed in the war. His only relative was an ageing grandfather somewhere in the North of England. Morda was comfortable enough here, but then again... he raised alternate legs in the air to meet the pointed joining of his arms. ...fourteen, fifteen. He could have been living with Harvil, and he might have been in that house.

He boiled a kettle for his wash and began to dress. He was due at the workhouse centre in the city at one o'clock; still looking for a job since his sixth month posting at the brewery had finished. There were 500,000 people living in London and yet he was unable to get the permanent job he wanted. With more and more people required to go into service for the Populite, it wasn't as if opportunities were scant, but there was a stigma attached to service from pre-war days when it had been illegal, and although Provlyn seemed quite comfortable in that Wimbledon house on Parkside, he felt differently. Harvil would have rather died; perhaps he still would.

"I understand you have been drawing a war relief pension for the last five years, but that in this period you have been employed only on a short term basis and that you have refused two jobs offered you in the last week." The grey-haired man behind the counter smiled. Morda looked skyward.

"There are three jobs I can offer you this week. One is an eight month clerk's apprenticeship with *Palby's* in Holborn; that's one pound and fifteen shillings a week, with a half day on Saturday. If you're successful there, they may give you a full time contract, subject to the government's new Employment Act, which comes into force next year. Then there are two positions on Lady Kennerworth's Estate; a butler and a footman. Both will pay two pounds a week. Before you answer, I must warn you that you only have two more refusals before fifty per cent of your relief entitlement becomes dockable monthly." He read the phrase from a printed blue card behind the window. Morda nodded. They were the only two people in the workhouse centre. Outside a tram moved noisily past.

"I nearly died in Manchester," Morda said. "And you'd still take away fifty per cent of my relief pension?"

"Not me sir. It's the government."

"Yes," Morda said, taking the job offer form. "Sure."

He left the building and crossed the road. Wasn't he just another part of this mass complacency? Laws were being introduced, it seemed, every week to stabilise the economy. The cause was always stability, but stability through change sounded like flawed logic. And *new* ideas? *New* was, perhaps, an effective euphemism for *ideas that people will have by now forgotten.*

It was raining. He ran across the street and jumped on the back of a tram that was picking up speed. He looked at the conductor enquiringly.

"Whitechapel, mate," he said.

Morda went upstairs and sat down. It was an open top, but he felt in a sudden frivolous mood. It was strangely pleasant to view the City of London from a tram rooftop, even if he was under an umbrella. Several important-looking women in dark suits congregated at a street corner, one waving her hands in exasperation at something. They are talking about money, Morda thought. His mind was a long way from the subject. He was thinking about Harvil again. Harvil, who would almost certainly be dead in a month or two, if not from his injuries, then surely from his offence, however it would be framed. *Treason.* Now *that's* a capital offence, my good man. And you are guilty. *It's the law. Sorry.*

Whitechapel Police Station, the words were carved out in the light concrete stone that comprised part of the red brick roof of the building. It set an idea running in Morda's head. He ought to stay on until the terminus and go home, but then *ought* was a word that had been giving him a lot of problems lately. He shot down the stairs quickly enough to leave the tram without losing his balance, and he crossed to the station entrance.

He was surprised, on entering, to find that the building was a mass of shiny silver machines and polished surfaces. He hadn't expected such a sophisticated enterprise... weren't those flashing lights behind the counter some kind of *computer?* Before he was able to continue his visual tour, a young police officer came out from behind one of the machines, eyeing him suspiciously.

"I suppose you have a good reason for being here?" she said.

"I believe you have a man named Harvil in the building," Morda replied. She continued to study him with apparent contempt, but eventually moved to her left to consult a tiny grey screen.

"So what if we have?"

"I'd like to see him."

"He's a Classified Twenty. Nobody sees him unless the Superintendent gives her permission. Which is unlikely," she added. "Just who are you, anyway?"

"Morda," said Morda. "I was a friend of his. I mean I *am* a friend of his." But it was no use. The look she was giving him suggested that his demands were untenable.

"You'd better fill in one of these," she said. She handed him a large light blue strip of paper which had gaps and sections ripe for personal information. He caught sight of several emotively titled sections: *Previous Convictions, Who is your partner?, Have you sired in the last ten years?, Is your father still alive?...*

"What is this for?" he asked.

"You've asked questions about a Classified Twenty. That makes you an interested party. Fill the form in please. There's no charge." Her voice delivered the words without irony. The first time he had entered a police station in his life, and he was having to fill in an

FD407C *(Revised: December).*

He completed the form, having given it some thought, substituting the details of Mordga Palapsis, a young man from Stepney he had served with in the war, wondering how the information was, if at all, to be used. The policewoman smiled at him; it was a rehearsed smile gathered, no doubt, at some Populite police training college. It made him feel helpless.

"In any case," she said, as he was leaving, "he's not here. He's at a nearby hospital. He is still quite ill." Morda made a note of her badge number, C 4501.

Once outside, he felt sobered. Harvil had been hospitalised some years before, after an activists' rally at the American Embassy, and Morda recalled that the security ward was above the Queen Edwina Ward at Guy's Hospital. He had never been inside the hospital, but he knew where he could find it, and what he might do when he got there. The resignation of everyone so far that day that he should have little or no control over his destiny was hardening his spirit and resolve.

"It's a little worrying, Home Secretary, I must agree. In separate factions, these fanatics are quite harmless, but recent incidents have led me to believe that some of these groups might be working together."

Provlyn worked some *Brasso* around the neck of a darkened candelabra on the far side of the drawing-room. He caught the day's visitor, Lady Arkandale, waving a discretionary finger in his direction as she finished speaking.

"Provlyn's alright, aren't you, Provlyn?" Challis said. He, in return, smiled pleasantly and continued polishing.

"The Prime Minister has called a cabinet meeting for next Thursday, so I'll raise it there, if it's not on the agenda already."

"Thank you," said Lady Arkandale. "Better to be safe than sorry." Both the women were dressed in dark suits, brown and black. It had become quite regular for informal meetings with other Party MPs at the house in the last few months. Provlyn found it rather amusing that he should be privy to such information at its most direct source, but he never passed any of it on. He was the soul of discretion, fully aware of his obligations in service; even Morda would not hear what he had picked up during the day. He was trustworthy and reliable; *a good servant*, as the saying went.

Morda occupied himself with intermittent visits to the coffee shops surrounding London Bridge station for the afternoon, biding his time until visiting hours commenced. The hospital was a fairly typical Georginian building, a bold architectural front of wide columns ill-preparing visitors for the grey corridors and overpowering smell of carbolic. He bought a bunch of carnations from the flower-seller boy at the entrance, surprised at his own tact, as he moved swiftly up the stone steps behind the small crowd, keeping to the back. The brown notice at the head of the stairs made it clear that the Queen Edwina Ward was on the seventh floor, alongside the word *eighth* the painted instruction, *Staff Only*.

By the time he reached the seventh floor, the crowd in front of him had thinned out to four or five people. He moved confidently into the Queen Edwina Ward, smiling at the suffering old men he passed, eyes racing for visual inspiration. He saw a small utility room at the far end of the room, but before he could get any further, he was stopped by a staff nurse.

"Can I help you, sir?"

"Yes," he replied, "I was looking for my... oh, there he is!" He side-stepped the nurse and moved to a seat beside the only unattended bed, inhabited by a man who looked as though he had journeyed there from the beginning of time.

"Hello Dad!" he said, with enthusiasm. The man in the bed beside him grinned, showing a wide rim of toothless gums. The young nurse smiled and moved off. Morda leaned across to the man.

"I bought you these," he said, putting the carnations in a plastic bowl he'd found under the bed. "I hope you get better soon."

"Prettiest thing I've seen all week," the old man began, but Morda shook his head.

"Not tonight, Joseph. You're not my type." He took hold of a small jar of capsules on the cupboard beside the bed. "The doctor says you need six of these," he said, pouring out a glass of water. "Sooner you get this lot swallowed, the sooner you'll get some well-earned sleep." He lifted the old man's head from his pillow and angled it towards him to block anyone else's view, and administered the handful of pills.

"Are you coming back to-morrow?" the man asked. Morda nodded.

A few minutes from now and he would have to take his chance. The easiest guard to pass would be after midnight, and he now had only one flight of steps to overcome. He moved swiftly from the bed of the sleeping man and into the utility room, blissfully dark, full of wicker trolleys which presented a wealth of choices of hiding-place. He finally settled down in between blankets on a blanket trolley, ready to move at the first opportunity after midnight.

After three unanswered taps, Provlyn reached in his pocket for the key. He stood in the darkness in the hall, wondering. He lit a lamp in the lounge and sat by the window. He had felt uneasy since they'd stopped by the ambulance the previous evening. Morda had recognised the injured man; there must have been a reason for his silence. His note from the morning lay crumpled at the foot of the stairs. In spite of the expressionless face seen in the mirror, he felt the tears. He moved towards the telephone. He had read in a national newspaper about keeping the police informed of suspicious happenings so they could be one step ahead of the criminal. But now the war was over, crime was virtually non-existent; all the criminals had been put to death for treason.

Perhaps Morda had found a job. But there was no note. The greatest fear was that he would leave. He had been talking in riddles lately. He had left many questions unanswered. He hadn't talked about siring for weeks despite the fact that they were eligible in March. Provlyn knew he would have to live permanently at Parkside if anything happened. Serboth Challis would look after him, and if this Reform Bill they often talked about were to be introduced, he would be in the right working environment to make the most of it. But he would lose the house; transfer of property was a complicated legal matter. He would have to give up the house.

He took down the letters from the letter rack and opened them. More forms to fill in. More laws changing.

Morda heard the hospital clock chime twelve, and moved the laundry basket out in front of him. The only light in the ward came from the threads of moonlight, but Morda's eyes were trained by now, and he had a good view of the obstructions in his path. The only sounds he could hear were of gentle snoring from some of the old men on the ward. These were the first of a new generation of old people who would be pensionless from the end of the month, thanks to the new changes in the law. A strange irony that the majority of those in favour of the abolition were of virtual pensionable age themselves. He crept out, relieved to see that the late shift ward nurse hadn't yet arrived.

The difficulty would be to pass whatever guard they had operating on the security ward. He felt his chest tighten as he held the steel banister. The chugging of the boiler room from below gave the dark stairs beyond an unwelcoming quality, but he moved on. Harvil was just thirty-four; an appalling waste of life if he were to die...

Two voices cut into the darkness from the next floor; Morda skidded back behind the lift shaft, cursing at the scraping noise his shoes made on the cold stone floor. After a moment, the voices stopped and a figure moved past him down the stairs in the darkness, wielding some kind of torch in front of him. He waited for the sounds to die and began climbing the stairs again, three at a time. He reached the top landing and saw the night light on in the security office fifteen yards in front of him. A silhouette sat in front of it, reading a book. Harvil would be there, beyond the office; he would soon know why the activists had been shot at.

The office door was slightly ajar. He was a few feet from the ward when he took stock of the situation. He needed something with which to render the guard helpless. It had to be temporary; he had no intention of killing anyone.

Listen.

He watched the shadow of the guard's tremulous lips, miming out the words on the printed page. Beside the door was a window-pole. Too clumsy. He knelt slowly and soundlessly forward to take one of the short sections of tubing that sat in a box to the right. Whatever they were for, they were of a substantial weight.

He had learned to move swiftly during his time in the North with the army, and, even five years on, he was able to act without compunction when the situation demanded it. He moved round to behind the other side of the door and tapped gently on it, twice. In the split second before the guard raised himself to see what was going on, he saw the figure in the ward sit up, and he lunged round the office door to deliver an unexpectedly severe blow to the back of the guard's neck. He toppled out of Morda's reach and fell to the ground, striking the front of his head against the side of the table. The whole incident was over in less than five seconds, but the silence that followed was like a wild screaming.

Morda moved forwards into the ward, taking the gas lamp off the table with him. He sat at the side of the bed and brought the lamp round.

"Harvil!"

He hugged the wounded man round his chest, surprised by the rush of desperate emotion he suddenly felt. Harvil's hand eventually drew itself up to the back of his friend's neck.

"You're dead if they find you here, Morda."

"Who's the *they?*"

"The police, the hospital guards... whoever."

"Why did they shoot you? What had you done?" Harvil leaned across and looked out of the window. City buildings reflected in the moonlight across the river, the dome of St.Pauls rising into the dark sky. All they could hear was the chugging of the boiler in the basement.

"They must have found the house a few weeks ago. Maybe

someone told them, I don't know. But we had all sorts of stuff in there: explosives, ammunition, stuff like that. I wouldn't be sitting here if Raptel had wired everything up; we were going to disappear and take most of Whitechapel with us, but they stormed the place before I could finish the job." His voice was like a low barking.

"I can't understand why you all want to destroy yourselves like this. They're both dead. They may kill you too..."

"They will. They told me yesterday. They're organising the trial for March; moving me to some High Security place to-morrow. Quite flattering really..." They both turned to the direction of the office, from where the groaning sound came.

"What did you do to him?"

"I don't know. I don't think he's badly hurt. Look, I want to help you... I want to help *us*. Whoever *us* is."

He stood up. The creature from the front of the ward was crawling slowly towards them, pulling on the leg of a hospital bed a few yards away to move himself forwards.

"I've taken an oath, I can only say that," Harvil said quickly, watching the guard's lumbering movements. "A few people know. You will too. They know I knew you. They'll find you, don't worry."

"I can't leave you here."

"I've lost blood, I'm weak. You'll be lucky to get home on your own as it is." He took Morda's hand. "I've done what I can; if you want to help, get out, get away from here!"

They had spent five years of their lives together, through the war, four of them living in the flat at Whitechapel. It had been knocked down since. Morda had often thought of Harvil in the last few years. Wondered if he might meet him in the city or pass him sitting at a table in a café. A meeting that would now never happen.

Morda had picked up the short section of pole and was holding it tentatively above his shoulder. He moved backwards towards Harvil. There was a strange moment shared by them all; the two wounded men and him, almost silent. Then, in a desperate lurch, Morda threw himself from the bedside, over the stumbling guard and out of the ward. As he hurried down the staircase, taking two steps at a time, he tried to lose the recurring picture he had of the crawling man. Sticky blood was on the cuff of his jacket and the short piece of tubing was still in his hand, like a baton out of an unfinished relay race. He hadn't been seen by the guard, though; he was fairly sure of that.

As he took the last flight of steps, he slowed his speed to a leisurely stroll. The corridor on the ground floor was well lit, but there was nobody around. He doubled back the way he had come, remembering a small window at the side, just a few hundred yards from the entrance. The eradication of crime in the years since the war had many advantages, not least that of the removal of intruder identification devices from public buildings. He eased open the single pane and dropped soundlessly onto the ground outside.

It was Curfew, so no-one was around except a few police and government workers. He stopped halfway across London Bridge. The Houses of Parliament were lit up as was Big Ben, cast in a glowing gold. Parliament in session? At one-thirty in the morning? The moment he had crossed the bridge, he darted into the back streets, his heart pounding like a sewing-machine. There were no tubes or trams, but he would have to get back across London to Hammersmith in case they sent police to the house - Provlyn would know nothing of it, but no-one was likely to believe his innocence. He drew back into an alley as a battery-powered police wagon approached. It was one of the new models created in the wake of the government's energy conserving policy; a scarlet carriage with *Metropolitan Police* hand-painted in gold across the upper tier. He moved out again, into the night.

The journey back involved keeping away from main police areas and government buildings, most of which Morda knew from his involvement in the war, and when he was unsure, areas with the most dense stretches of street lighting were more than likely to be places to avoid. He had a scare when he cut through Kensington Gardens and was stopped by a Parks Security Officer, but miraculously he was allowed to go after he had explained that he'd fallen asleep in the park after having several drinks at a nearby pub.

Hammersmith, like most London suburbs, had several listed

office blocks which had become derelict. The problem was, he had read, how to demolish them without damage to the surrounding houses and shops. Their house in Grove Mews was on a list of at risk property he had seen with Provlyn at a recent exhibition in the Town Hall. The National Clearance Act had given all local government housing departments the obligation and authority to demolish all buildings above four storeys in each borough. The Act had not gone on to explain how this was to be done or whether compensation would be offered to those losing homes in the process; the authority to remove seemed to be all that was really necessary. Morda suspected that Town Hall Exhibitions of demolition plans were something of a sham; a way of suggesting that the word *consultation* might have some genuine meaning for those with supposed access to it.

Doubling through the back streets behind Hammersmith Grove, Morda was able to reach Grove Mews without any further problems. It had been Harvil, who, with the aid of monies of unknown source, had bought him the house when they had parted.

"You want to get out of London," he had said. "Whitechapel's becoming so *busy*, lately."

The house had belonged to a friend of Harvil's, an old man who had lived there most of his life, having died three months previously of tuberculosis. With only rates to pay, Morda had found it quite easy to get by, even though he was sometimes limited to the fifteen shillings a week provided by the war relief pension. Now, however, he might have to surrender half of that, as well as pay the new Toll Tax, which promised to be double the yearly rates sum.

He slipped the key gently into the lock and went in. Provlyn was asleep in the armchair by the fire, an unused cigarette in his hand. The lamp flickered weakly, throwing a gentle light over him, making him look peculiarly handsome as he slept. Morda remembered how Harvil had often returned late from one of his meetings, and finding him asleep had carried him to bed, like a father might carry his son. He drew a stool up to the chair and took Provlyn's hand.

"You should be in bed."

Provlyn looked up.

"I was dreaming," he said. "You were in a building that was on fire. It might even have been this house. I was watching you from across the road. You didn't try to leave, though. You were just watching me, as if you wanted to see what I would do."

"What did you do?"

"I woke up."

Morda looked into the fire. He was thinking about Harvil.

"Did you get a job?"

"No job. That is, I decided not to take what they offered me. I believe I'm running out of refusals, now." His eyes grew small. "Have you been crying?"

Provlyn got up and walked out into the kitchen.

"Do you want a tea?" he said.

Morda watched the fire until he returned. "I went to see the man they shot."

"Which one? They shot three, didn't they?"

"I went to see the one who is still alive. He was in a security ward; I had to use some force to see him. They wouldn't have let me otherwise." Morda sipped thoughtfully at his tea. He sighed deeply. "He was a good friend of mine. But there's no point in crying. He's as good as dead. And you were right. He is an activist, even if you might not know what that means. I know I don't."

Morda felt uncomfortable and moved across to the front window, watching the still scene outside through the curtains. He wondered why he had never spoken of Harvil before. It made his words sound like a betrayal when, in fact, they were just a few paragraphs out of his past, necessarily screened.

"Lady Arkandale was at Parkside today. The conversation was mainly about fanatics." Provlyn stood up and turned towards the bedroom. Morda pulled him back and drew him face to face, breathing tightly, eyes harsh.

"Provlyn, this was someone I *loved;* this was someone I lived with for five years of my life! You don't think I was a virgin until I met you, do you?" He shook him, but gradually his arms tightened round him and they kissed. Provlyn's cheeks were wet.

"I left him *because* of what he was becoming involved with. He was spending more and more time out at night, breaking War Curfew when we were working in London. I knew they'd get him one day. And if they got him, they'd get me. They don't take any chances. I'm sure you've heard them say that at Parkside. So I left him. I hadn't seen him for five years until yesterday."

Provlyn looked up at him in desperation. "Why didn't you tell me any of this before?"

"I didn't tell you at the beginning because I was trying to make sure I severed all links with that part of my life. A few activists knew me from when I lived with Harvil in Whitechapel, but fuck the Queen, man, there wasn't any way I could tell you once you'd got that job at Parkside! They might have been watching me, they may have become suspicious. And you couldn't tell them what you didn't know."

"But I know now."

"Yes," said Morda. They went upstairs. The clock at the top of the stairs chimed five. Provlyn lay on Morda's bed, his head on his chest.

"You lived together for five years. Did you ever think of siring?"

"We had talked about it, but it could never have happened. We only had a flat, and although I loved him, I wasn't sure that we would stay together."

The response seemed to satisfy Provlyn, who eventually fell asleep holding him, his night shirt unfastened around his shoulders.

February

Provlyn pulled the carriage doors shut behind him and adjusted his cap. He was supposed to arrive at the Parkside home each morning before eight o'clock and it was now twenty minutes past seven. He moved self-consciously to a set of vacant seats in the corner, secreting himself behind a copy of *The Times*. The atmosphere was smoky and stuffy and people seemed more bad-tempered than usual. It may well have been the fact that it was the second full week of the implementation of the Democratic Transport Act, one of the results of which was to provide two carriages for women only (other than during peak hours), but if these were full, the other carriages would still be available to them. As very few women travelled on public transport in any case, it seemed something of a speculative gesture; at this moment there was one woman sitting alone at the end of their carriage. Provlyn wondered if she was overspill or a conscientious objector.

The newspaper was running another story on the government's proposed First Reform Bill, and showing how it would make the nation, *once again,* the most powerful country in the world. It all sounded quite grand, but since the World Service had been discontinued four years ago, there was very little day-to-day contact for the average English person with any other countries in the world other than Wales and Scotland. Morda had been to France once, as a child, but his memories were blurred and distant. Provlyn's grandfather, however, who lived in York, remembered a war fought against them, and had interested him with several tales of the intrigues of battle before the death of his father and his move to London.

Inside the paper in the local section he was drawn to the headline *Attempt To Free Activist Leader Foiled By Guard.*

'*Up to three Republican Activists may have been responsible for the attempt to free the only surviving member of the Sidney Street Siege in the early hours of this morning from a London Hospital, which resulted in the death of a security guard. Police have confirmed that they have launched a full scale murder investigation. The incident has renewed calls up and down the country for the banning of all activist and unionist activities.'*

Provlyn looked at the photograph of the security guard. Just how easily would they be able to link it to Morda? They had drank together in Whitechapel on several occasions, but if what he'd said about Harvil was the truth, the only chance of information being fed back to the police was through Harvil himself, or other activists.

They were pulling into Earls Court station. He had less than half an hour to get to Wimbledon; he knew Morda would still be at home. They had arranged to meet that afternoon at Parliament Hill Fields for a picnic. His mind raced. Perhaps he would have a moment to phone from the call box at Wimbledon Station. He crossed the bridge to where his train was already waiting. He sat in one of the front tabled carriages; he would have no time to phone. As it was, he would be desperately lucky to get to work on time even if he ran all the way from the station. He pushed the newspaper under the table, ready to forget the whole episode.

Morda looked at the clock. *Ten to eight.* Who would call at this hour? Provlyn forgotten his cigarette papers? He put on his dressing-gown and came down the stairs. Outside, an official of the Royal Mail, his van parked a short distance ahead, waited for him with a chit to sign. Morda had the unnerving feeling that he had seen him somewhere before.

"If you'd just sign this, young man. It's a Recorded Delivery. Looks rather important, I'd say."

"Yes," said Morda, scribbling an illegible signature on the form underneath his printed address. He dropped a florin into the man's hand. It was something Harvil had taught him; *always tip tradesmen to keep them from talking about you.*

"Thank you, sir."

He watched him drive off to the top of the road. He looked up the street. There was no-one around. He went back inside. He had feigned sleep an hour or so earlier, when Provlyn had left. He had not slept at all well. It had been a mistake to look for Harvil. He hadn't been able to do anything for him.

He poured himself a glass of soya milk from the larder.

'THIS IS A REMINDER : *You are required to attend a war relief medical at Barclay House at Bloomsbury this morning at eleven o'clock. Please be prompt. Any contingency arrangements with your employer will have been attended to.*'

A reminder? He went into the front room for his diary. *February 1st. Birthday of Queen Edwina VII.* No appointment. What had Harvil said? '*They know I knew you. They'll find you, don't worry.*'

He put the kettle on for his wash. Perhaps this was because he hadn't come back to them about yesterday's job. But it was just a job. Even in the eyes of the law he had one refusal left. He looked at the date stamp at the top of the letter: *20th January 1909.* He might have forgotten to write it in his diary. It was possible. But such lapses of memory were highly unlikely.

The phone began ringing. He jumped.

"Hello?"

"Am I speaking to the occupier of 43 Grove Mews, Hammersmith? Are you Morda...?"

"Yes... speaking." The clipped voice was that of a young woman.

"It's about your war relief medical. I'm glad I caught you, only there's been a change of venue, I'm afraid. Could you make your way to Guy's Hospital, please. Report to Reception in the West Wing by ten to eleven. You'll be given instructions from there on." There was a weighty pause. "Do you know Guy's Hospital?"

"Yes, ...thank you."

"Nearest tube London Bridge."

"I'll be there. Goodbye."

He walked to the window. The road was clear.

"You're in a bit of a state."

"I've run all the way up the hill. Am I late?"

"No. Just as well, too. It's her at-home today; half the bloody cabinet round I'll bet. They get more things sorted out here than they do in the House of Commons!"

Chatwick took Provlyn round to the cloakroom. He had been in service since the war, even in the days when it was illegal. For his services to Serboth Challis, he had been made Head Footman. Provlyn had often speculated that he was probably earning £5 a week! It would be a particularly good salary as he had his own quarters there. Like Morda, he was unsired; he had no immediate family to worry about. He had often spoken about his *friend* when they had discussed what they did at weekends, but he was discreet about his private life. Provlyn had been reticent enough about his for it to be generally concluded amongst those in service there that it was non-existent.

"You had better make up some sandwiches for the guests, with a pot of tea for when they arrive at nine. They'll be taking it in the lounge."

Provlyn changed into his work suit and busied himself around the kitchen. In addition to the day's duties, there would be coals to take to the sitting-room and lamps to trim. This week he was to keep the clerks' rooms tidy. There were three clerks who worked at the house, organising its financial upkeep and the regulating of Serboth Challis' political affairs, her social calendar and, though it was never mentioned, her personal security.

On the stroke of nine, Provlyn wheeled in the morning tray and set out the plates for the guests. There were seven women, all wearing dark suits with long dresses, all with serious expressions. One of them moved towards the tray to collect a plate of sandwiches before he had finished setting them out. He moved back to give her room and she smiled at him. It was a laboured expression giving the opposite effect expected from a smile. He felt his heart lurch when he realised this was Lady Herben Asquith, the Prime Minister. He moved swiftly round the rest of the group, serving tea and laying out sweetcakes. When he finally eased himself out of the room he stopped in the hall, watching his reflection. He looked pallid and could feel how moist his neck had become under his collar.

"Are you alright, Provlyn?" Chatwick asked, coming up from the basement with some clean towels.

"Yes," he said. "Just feel a little giddy, that's all. You didn't tell me the Prime Minister was here."

Chatwick smiled and raised a finger to his lips. Provlyn passed him and went downstairs. Just two more hours and he could escape; he felt stifled. After he had cleared the clerk's room of cigarette ends and wine-stained glasses, he took the newspapers downstairs for ironing. They would, no doubt, be handed round the lounge for critical comment.

Activist Death Plot Backfires.

'An attempt by activists to silence one of their own leaders who was being held for questioning by the police, backfired in the early hours of this morning when a security guard was killed. Police believe that the assailants were members of the extreme unionist group CYNID, responsible for the anti-populate attacks in east London at the end of last year.'

"You're paid to iron the paper, not read it!" a voice called out behind him. It was Dorjess, the senior of the three clerks, a balding red-faced man of about fifty. He often came downstairs in the hope of finding unclaimed bottles of wine, or to pilfer food returned from the upstairs lounge.

"Yes, sir," Provlyn said.

"You are very young," he continued, moving beyond the iron so they came face to face. "And attractive. But you could learn your place a little more successfully, don't you think?"

Provlyn had managed to reverse the pile of newspapers so all that was visible was the Sports News. He continued to iron them.

"We'll make a man of you yet, Provlyn," Dorjess said, moving his hand round and stroking his behind. The sour smell of his breath made Provlyn feel bilious. He smiled weakly. Dorjess took a half bottle of wine vinegar from the open larder and moved off.

"But that's..."

"No-one will miss it if you keep your mouth shut."

"Yes, sir."

He picked up the papers hurriedly and moved into the back half of the lounge, the room dividers having been pulled across since he had last been there. The conversation continued as he entered the room after a short pause.

"Is there a movement?"

"Well, somebody killed him, whatever they were there for. The activist wasn't strong enough to get out of bed, let alone beat a security guard to death."

"It is just a few people working in small groups," an unrecognised voice said. It was almost certainly Lady Asquith. Provlyn looked desperately for the newspaper rack; the longer he was in the back room, the more suspicious it would seem.

"I must say there is a danger in all of this *laissez-faire* nonsense. If we are to bring in these historical reforms, the country has to be ready for them. We have to set ourselves the target of quashing the activists." The Home Secretary spoke in the measured tones of historical experience.

"We cannot let a few scaremongers frighten us. We have a duty to the people to address the task of the socially creative Reforms we have been following. We haven't time to stop..."

They looked up at Provlyn, who carried the silver suitcase-shape, filled with the day's crisply ironed newspapers. Serboth Challis stood up to take them from him.

"Thank you, Provlyn." She handed one out to each of the visitors.

He bowed and left the room.

It was a little macabre returning to the hospital in daylight, but Morda confidently mounted the steps of the Main Entrance, showing his admittance card to the police officers at the door. Would they have been there this time yesterday? His heart had lifted awkwardly to the base of his throat by the time he approached reception. The whole reception area was deserted apart from a young woman at the desk who looked enquiringly at him.

"I have a war relief medical at eleven o'clock, I believe."

"Your name?"

"Morda. Unsired," he added.

"If you would like to sit down, Morda, I will tell the Hospital Doctor you're here." She moved to the left of the counter and pulled out a small switchboard housed like a drawer in the desk. He was reminded of Whitechapel Police Station.

"Sit down," she said. It was unpleasantly like a command, but he moved to his seat. He had once read an article about air travel, that had related the impersonal quality of the airport lounge. The article was clearly written to support the phasing out of world travel, what with its emphasis on world resources, but the description of the airport lounge had stuck. Looking round the vast pink walls and dark brown carpet, he felt lost. He felt like the last airline passenger in the world.

"The Hospital Doctor will see you now."

He looked up, and out of a door in the wall it seemed, way across the hall, a white-coated woman raised her arm. He moved across towards the opening. The room he entered was quite as expected; small, with two couches, one raised with a lamp, one by the wall.

"I hope you found the hospital without too much bother," the doctor said.

"I've been here before."

"Oh yes? Tell me about it."

"It was just to visit some friends from my battalion. I had been serving out with them in Liverpool when we were ambushed. One of them saved my life."

He shook his head at the memory, not least because he had not actually visited them at all. But he was now convinced as far as he could be that his unexpectedly prompt reappearance at the hospital was just a coincidence.

"Now you were awarded your war relief pension, according to your forms here, because you saved the lives of three army generals. It says here that you intercepted a gunman in the Manchester Barracks who had broken through the security cordon at the gate, on a mission to kill the three generals staying there. You were shot in the foot." She had already unclasped the right trouser leg of his suit and was examining the base of his ankle.

"I was shot in the chest as well, but the injuries weren't as serious," Morda said.

"Have you worked since?"

"On and off. It's difficult finding something I can do well in this condition."

"The country has full employment, and I don't imagine there are many jobs that require the use of your foot."

"But I can only stand on it for a few minutes at a time. And most jobs these days require you to stand up for at least two hours or so in the day."

The Doctor frowned and began examining each bone in the injured foot.

Morda generally felt slightly awkward in the company of women; it wasn't that he resented their superior social status, just that he felt uncomfortable in their presence. This doctor was quite handsome and reminded him, in an oddly repulsive way, of Harvil; but it didn't do to let such thoughts develop any further. He knew women were different, but he had never seen one in any state of undress. He had yet to meet a man who had. It was deterring enough simply to be aware of the severity of the punishment for any kind of proven relationship between individuals of the different sexual classes.

Provlyn had felt decidedly uncomfortable for the latter part of the morning, one reason being a developing reluctance of Serboth Challis' guests to continue their conversation when he was in the room. They no longer ignored him, like before, but looked instead at Lady Asquith, who had presumably set this group secrecy in motion.

Provlyn felt profoundly irritated by the sudden self-consciousness which had descended upon him. He was unable to perform a single duty that morning without the feeling that he was being watched. Any voices he overheard he tried to block out for fear of hearing something else that would be a burden to him. Morda had, he knew, been a little disappointed when he had taken the job nearly eleven months ago, but at the age of nineteen he was eligible for several new professions, going into service being one of them.

He had found the idea of being a butler or footman rather romantic; the free uniform, working in a large house, having the chance to mix with educated people. These were all things he thought he might enjoy. And he had. Nearly a year later he was First Junior Footman, thought of very highly, so Chatwick had told him, by most of the people upstairs, even Dorjess. He had found it difficult to understand why Morda did not wish to mix with the Populite, why he always made the distinction so pronounced.

"Isn't it your afternoon off, Provlyn?" Chatwick said.

He looked up at the clock in the hall which he had been polishing. It was half past one.

Up above the dwindling shapes of the city horizon, Morda sat on a wooden bench, cradling a small plastic box of sandwiches and a flask of coffee. He could see the figure running towards him from the Hampstead side of the hill. Such unfathomable innocence in someone already twenty! He wondered how much they needed each other. It might be a lot more in the near future. He took out a cigarette that he had rolled himself on the tram journey there, and lit it. He seldom smoked, other than to share the first few puffs.

"I'm sorry I'm late," Provlyn gasped, kissing him. Morda pushed him to the ground and they wrestled over and over in the grass.

"Sit up, boy," Provlyn said, eventually, when he had pulled free. "You'll break the cigarette."

Morda laughed. When they had first made love, Provlyn had developed the unfortunate habit of calling him *boy,* a term of reference that was later to induce much impotence through its side effect of paroxytic laughter. He divided up the sandwiches and poured out the coffee.

"I meant to tell you. They called me in for a check-up this morning. The relief is guaranteed for another year, but apparently I am not eating enough." Provlyn moved slowly to his briefcase and took out a folded newspaper which he threw across to him.

"Have you seen this?"

Morda read the article with wonderment. The crawling man, then, was dead.

"I didn't know I'd killed him. I didn't mean to."

They both looked out over London, the capital city, the winter trees now blowing more frequently across the view.

"What are you going to do?"

"There isn't much I can do, is there?"

He could not bring himself to say he had been back to the hospital. He lay back and looked up at the sky.

"Do you think I should leave my job at Parkside?"

"Don't be an idiot, Provlyn. I may not like you working there, but you can't leave now." Morda felt a weakening in his bowels. This was a prime position of impotence. He could not tell Provlyn about what Harvil had said; there was, indeed, no action he could take to resolve the situation. He would have to wait to be found, and hope that the activists found him first.

"They were talking about it today. She had an at-home and most of the people there were from the cabinet. Lady Asquith, the Prime Minister. And the person serving them sandwiches is the lover of one of the activists that they were discussing. I was so scared that they would ask me what I thought about it all. Chatwick is bound to ask me in the next few days."

"Do you have an opinion?"

"I still love you, if that's what you mean."

"This isn't about love, though, is it? I have killed a man."

"You have been very good to me."

"You owe me nothing, Provlyn. They have offered you the chance to live in there; the money would be better, and there would be no risk of getting involved with anything that might happen to me. You ought to think seriously about taking up their offer."

Provlyn looked at him mournfully.

There didn't seem to be anything Morda could say to him. Strangely enough, though, he felt he had struck a blow for something good. He had killed four men in the Civil War, killed them for his country and the continuing establishment of the Populite's hold over the Populace. He had fought for people who sought to consolidate their power, power that would, in the years to come, be used against the people who respected it. The men he had killed had thrown themselves selflessly into the cause of freeing the Populace, in the same way that he had sought to free Harvil. *'It's difficult to feel any sympathy for them,'* Provlyn had said. But he had to go on while there was something to fight for. He thought back to the Doctor earlier that morning; he realised what he was beginning to feel then. A hard revulsion at the existence of unquestioned and unearned power. Had it always been like this? Yes, of course it had.

He moved across to Provlyn who was sleeping, lying face up on his pillowed scarf. Provlyn was privileged, too, in a way. He had been sired at eighteen months, even though his father had died when he was fifteen. No wonder the government was keen to keep the institution of siring alive. All the advertisements, the propaganda; if the Populace could exist in comfortable, loving groups, they were less likely to feel a need to question other aspects of their existence. Provlyn was part of it, too, but he did not understand. He was desperate for the two of them to sire a boy. It would set a seal on their relationship, giving him the security he needed, and it would make him feel a worthwhile member of the Populace. Once you had sired, you had to sign registration documents to offer the child a joint home for at least fifteen years. It was a pledge of fidelity; and every insecure member of the Populace jumped at the first opportunity to sign one. Five years gone, another fifteen promised away... Proliferation.

He crouched over Provlyn and kissed him gently on the nose. There was something to be said for companionship, even if it was open to exploitation.

"I think there are better times ahead," Morda said, looking out at the city. "I just hope we're around when they get here."

As far as could be seen, there was just grass and trees, nobody in the park at all. Morda walked over to the small metal plaque, erected on wooden feet just by the edge of the hill which allowed the commanding view of the city. It offered a facsimile of the climbing shapes against the skyline, listing each by name. It was noticeable, however, that several of the towers were absent from the horizon. The Post Office Tower, The Brandon Building, The Crystal Palace Transmitter Tower, removed from the skyline in the changing shape of the city under the corrective push of the National Clearance Act.

Underneath the old plaque, the inscription stood: *Made in and paid for by the City of Hampstead, 1995.*

They got back to Hammersmith as it was getting dark; the rush hour was in full flow, the ordinarily empty suburban roads jostling with men returning from their various city jobs. There was talk of a revolution in industry which would bring jobs to the suburbs; it was another part of the campaign to conserve limited national resources. Several city clothes industries were to expand, building centres for communal work, *'factories'* as they were to be known. The papers were full of the advantages this expansive programme was likely to bring the country. Morda speculated that these were the kind of jobs he would soon be accepting, if he refused at his next work interview.

They bought an evening paper from the news stand in the Broadway, *The Informer,* as it was known. There were several luxuries that not everyone could not afford, but at one farthing, everyone could buy a newspaper. It gave people a feeling that they were keeping in touch with what was going on in the important areas of the country; with the Populite and the Royal Family; listings of local dances and theatre seasons; even overseas information when they ran the features on a Tuesday.

Morda tucked the paper under his arm; he had already seen the headline, but the street was not the place for a political debate. He took Provlyn's arm as they crossed into Hammersmith Grove. They were passed in the street by several other young couples wandering idly, chatting about their day, some already off to the Palais for the early evening dance. It was the only dance hall for several miles and was full every evening for both sessions. Tonight's show promised *'Alexander's Ragtime Band'* until nine-thirty.

The house smelt different when they returned, like sweet blossom, the upstairs window open. Morda recalled his haste in leaving earlier in the day.

"Come and look at this!" Provlyn called from the front room. *"Republican Activist Harvil, involved in Tuesday's siege at Whitechapel, died this morning at ten o'clock, it is thought from internal bleeding. After* extensive enquiries, police have confirmed that he was the man who attacked and murdered the security guard yesterday evening, and not the activist group suggested in our early editions."

Provlyn's face lit up.

"So. Maybe I wasn't there after all," Morda said.

"You didn't mean to kill him. It's only justice, in the end."

"But it only happened this morning, and yet *it's already in this evening's paper*. Don't you find that a little odd?"

Provlyn was already in the kitchen. "Would you like some vegetable soup? I bought some fresh bread from the baker's in Wimbledon..."

"Whatever," Morda said. He was thinking about what he had said earlier. There was something he could do. He could get a job. He could ring the workhouse centre to-morrow and take the apprenticeship at *Palby's* the following day. It wasn't wise to stay in the house all day; it would be safer at night. There would be more money for both of them, and if he had to lose his relief, then it wouldn't put unnecessary pressure on Provlyn. Harvil was dead; he would want Morda to be working, keeping his mind active.

"I understand you rejected this post when it was first offered you, Mr.Morda," the elderly clerk said, staring at him from behind the Administration Counter in the foyer. Morda touched the sheet of security glass which separated them. He straightened his thin tie and nodded.

"I had no idea I'd be working for *Palby's*. I thought it was just a tiny office in Aldgate."

"I have prepared your employment file," the clerk continued, humourlessly. "Please pin this security tag to your lapel. If you continue behind you to the stairs and go to the second floor, you will find the Chief Sales Accountant there, who is in specially this morning to see you."

"Thank you very much," Morda said. "And it's just *Morda*, by the way." He smiled at the clerk who looked rather offended by the revelation. It may just have been the way he had said it.

The outside of the building looked like any other city establishment, but inside it was rather plush; a heavy pile crimson carpet with glass tables and steel furniture. His suit began to feel a little shabby. He would use his relief at the end of the week to buy another, if he could find one cheap enough.

He mounted the stairs at the end of the foyer, looking down on the ground floor below. *Palby's* had been one of the major shopping chains of the last hundred years. Morda recalled the grand closing of their last shop in Regent Street two years ago. The majority of departmental stores, as the larger shops had been known, had moved from retail sales to investments in the new factory industries. The pound had been devalued three times in the last sixteen months, and longer term investments had become more fashionable in the financial world. But where had all the merchandise gone? This was something he could pursue when he had settled in at Palby House.

"Good morning, Morda. My name's Rocassa Milo, Chief Sales Accountant at *Palby's*. I'm pleased you've come to work with us and hope you'll enjoy your stay here." The Chief Sales Accountant was surprisingly short for a woman, barely five and a half feet tall. It was the first time in his life Morda could ever remember looking down at a woman, even if it was only from a superior height of about four inches. He shook her hand and was led through a short corridor, offices of corrugated windows on either side. Fuzzy shapes clattered away at typewriters behind each glass panel, but there seemed to be only one person in each office. The image he had built up of an open plan room of bubbly workers exchanging ideas and phone numbers fizzled away to nothing. At the end of the corridor they turned right into an office that was a little smaller than the rest. Rocassa Milo slid out the white 'Vacant' sign and pushed home a piece of card she took from her bag, with 'Clerk 15 : Morda' printed in bold black letters on a green background.

They went into the office, a room of about eight square feet with a wooden chair and mahogany table on which was a robust grey typewriter and a black bakelite telephone with silver dial. She handed him a bright glossy document with *Palby's* printed on the front in the same bold lettering as the card on his office door. He flicked through the sections of shiny pages, all covered with bold print and photographs of the history of the company. He stopped at the last section, titled simply, *The Future*.

"That's where you fit in," she said. "I would like you to read very carefully through the document, and when you finish, please telephone exchange forty-three and they'll send you some work."

He looked round at the glass, the walls and the desk. It was something of a disappointment after the plush carpets of downstairs. Her raised eyebrowed smile suggested she had intuited his thoughts; the expression invited any questions he might want to ask.

"What will I actually *do* here, if it's not a stupid question?"

She looked curiously at him.

"You'll be a clerk," she said.

He sat over a cold tea in a small café in Bloomsbury. He had felt physically repulsed for most of the morning. It had taken him nearly two hours to fight his way through the drivel of a document, and then he had been given three files of debentures to correlate. The dullness of simple addition and book-keeping would have ordinarily had him rushing back to the workhouse centre demanding another job, resigning after half a day. But he fought through the first file, a groggy trembling feeling in the pit of his stomach. He was despairing in the sweat of his wet page-turning fingers that it would be given outlet, but he could not push it away. He wanted to somehow sick up the feeling so it would leave him. The sheer drudgery of the task in front of him allowed it shared space in his thoughts. The document. The glossy booklet. He had crossed his legs tightly under the wooden table. He had begged a sea of faces to rise up and watch him from the corridor, but no-one seemed to be around. In the end, he began to push his elbow along his front. He put the file down, his heart racing a bile to the back of his throat. He knocked two further files to the floor, but no-one came. The booklet. He thumbed clumsily through the pages, which stuck frustratingly to his wet fingers, looking for the one that had caught his eye. At the back of the booklet, after a struggle, he found it.

'*Our Chief Sales Accountant, Rocassa Milo, is seen at the grand closing of our Kensington store, one of five we closed in our investment drive to join the revolution in Industry.*' Positioned above the paragraph, a photograph showed Rocassa Milo fastening a measure of red tape around the main shop doors. She looked radiant, handsome, *she was smaller than any of the other women in that photo!* Her height, it must have been her height that had triggered this shameful feeling he was having. He pulled at himself desperately from under the table to free his desire and soon, mercifully, it was over. He took a handkerchief from his pocket to clean himself up. He felt nauseous, gripped by a sudden terror that he had spoiled the book in his frenzy. But it was untouched.

He sipped at the tea. It tasted like sludge. A friend in the army, Charness, had told him about the castration meted out to a boy from his boarding school, for having a picture of a woman in his locker. There was no evidence of who she was or how it had got there; he had said nothing. Charness had said someone had planted it there, some jealous kid whom the boy had spurned. There was no evidence that the boy had even had any feelings for her. But now he had done this he felt a clammy shame upon him. He wanted to confess to Provlyn and be punished. That single act had destroyed his command of reason. He had pushed the handkerchief down the lavatory in the café. It had gone down comfortably enough, but he had not been able to equivocate what he had done in his mind.

"I picked some aubergines up at the village market this afternoon. We could have a *ratatouille*," Provlyn said, from the kitchen.

Morda sat at his desk with a sheet of figures in front of him. He was trying to calculate whether he could afford the £3.15/- needed to buy the dark blue double-breasted suit he had tried on after work in the Piccadilly *Trocadero*. He had two pounds saved from his first two weeks in the job, with his relief still to come.

"We don't have to have a cooked meal if you don't want," Provlyn said.

"I am quite hungry," Morda said.

"It's good that you're working. We could send off those Toll Tax returns this weekend, instead of leaving them till the end of March."

"We might as well leave them as long as possible," Morda said. "I don't see why the government should get any interest on our money, simply because we're stupid enough to send it in early."

"But it was due in January."

"No-one else in the street has paid theirs. We'll pay it in March."

The rest of the evening was spent in an atmosphere of restrained silence, Morda working at his desk, and Provlyn reading the morning and evening newspapers. There had been no further news in the past few weeks about the activists, and the story seemed to have died. Morda had begun to bring work home with him, but had not discussed it to any real extent. He still asked what had been said at Parkside by any influential people who had visited; he still spoke of the better times ahead, but was not so keen to elaborate.

They had stopped going out to the public house so often; Morda would bring drinks back with him, bought from the off licence round the corner. It seemed to Provlyn that he mainly drank before and after they made love. He hadn't complained, though. He had been just as active as usual, even if he did seem to want to dominate most of the time. It was all the same to Provlyn. He longed only for Morda, in any way he could have him.

That morning, however, a letter that he had been waiting for these last three months had arrived. He had tried to find a convenient point in the conversation to discuss it, but up until then there hadn't really been any to sort a moment from.

"Our siring registration forms came back this morning."

Morda stood up from his desk and closed the file he was working on.

"They've suggested two dates at the Siring School; the fifteenth or the seventeenth of next month."

Morda looked at him nervously. It had become like the situation with Harvil. He had been desperate to sire a boy, to have some new hope in his life. He still was striving for that same hope, but was it fair to expect a child to provide it?

"Do you still want us to sire?" Provlyn stood by the window, where Harvil had told him they had kept an old radio, playing out tunes transmitted from the South London Broadcasting Station.

"I have been thinking about it a lot lately."

"And?"

"I don't feel I should put any pressure on you. I can't pretend I don't want it, but if you even have the slightest perceptible doubt... I couldn't have us sire because you felt you *owed it to me*."

"You want me to make the decision? Haven't you got the confidence to tell me you want it? That's usually the way these things get done." Provlyn sat in the armchair, waiting. Morda moved to the armrest.

"It's fifteen years," he said.

"I want you."

Morda slid into Provlyn's lap and they kissed. For all his dreams and visions of change, there was nothing in his empty life he had yet been able to give himself to. Stability came with its own price tag. He had recently found the list of activists Harvil had given him when they had split; it had been left at the bottom of a biscuit tin in the larder. He did not recognise any of the names, though it was possible that they had used codenames. Any one of them could be looking for him at this moment, outside now perhaps.

He felt the younger boy's hands working their way under his shirt, pulling him closer as they embraced. The stirring beneath his chest gave him the courage to speak.

"I love you," he whispered. "Let's find one. Let's find ourselves a boy."

Provyln sighed deeply, though whether from pleasure or relief it was difficult to tell.

March

Morda had almost completed his first month at *Palby's*, and he was beginning to feel events in his life settling again. The newspapers were talking about a 'Stabilising Britain' under the Liberal Government, with a significant move away from the lifestyle that had been encouraged by events and developments in the United States. One of the top American departmental stores, *Selfridges*, had closed the day before yesterday, leaving another section of Oxford Street broken up into small clumps of building work. Elaborate shop fronts were being converted, gradually, into modern workshops, as they were being called. Some areas of the West End were being knocked down altogether, rolled out for hurried turfing to catch the front end of spring.

London's appearance had changed drastically since the end of the war, five years ago. A workforce of nearly two hundred thousand builders from round the country worked long hours to meet the demands of the Clearance Act. Many streets were cobbled over using quick-setting concrete, sometimes changing the appearance of a square overnight. There had been scuffles in Islington a fortnight ago when a young man, after an altercation with one of the concrete supervisors, had been thrown into a mixer and had lost a leg. Only the city seemed to have its external appearance preserved; it was noticeable that it contained mainly historical buildings and, above all, seemed to be the centre of all government operations, at all levels.

Morda felt less than convinced about the amount of *progress* that was being made in the country, however. The motor car, criticised for its gluttony where natural resources were concerned, could be counted in ones and twos throughout the city. The last Model T was reported to have been run off the production line in Leeds, and trams and trolleybuses were now the only transport an ordinary person could hope to employ to get themselves round the city above ground. Very few people complained, however, pleased with more parks and less shops, pleased at the increasing availability of service and industry jobs in and out of the city, pleased in the knowledge that the country was *getting back on its feet again,* and conserving the majority of its energy in the process.

It was a miserably dark afternoon, with storm clouds scuttling into position overhead. Morda had taken the afternoon off to meet Provlyn at the School for Siring in the Caricott Building on Shepherds Bush Green. It was an anonymous grey monolith next to the tube station overlooking the site of an old motorway on which two boys were playing a game of had. It was hard to imagine the sophisticated machinery that had once whisked people at eighty miles an hour along that cracked road. There was not a sound to be heard as he stood in the forecourt of the building, reading the notice on the window.

Attention - All siring appointments booked after March 20th should go to Nuneaton House in East Finchley. A tram can be caught direct to the building from outside Notting Hill Gate station.

The reason for the change of venue was clear enough in the number of hard-hatted builders' foremen parading round the front of the building.

Provlyn was late. Morda bought an afternoon *Informer* from the newsstand. He felt certain that a siring was the most noble thing he could do now with his life. Even though it was only two months since the killing at the hospital, he was returning to the calm demeanour he had possessed for most of the time he had been living at Hammersmith with Provlyn. Moments of instability fed by bad dreams or acts of deception he had felt forced to practice threatened him sporadically, but the thought that he could be a father in the next two weeks made him feel genuinely important. Such complacency would have blown away with the wind had he caught sight of the headline on the third page of his newspaper, but at that moment, Provlyn arrived.

The Caricott Building was reputed to be almost three-hundred and fifty years old, and had acted as a School for Siring for nearly seventy years. It was meticulously clean and empty inside, its walls a gentle fawn, decorated with several prints of local scenes hung every few yards. There was a painting of the Shell Building (since demolished), one of the National Theatre (to be demolished in May) and one of Nuneaton House, its replacement-to-be at the end of the month. All this was lost on Provlyn, who was clearly overcome by the moment.

"I wonder if it'll be a girl or a boy," Morda said, fatuously.

"We won't even be signing anything today!"

Provlyn was keen that the event should be conducted with an air of respect. Morda watched his serious expression in the lift with some amusement.

They got off at the eleventh floor surprised, again, to see a clean but clear corridor. At the end was the sign *Siring*. They entered a small office with a single desk clerk with his back to them, filing a handful of documents into a filing cabinet drawer. Morda looked out of the window to their left. The view of London was comprehensive and astonishing. Like the scarred face of the survivor of a horrific accident, the vista showed hundreds of tiny pocked changes to the city's layout. Even as he watched, south-west, a cloud of grey-brown dust lifted high into the air; probably somewhere past Chiswick or Putney. He nudged Provlyn, but before he could look round, the clerk spoke.

"You must be Morda and Mr.Ranshell. Provlyn, is it?" He consulted a single sheet of paper filched unceremoniously from his top pocket. They both nodded.

"You'll probably be the last people to sire from the Shepherds Bush office," he said, shaking his head. "We're off to Barnet, soon. They think it's an idea if we're a little more provincial. Can't say I care much, myself, though it'll be quite a journey for some people. 'Course I'll have to move if they want me to stay on. Can't travel up from Barons Court every day now, can I?"

"Hasn't that been sorted out, yet?" Morda asked.

"They haven't told me what's going to happen. I expect I'll hear in the next few days."

"Oh," said Morda.

"About the siring," Provlyn said.

"Yes. Well I'll take it as read that you've lived together for five years and have signed a fifteen year clause certificate."

"It's here," Provlyn said, fumbling for it in his jacket pocket.

"The law states that in cases of siring, the older man will be the father, though in this case, sir, as you have not been sired, you will take the nominal role of First Friend and your young man here will be the father."

"I thought the law had changed on that First Friend crap."

"Morda..." said Provlyn.

"You knew about this," Morda said.

"What difference does it make *who* the father is? We've signed the forms, we'll live together! Why should it make any difference?"

Morda left the room.

"I'm sorry. We have discussed this, but, he gets touchy about being unsired. Could you show me the file please?"

Shaking his head, the clerk took Provlyn through to the office behind the reception room, where several filing cabinets were bunched, a little untidily, together. Those placed at the back were in such a position as to be virtually unreachable other than by being broken open from the top. From one of the front cabinets, the clerk took a brown velvet file.

"Numbers 104 to 112 are available except for 110 who, unfortunately, died yesterday."

Provlyn took hold of the book and turned the pages. The first two that were not deleted were both Caucasian, one a blond boy with blue eyes, the second a boy with red hair. He noticed that these were, in fact, numbers 5 and 6.

"You'll need to look further on," the clerk said, moving the pages hurriedly.

Towards the back of the book, Provlyn found the relevant section with children of his own skin shade. What had happened to 5 and 6?

After some consideration, Provlyn settled on Number 107. *Age seventeen and a half months. Eurasian extraction. Birthdate: September 29th 1911. Circulated: February 8th 1909.*

"May I take this?" Provlyn asked.

"You have a week to decide. And perhaps you'd be good enough to sort out your differences for next time? I shouldn't tell you that, but the Siring Officer will be here next week, and they'll veto it if you argue at the interview. There's still another three to get through yet!"

"I know. Thank you." Provlyn detached the filesheet. He had worked hard enough to get Morda to this stage. He had to calculate a strategy to get him past the next three.

Morda's drink sat, untouched, on the pub table, where it had been now for nearly ten minutes. Provlyn shifted about uneasily on the plastic-covered seat, watching the gloomy expression.

"Don't you think we might grow to love him?"

"You might. You'll be his father."

The filesheet had, unfortunately, only made things worse. At home in his Personal File, Morda still had the filesheet on Child Number 446. *Age seventeen months. Caucasian extraction. Birthdate: January 20th 1938.*

Circulated: 6th May 1937. It had been returned to him from the Records Office at his Boarding School when he had left, aged sixteen. He had experienced no sense of rejection as a child; it was only when he had learned about siring that he understood that he had not been selected. He had been on the siring files for nearly four years, but, in the end, as he was over-age, he had been sent on to Boarding School. Morda had promised himself that if he could find someone he loved enough to stay with, he would sire as soon as possible. That pretty face on the filesheet was not unlike a younger version of Provlyn. What respect would it have for a *First Friend* who was older than its father?

"It seems to me that you only discover what laws there are in this country when you do something that challenges them."

"I didn't mean to deceive you, but it's the only way they'll let us have a child. We could always let the child think you were the father."

"Yes," Morda said, bitterly. You *could* tell a child anything, but you had no final control over the truth. It was something that would pay you a visit, sooner or later.

All your shopping under one roof, the display sign said, but the roof was no longer there. All that remained of the store was an isolated unit at the end of the block, covered in dust and rubble. Although there had been a huge clearance of shops and blocks of flats at the top end of the street, the area had not been sectioned off. Large hoarding stands repeated the phrase every hundred yards - *A Revolution For Industry.*

Morda shuffled through the dust and bricks back to the edge of the pavement. He often set off early for work along with Provlyn, who was now starting work at half past seven; he received no extra money despite the fact that it was the third time his hours had been slightly extended. He would receive, they had said, a new contract fairly soon reflecting these changes. He had chosen to see this as a euphemistic promise of extra money. Morda had said if his eyes were any wider they would fall out.

He walked up to the end of Tottenham Court Road. The only other people in Oxford Street were people from the demolition company. He noticed that his shoes were dusty. No matter; he would have them cleaned at that new heel bar round the corner from his work.

He had so far only made the acquaintance of one of the employees from *Palby's* in the time he had been there, and that was Pridge. He remained an acquaintance due to his wanton dullness and bad breath, compounded, perhaps, by the yellowest teeth Morda had ever seen. They were, on close inspection, almost orange. His hair was a flattened greasy grey, as if it had been steamed down with an iron. In fact his only redeeming quality was as a link with the past, and the episodes in his life he occasionally chose to chronicle.

As Morda entered the café in Bloomsbury where he usually got himself an early morning tea, he heard Pridge call him over from a table stored away at the back of the small room, despite the fact that the café was almost completely empty.

"I had such a shock last night when I read this story about that killing in yesterday's paper. Take it. You'll soon see what I mean!" His face was an animated grin. Morda, however, was not smiling.

Stepney Killing - Rival Activists At Work?

'A known member of the East London Workers' Union, Mordga Palapsis, was found brutally murdered last night in a flat in Stepney. Police have said they wanted to interview him about the recent siege in Whitechapel. The assailants are thought to have been from a rival group.'

"That East London Workers' Union closed its membership three years ago," Pridge said, shaking his head. "Anything to link him with the activists, eh?"

Morda nodded, but his head was throbbing. Yesterday at the School for Siring. It was the only reason why he had missed the story. He could see the smiling policewoman and the form he had completed, sending Palapsis to his death. It had taken a while to find him, but they had got him alright. A man who had, as far as Morda knew, never been a member of any political organisation. Just a quiet guy in his battalion, unfortunate enough to have a similar name.

"See - I thought it was you!" he said. "With a name like Mordga, see, that's only one letter's difference..."

Morda drank the rest of his tea and left.

Provlyn looked up the stairs and listened.

"What are you doing?"

"Could I have a word with you, Chatwick?" he said. "I wanted to ask you something in private."

Chatwick drew up a chair and sat down at the table. Provlyn looked up at him through splayed fingers.

"If I ever wanted to sire a child, would I be able to get my hours here reduced, so I could have some time at home to look after it?"

Chatwick's face grew unexpectedly serious. He looked at the ground for a while before speaking.

"Do you have a *friend*?"

Provlyn continued to stare at him.

"Because if you do, they'll want to vet him. You're in the company of some of the most important people in this country, Provlyn. People who will decide just what happens to all of us in the next few years. These people have an enormous amount of power and influence. They have to be able to trust you, as well as whatever friends you might have. Would he be prepared to be vetted?"

"It was just an idea."

"I don't want to spoil your ideas, but, they checked a friend of mine once. I think I've told you about him. He didn't have any kind of history as far as I knew."

"What sort of things did they ask him?"

"I don't know." He looked at the floor.

"You still see him, don't you?"

"I never saw him again. I was later told that it might be a good idea to just forget him."

Provlyn bit his thumb. He had the uneasy sensation that he had just committed an unconscious act of betrayal.

Behind the door at the top of the stairs, on a personal errand of wine tasting, Dorjess stood, a smile at the edge of his lips.

Morda had found the address in his *1915 diary*, which he carried in his overcoat pocket as evidence that they had been in the war together. It was now half past six which only left him a few hours until Curfew, but he had become rapt by a morbid fascination, etched on his conscience. He had to find someone who knew Palapsis, someone who might have an idea about what had happened to him, someone who could relieve him of the gnawing feeling that it was his fault alone. He sat in the empty train carriage, reading through the old diary, remembering the unfortunate soldier. He had been a quiet, likeable man, who had never spoken much, but had, on one occasion at least, shown extraordinary courage.

At the beginning of the 1918-14 Civil War, just nine years ago, they had both been drafted to the outskirts of Liverpool where much of the unrest had been centred. Three Conservative politicians had been killed by a car bomb on their way to a political meeting in Leeds, after crossing enemy lines. The East London Workers' Union had been operating in unison with the Northwest Workers' Alliance and the Scottish Freeworkers Association in an organised plot of terrorist attacks to overthrow the government. They had seized Liverpool and Manchester, and their ranks had grown, supplemented by the disenchanted, the desperate, and those who felt they were siding with the first ruling force of the new Republic. It had been the first unrest in the country since the civil unrest of 1945. As before, they had become known as the republican activists, partly because of the stated aim to overthrow and abolish the monarchy, and partly because of a declared aim to break down the barriers between the Populite and the Populace, and move more men into positions of authority in the country. Even so, in number terms they only amassed twenty-five thousand, barely half the population of London, and it was always going to be a coercive overthrow, as the movement was exclusively male.

The army had gathered five hundred soldiers, including Morda's battalion, to storm Kirby, from where many of the republican operations had been planned. Travelling in low trucks and lorries, they had found most of the people in the town to be civilians. Only six officers of the NWA had occupied the Town Hall, all of whom were eventually sentenced to death or shot.

When the remains of their battalion had reached the Town Hall, four soldiers including Morda and Palapsis, had been sent around the back to hold cover on the two rear exits of the building. As they had crept round to take up positions, the last one (if Morda could read the scrawl in his diary his name was *Astor*) drew his rifle on them and told them to drop the guns. He had declared himself a republican in sympathy with the NWA and operating on the inside for the East London Union. Moving them round to inside the first exit from the building, his plan had been to alert those in the building to the raid, none of them aware that there were only six inside.

"You work for E47 Division?" Palapsis had said, watching Astor with interest. He looked over his shoulder behind him, grinning. "It's alright.

We're all with East London."

In the few seconds' hesitation this had caused Astor, Palapsis had thrown himself to the ground, rolled over, picked up his hand gun in the process, and shot the man in the head, all in one movement. It happened so quickly that Morda and the other soldier still had their arms raised; the first time Morda had ever seen a man shot in cold blood. It had been fortuitous that Palapsis had been, before his call up, a member of the ELWU; a stunning piece of luck for the three of them.

He could still see the expression of surprise, a still life on the dead soldier's face as he hit the floor. It was a story he had told Provlyn on several occasions. And this servant of government, who had never been rewarded for his bravery, had been butchered in his own flat by an unknown intruder; the smiling police officer, perhaps.

He came out of Stepney Green station; he had not seen Palapsis since the end of the war, but had a clear picture of him, rugged, handsome... a little fresh-faced, perhaps. He would have been thirty-three, now. Morda was fairly sure he had had a lover, then, though five years was a long time for a friendship to last; he had only to think of the fifteen he was preparing to surrender to Provlyn.

He would certainly have been living in the same flat; how else would the police have found him - he was sure they had. Two days after the event, his arrival would attract suspicion. For all he knew, the same policewoman could be there, keeping a check on anyone coming to pay a last visit.

The flat was on a small estate of six three-storey buildings, each housing twelve flats. There was no obvious police presence, so he climbed up the steps to Flat 19. He noticed that it had darkened since his walk from the station. He wondered, if he had a lover, whether they would still have been staying there that soon after the murder? He lifted his feet so as to approach the doorway in silence. It was only when he had got within a few feet of it that he realised the door was slightly ajar. He looked down below into the street, but there was no-one there as far as he could see. He stood, motionless, watching for a movement from the door. He knew now that coming to the flat had been a mistake, his own guilt leading him, once again, towards danger. Looking back behind him, into the darkness, it was a long way to the High Road from where the distant lights shone, and just a few feet to the flat, a front room light on behind the curtains.

"Are you coming in or are you going to stay out there all night?" a friendly voice said from inside. A young man appeared from behind the door, thin, dark-haired, around twenty. Morda breathed a sigh of relief.

The man was wearing a suit that a footman might wear. Morda had seen them coming to the door during the day in some of the bigger houses in Hammersmith when he had been out of work. It looked decidedly wrong on someone in a flat in Stepney. Footmen were never allowed to take their working clothes home. He turned sharply, bumping into a hunched figure standing behind him, sending them sprawling across the balcony into the wall of the flat behind. They meant to keep him there. He staggered up from his falling position, kicking himself free to reach the stairs at the end of the landing. He heard two screams and someone cry, *"Stop!"* but he ran off into the darkness. He almost lost his balance as he hit the foot of the stairs, but tripped his way into an accelerated running. It was an irony in his favour that the reason he could escape was due to the limited lighting in street areas, mostly from the newly installed cheaper gas lamps.

In the dark overcoat he could, at any other time of day, have walked quite inconspicuously back to the station once he reached the High Road, but he was the only person around; he would be remembered. He decided it would be safer to follow the back streets towards the city, and get a train back from there, where the lighting was better and people would be greater in number.

Finding himself eventually in the streets around the Barbican, he decided to get a train at the next station he passed. At half past eight, as he boarded a train, he was still in a position to beat the Curfew, but he felt exasperated with himself for being so asinine. His elusive romance with the authorities had taken him to within a few feet of being caught; he was certain he would have been named as Palapsis' killer as well as that of the hospital guard and probably Harvil, too. They might have been activists, laying in wait to find out who had *named* Palapsis. Palapsis might have been working for them after all - Morda knew nothing of his movements for the past five years.

But at least he knew now, if he had been in any doubt before. There was still a war on, a civil war. If you looked hard enough, you could see it in the demolishing of the buildings, the creation of service jobs, the

44

Revolution for Industry; but the knowledge was a kind of impotence, because there was still no-one he could tell, no side he could join. He passed his handkerchief over his forehead to catch the sheen of sweat. Looking at the handkerchief, he was reminded of the fate of its twin, in his first week at work. He felt the hardening below his chest as he sat in the empty carriage. It wasn't really a death wish, or a desire to placate his conscience. For the first time in his life he became aware, with the sturdy erection he felt below, that he was somehow different. All of this was *different,* wasn't it? That had to be why he could find no genuine confidant; because no-one else was like him. It was, he realised, as he moved his arm against himself, even in the throes of this perverse pleasure, something which, were he not to exercise proper control over it, would eventually kill him.

He lay in bed listening to the remonstrations, his eyes growing heavy in the heat given out by the bedroom gas fire. Provlyn soon lay on his chest, finally quiet. The vagueness of his note, another evening wandering off. This was not the way a *First Friend* should behave. And problems at work, too. No chance of giving up the job, more pressure to start earlier, promises of pay that were not being realised. Morda turned over.

After a while, Provlyn slid across, pressing himself up against him, kissing the nape of his neck. He moved down slightly, pivoting himself.

"No," Morda said.

Provlyn drew back and turned on his side.

"What's the matter with you?"

"The matter with me? Nothing. You're the one who has the problems, as far as I can recall."

"We haven't made love for six weeks."

Morda folded the pillow under his head and sat up.

"Just remember I'm prepared to give up fifteen years of my life for you. I just decided to visit a friend I hadn't seen for a few years - I left you a note, didn't I?"

"You're not consistent," Provlyn said. "Sometimes you become moody, unpredictable; you talk in riddles, only half answer my questions. Then you tell me how much you're worried about me. If you want the truth, half the time I've been living with you has been spent preoccupied with wondering whether or not you'll be here this time next year." Morda looked over at him.

"What *do* you want from me other than security?"

Extensive silence. Morda could hear a record-player playing next door. Provlyn stared hard at the filesheet from the Siring School.

"I found out today that if I want to sire and keep my job, there might be problems."

"Oh?"

"They'll want to vet my partner. It's alright. I only talked about it with Chatwick, and even then, only hypothetically."

Morda's expression changed. To think that he was the one who had encouraged the pursuit of full time employment. Everything that moved with the stamp of government authority over it travelled in and out of that house at some time or other. If they didn't know who he was now, it was clear that they would soon be on to him. The siring application was already being processed: they had signed the fifteen year agreement forms. He was feeling nauseous. With his back to Provlyn he tried to drain the anguish from his face.

"Don't make any decisions yet, Provlyn. Just don't talk about it at work. London is becoming awkward for the unorthodox. Tomorrow evening we'll go for the second interview at the Siring Centre and see what happens. They may still decide that it's inappropriate for us to sire. After all, a father of twenty is very young."

"I'm not sure I feel safe any more, that's all."

"That's the best attitude you can have. Then you're always prepared for the worst." Morda drew the bedclothes over him, pulling himself up to Provlyn, a deep warmth in the bed. Cold spring nights invariably triumphed over disagreements to make the second single bed redundant.

At ten o'clock the following morning, the service staff of 47 Parkside were assembled in the upstairs lounge to be addressed by Serboth Challis. She was dressed for the House Of Commons in her dark brown suit with the fawn blouse. She looked distant, authoritative, and a little haughty. Chatwick bowed deferentially to her, and left the room.

"I'm sorry if this meeting is a little sudden, or if it has caused any of you undue concern," she said, choosing her words with care. "However, I am in possession of the changing clauses in the Reform Bill the Liberal

Party have been working on, many of which, I am sure, will become law in the early years of the next century. You might regard this as a somewhat pre-emptive measure, but I have decided that, at the beginning of April, I will be offering all of you firm contracts for your employment. These were promised before when you were asked to undertake longer hours, but signing them will guarantee you a weekly increase of one pound ten shillings, as well as access to our local Doctor for any treatment you might need. All you will be expected to give the household is an undertaking that you will stay in employment here for ten years."

Even in the silence, there was a perceptible fidgeting at the extent of the demand. The staff were all male, half in their fifties and the remainder in their early twenties. Service jobs were still in their infancy in the country, and were only attracting the very young and inexperienced, or those too old to embark upon a new profession.

"You may study the contract in your own time. I have left a copy in the hall for those of you who are interested. If you are not in a position to sign, there is no question of you losing your jobs, but naturally you will not qualify for the benefits, financial and otherwise."

She marched briskly out of the lounge. She could be heard moving downstairs to the waiting car. In the lounge, the three clerks were discussing their future in jovial tones, their greying beards twitching with the movements of their mouths. It was a fair certainty that the sum of ninety shillings would not be the limit of their reward for signing the contract. There were four other footmen apart from Provlyn; Chatwick, the chef and two cooks made a staff of twelve. What was in it for Serboth Challis? If she were to lose the next election, due in three years, would she be able to afford to pay all of them? More to the point, could she justify employing all of them, if the Liberals were relegated to being a mere Opposition Party.

Provlyn busied himself in the pantry, preparing the order of vegetables from stock for the cooks, his mind on the second Siring meeting. He had a feeling that Morda was quite taken by Number 107, even if he had darker skin. Morda himself had spoken about being *orthodox* in London, and the majority of the Populace were of Eurasian extraction, including himself.

It was quite an experience to have access to the pantry at *Parkside*. At first he had needed a Vegetable Guide to recognise and differentiate between the various vegetables: aubergines (fat purple objects), courgettes (like cucumber only a lighter green and more resilient, if they weren't ripe), krats (like small carrots, but yellow) and warlochs (looked like a beetroot, but was somewhere between an onion and a bulb of garlic). He was now at the stage where he could recognise them in the dark, just through touch and smell, and had great delight in introducing Morda to new recipes he might try out on weekends off, when he was allowed to take some of the excess food home.

"Are you going to sign it, young man?"

Provlyn jumped. Behind him, Dorjess had arrived, and was sitting on the edge of the downstairs dining table.

"I'm going to think about it this weekend," Provlyn said, watching him. Dorjess moved into the centre of the room, biting into an apple he had found on his way in.

"I think you ought to sign it," he said, nodding gravely. He moved to within a few feet of the pantry, and looked in.

"Why should I?" Provlyn asked, nervously. He could smell the sour breath above the freshness of the vegetables.

"So you're not tempted to sire for another ten years." Provlyn swallowed hard. He could feel tears lurking behind his eyes. Had Chatwick told him? It was unlikely. He must have been hanging around at the top of the stairs. It wouldn't have been the first time. He turned to the wall. Dorjess moved up slowly behind him.

"Guess what?" he said. "Our lunch hour is due in a few minutes. I'm sure Lady Challis won't mind if we take it a little early today. We can celebrate the fact that my two esteemed colleagues have decided to lunch out." He twisted Provlyn's wrists together as if they were caught in a washing mangle. He pushed him towards the stairs. When he spoke, his voice was low and bitter.

"Move up there to my room. Anyone stops you, you've been told to make my bed again; I wasn't satisfied with it." He lunged at Provlyn, pushing him up the stairs. They both came out on the landing, but it was empty; the Commons was sitting that afternoon and it was Chatwick's shopping day. Dorjess had planned his move quite carefully, it seemed.

He pushed him into the room, locking the door behind him.

"On your knees," he said. "I've washed it specially for you."

Provlyn felt an involuntary retching, rising in his throat. Morda had always taunted him that he did not know what it was like to feel shame. In front of him the fingers fumbled with the black buttons. The tears ran down his face. He moved towards it, and, eventually, took it in his mouth. He closed his eyes, wanting the blackness to engulf him. Heavy hands pulled the hair at the back of his head, pulling him in further. He tried to imagine his death; would it be like this?

A business-like rap on the door.

"Mister Dorjess?" a voice called. "It's a telegram for Lady Challis, sir. I need you to sign for it because there's no-one else in."

Dorjess pulled himself free and worked furiously with his buttons.

"I'll be there, boy. Just a moment." He kneed Provlyn forcefully in the shoulder.

"Wipe your bloody eyes, you little shit. And get working on that bed."

He moved towards the door and opened it.

"Afternoon, Mr.Dorjess," the post boy said. "After you've signed this, Jenner down the road at the Post Office asked if you'd spare him a moment with his accounts." Dorjess nodded and signed for the telegram.

"Thank you," he said, and closed the door. He lowered himself level with Provlyn, pulling him up face-to-face by the collar.

"If there's any trouble this afternoon, I'll have you followed. I've got friends who'll see to anyone who's stupid enough to want to sire with a slut like you. One way or another I'll make sure it doesn't happen." He left the room, closing the door forcefully behind him. Provlyn dropped to his knees and wept.

Morda stood outside the Caricott Building. Provlyn was late for the second week running, despite having stressed the importance of the second appointment all the way through breakfast.

Their appointment was at half past six, so he moved in to the building, alone, at twenty to seven. It would not look particularly impressive to arrive much later; it was bad enough arriving without the would-be father, but any further delay would guarantee an authority refusal of their application.

The building was as empty as before, and Morda felt a little chilly inside the foyer; perhaps they were no longer operating central heating in the building. He took a sheet of paper out of the jacket of his new double-breasted suit, purchased that lunch-time with his latest wage packet. He scribbled a short note to Provlyn and clipped it over the Notice Board at the front of the building.

In the lift, he had to remove a piece of card that had been placed over the floor guide to the building. *Siring Interviews (Second Appointments)* were listed on the twelfth floor. The lift functioned smoothly enough to suggest that there might be people behind the doors on the ground floor simply changing the scenery while he waited to convince him he had travelled twelve floors. It was difficult to see what reason anyone might have to destroy such a building.

Alighting at the twelfth, Morda turned into the corridor, catching a sight of himself in the polished glass. He might have been a top clerk, working in the Houses of Parliament. Noises came from behind a door labelled *Appointments,* so he knocked and went in. A typist clattered noisily away at the back of the office. He rang a service bell at the counter and the clerk they had seen the previous week appeared. This week, however, he was dressed in a well-cut checked suit, carrying two files under his arm. He looked a little distressed to see that Morda was on his own.

"He'll be along any minute," Morda said. "He was, er, *working late* today."

"If you'd care to come through the office to the interview rooms."

The clerk led him behind the counter through to a large room with a large mahogany desk, behind which sat a young woman. She was in her mid-twenties, but had the demeanour of many of the female bureaucrats Morda had dealt with in his life. The conciliatory handshake, stern protocol, sibilant speech, they all combined to establish his place as the underling requesting service of the great machinery of authority.

"I'm Keleh Cheragan, Siring Officer for west London. I gather you are Provlyn Ranshell. Please sit down."

"It's Morda, actually. Provlyn has been delayed." He watched her expression for signs of disdain, but she merely continued to flick her way through their file. He could see his squiggly signature at the foot of the page.

"I take it the clerk has explained the procedure to you." She didn't name him even though he was now in the seat alongside her. "Siring is a central function in British society, and is at the heart of every community in this country. Regretfully we cannot place every boy who comes under our jurisdiction, but for every boy placed, and our success rate is over eighty-five per cent, the community is more homogeneous and therefore more secure. I will be asking you a few routine questions, before I decide whether or not to invite you to the next Siring Trials in April. These will be held at our new west London centre in Barnet." Morda nodded.

The sound of distant carpet footfalls and a panting whispering voice from the office behind heralded the arrival of Provlyn who came briskly into the room, cutting rather awkwardly into the atmosphere of professional interview.

"I'm terribly sorry I'm late," he said, "but I work in service and they chose today to negotiate new contracts for all of us." He smiled nervously and took the seat next to Morda, who caught sight of his folded notice sticking out of the left hand jacket pocket. Although he looked quite neat, Provlyn had been unable to hide the fact that he had obviously been running for most of the journey. Morda felt additionally disconcerted at the fact that he was wearing his grey suit, something he had not taken into work with him that morning.

"As I was saying," the Siring Officer continued. "Just a few routine questions." Morda looked up at Provlyn and took his hand.

"Have either of you sired before?" They both shook their heads.

"Have either of you been convicted of a criminal offence?" They both shook their heads.

"Are either of you employed by a firm with a holding over your tenure of employment that might be detrimental to siring a child?"

"I didn't sign the contract," Provlyn said. They both shook their heads.

"Finally, are either of you a member of any of the following organisations?" She read out a list of society names with an explanation of what the appropriate acronyms stood for. Many of them Morda remembered from his days with Harvil. As she worked her way through them, Morda thought how useful it might be to have a copy of that list. It wasn't something you were likely to find published in *The Informer*. At the end of the list, they both shook their heads.

"You understand," she said, "the seriousness of what you are about to involve yourself with. It is a decision that will have ramifications for your relationship and the rest of your lives. It is not a situation that should be entered into lightly."

"*Fuck the Queen,*" Morda said, under his hand.

"I have had a look at your history, gentlemen," she said. "You have a house, I believe. That's a little unusual, isn't it?"

"It's a little tenement house, actually," Morda said. "I bought it quite cheaply after the war, when the prices went down." He looked at Provlyn who nodded, on cue. This was the moment; there would have been no point in ducking it. If they knew about Harvil, everything would stop here.

"Very well," she said, smiling for the first time as if she had just received confirmation that they were not criminals after all. "I think we'll put your names forward for the Trials in April."

Morda hugged Provlyn. It was more important a victory than he could ever understand. He had put himself in a position where the authorities had looked closely at him - found whatever information they had had the power to access. His army record was sound; his right foot was a testimony to that. He looked across at Provlyn: he didn't look particularly happy for someone who had just been assessed worthy of being a father, but success affected different people in different ways.

They eventually signed the Siring forms which the clerk witnessed, and left the building. Provlyn took his arm as they crossed the road, but they didn't speak.

Morda looked back at the grey building, two of its many windows lit against the darkening sky. It would soon be another Clearance Act casualty, replaced by a strip of grass, or a few houses, spread out over the area. But it wasn't something that bothered him much at that moment.

April

To celebrate their second year as a financial investment house, *Palby's* had hired caterers to provide a five course dinner for all the clerks and management working at Palby House.

Morda was meeting Pridge for a preliminary drink at *The Electric Lamp,* a nearby public house, half an hour before the meal. He had usually found Pridge good company and, in an odd way, he found conversation with an older man - even Pridge - quite edifying at times. It furnished his otherwise limited sense of history, opening up an instant link with the past.

Pridge was forty-eight and had, in spite of his monotonous voice and dreadful teeth, led a full life. He had lived through the 1945-39 First National War as a child, spending most of the time in the country - he was evacuated to Staines in 1944. After the war he had been a taxi driver in London, and had lost nearly four thousand pounds after investing in a fleet of taxi cabs in 1933; the Resource Act of 1932 had increased the price of petrol by 300% overnight, and banned any member of the Populace from owning more than one car. It was scarcely surprising that he was an outspoken critic of the government's new Reforms.

He had joined *Palby's* as a company chauffeur in 1930, and had ended up on the shop floor in 1927. Eighteen years on and he was just another clerk, of no higher grade than Morda, despite his unquestionable experience. It was company homage to the popular equality requests of the republican activists in the war. *'All clerks will be paid the same wage,'* had been the proud boast of the chairwoman. It was rough for the old, Pridge had been telling him, and tonight was another outing for his discontent.

"People's Budget my arse," he was saying. "Anyone who earns over five thousand a year will be getting another sixpence for every pound they earn; that's what they'll be saving by abolishing pensions at the end of the year."

"How can they justify taking away pensions?" Morda asked,

leaning forward on his seat. His tone of disbelief was deliberately couched to elicit the most contemptuous response possible.

"It said in *The Informer* today that the number of people living beyond the age of sixty is declining every year, and that to save money for people who will never live to spend it is a nonsense. It said that the prosperity and stability of the country depends on the propertied classes, so the extra revenue should go back to them. But it won't stop old people having to pay this effing Toll Tax."

He stubbed his cigarette out emphatically on the edge of the table. The few people around in the pub were all listening to him.

Everyone felt aggrieved at the government's reforms, but these were all people who had voted for Lady Asquith's party. Only the activists fought back in any effective way, but they were rarely discussed in public, and if they were, the comments were invariably derogatory. These were the ironic manifestations of the freedom of speech. You were free to verbally denounce anyone you wished - venting feelings this way even gave people a sense of political acumen. They knew what was going on in the country, no-one could impede or influence their judgement. It was a pity that it made no difference in the slightest to the way the country was run.

"Have you ever been in trouble with the law?" Morda asked in a confidential tone. Pridge chuckled to himself.

"You'd never believe me," he said. Morda moved back slightly; the confidence was drawing him within range of Pridge's breath. He leant back on his chair.

"I was once arrested, in 1937 I think it was, in Regents Park. This was when it was just a tiny thing then, with a plant centre. Not like that vast safari land they're turning it into. Anyway, I was on a first date with this young chap - seventeen he was - I'd met him a couple of times in the army, and out of the blue these three policewomen suddenly surrounded us. 'Get your dirty hands off me,' I said. I was a bit lairy in those days. But it didn't make any difference; they took us both off, separately, to Paddington police station. They wouldn't talk to me in the car, I had no idea what I was supposed to have done. It was only when they charged me with gross sexual misconduct that I began to cotton on." Morda moved uneasily in his seat.

"What did they think you'd done?"

"It was the boy, Dorla. He was a pretty one. They thought he was a, well, a she." He shook his head. "I was so embarrassed. But not as embarrassed as Dorla. He never did tell me how they found out."

He finished his drink and put his brown hat over the field of flat grey hair. Perhaps it was the hat that made it appear so flat. They moved towards the door together. Across the street, people were still arriving, mainly in carriages, but there were a few cars parked outside the building.

Morda was glad he had had his only suit dry cleaned for the occasion; it seemed that everyone had dressed up for the evening. He recognised the majority of the male faces. They had been seen in the washroom, passed in the hallways en route to lunch or leaving. Pridge was the only one he had spoken to at length, the only name he knew. He could see the bespectacled clerk who had first interviewed him at the Administration Counter. He looked something of a flaccid penis in his baggy dark green corduroy suit, especially tailed off with a pair of featureless black shoes. And he was alone.

The open plan foyer had been turned into a large restaurant with eight tables, each seating sixteen people. Eight low gas lamps added to the effect, alongside sprays of carnations in tall vases and placenames at each seat. Morda lost Pridge for a moment before his yellow smile beckoned him to a seat.

The last time Morda had attended such a large function was for the General Armistice of 1914 and, largely political as it was, the food had still been fairly basic, though they had all been given half a bottle of wine each. The sense of belonging was overwhelming, though this was presumably one of the aims of the meal. It was also apparent that tables had been divided into company sections, and not rank. There was no obvious managers' table. Morda could see several important-looking women collecting trays of drink at the rear of the ground floor where the caterers were situated. They were all wearing long elegant dresses and one or two of them were wearing face paint.

"Management mixing with the workers for a change," Pridge said, sardonically. He had opened the only bottle of wine on the table and was already filling his glass. Morda covered his with his hand.

"I'll wait to see what's on the way," he said.

"I'd enjoy it while it's here," Pridge said. "It may be the last company meal they lay on for us."

There was no doubt about it. The nine or ten managers were sitting with their own sections. Morda looked furtively about the placenames and was soon, as he had feared, struck with a name that cut both dread and ecstasy into him simultaneously. *Rocassa Milo*. There was nothing really strange about it. She was the Chief Sales Accountant, responsible for all fifteen employees on the second floor. Her name was on a small piece of white card positioned just four feet to his right.

He felt drunk. His forehead was suddenly wet. That odd revulsion was returning to his throat. The upper part of his body reeled with headache and nausea, but the exquisite anticipation of lust was visiting him elsewhere. It was like dotting an imaginary line around his waist ready for one of the caterers to deliver a swift slice to the midriff with a razor sharp cleaving knife.

"You look a bit sick old man," Pridge was saying. "Knock this back. Some of the best red vinegar I've ever tasted."

He had only seen her on one other occasion since that first day when she'd come in to show him what tasks he would be likely to be undertaking. She had been in the foyer, talking to the taller and less friendly Sales Manager, Velche Fridlyn. He had watched from the top of the stairs, on his way to the washroom, and when he had eventually got there, he had locked himself in one of the cubicles for some time. As before, it had not been a comfortable pleasure. When it had visited him before in the company of women, it had just been the upper half, the nausea. He closed his eyes. He ought to be thinking of Provlyn, at home now. He hadn't been in to work for a whole week. He wasn't sick. They were asking him to do too much, he was sure. The hours were getting longer, and he still hadn't signed the contract. And it was the first Siring Trial tomorrow night. All this on top of his personal wardrobe, ready to tumble down on top of him the moment he went to sleep.

Rocassa Milo. They had not even put her title on the place-name. He looked around the hall but he could not see her anywhere. The women with drinks were almost all sat at each of their Departmental tables, serving each employee with a generous flute of champagne. The meal was to be served at a quarter past eight. He drank some of Pridge's proffered wine. It was foul.

"Thank you," a voice came, from behind them. "It gives me great pleasure to welcome you all to Palby House for our annual dinner. If you've spoken to your friends about it, you'll probably realise that we are one of only three companies still upholding this company tradition in London. Next year we may be one of the only three companies!"

A burst of polite laughter rippled gently round the room.

"Who is that?" Morda asked.

"The General Manager," Pridge said. "Shh. You'll enjoy this."

"All joking aside, I am sure you are aware that we will be one of the few companies helping the government in its Revolution for Industry campaign starting next year."

There was a great cheer - a fair percentage of it coming from the heads of each table.

"As employees of *Palby's,* you can be sure that you will all be given a first option on each of the new Industry positions as and when they come up. This will give you and your sired ones a guarantee of a comfortable and secure lifestyle for many years to come!"

Another cheer came, this time from the back of the room. Was there a scream amongst it all?

"So thank you all for coming here tonight, and I hope you enjoy the meal *Radjkins* are putting on for us. Thank you."

The employees duly applauded, Pridge and Morda with them.

When he looked round, Morda found an iced dish of vegetable cocktail in front of him, and a glass of champagne. He turned his head round and back again, lowering his eyes to his meal, but he had seen her. He began to mechanically fork up food pieces to his mouth from the dish in front of him. It tasted like a cold nothingness, but he forked it up until it was gone.

"You haven't touched your drink," a voice said at his side. "It's a wine from Eastern France, from a little province called Champagne. You won't see much of that in London these days."

He could hear a smile in the voice. He took the drink and raised his glass, but did not look round. It tasted exquisite, both bitter and sweet at the same time, the bubbles fizzling out a few seconds after each swallow.

"How have you been getting on?" the voice asked.

He still had the momentary picture of her under his eyelids from his earlier glance. She had narrow eyes, but deep brown pupils. Dark hair tucked under an orange cap - she must have taken it off by now. Most odd was her neck; narrow, but full, so unlike a man's. He looked up and turned slowly round. She wore no face paint.

"I'm finding it very pleasant here," he said, trying to speak quietly. His nausea had him look round for Pridge, who had finished his first course and was busy rolling a cigarette. "It's kind of the managers to patronize us this evening," he said, surprised to hear the words leave his mouth.

"We have a very efficient workforce," she said brusquely. "It's a pity, really, that not everyone here feels they are entitled to the occasional reward. Those of us that do currently hold the balance on the board. Let's just hope that continues."

She shouldn't look at me so long like that, Morda was thinking. She isn't helping me get rid of this sickness at all. He looked around for something to do, and massaged a further few minutes out of his third-full champagne glass. He thought of the picture. He was glad when they had come round to collect in the company brochure a few days later. It hadn't completely terminated his clandestine visits to the washroom, but he had found the absence of source material a great help.

The thoughts he had been having about her had been vague, unstructured. The sexuality came out of the thought of being alone with her. If the guests were all to leave the hall, even as they were getting up from their chairs, he would mess himself. And all he could see through the vague notions of awareness and frustrations of desire were the opening rear doors of a police van and molesting strong arms pushing him into the back. Darkness. A long journey.

He looked up. She was still there. Had this not happened in the whole of history? It was never in the newspapers. Nobody ever discussed it. This whole society. Maybe it happened in other countries, but it was impossible to know. Nobody needed to. *Nobody wanted to know.* He was just another clerk. Above all, *he was a man.* He could not make it happen. This was where limitation stepped in, where The Law finally raised its hand aloft.

Large silver plates of food were being brought across to each table. Provlyn had told him about the different vegetables cooked at Parkside. He had often brought some of them home with him. In front of him now were sweet potatoes cooked in vegetable oil, sprinkled with parsley; a thick dark warloch sauce (he recognised the smell from something Provlyn had once cooked); a dish of krats on a bed of cauliflower cutlets, and a bowl of small brown cube-like things surrounded by onions.

One of the clerks from the top end of his corridor had started to dish out plates of food for the other people on the table. The various smells were mouth-watering enough to make him feel a little more relaxed. He realised, however, that it was his plate that was being arranged.

"A bit of everything?" the clerk was saying.

"What is...?"

"It's *meat,*" Rocassa said. "From North America. Try it."

He looked at the others, all of whom had portions of this substance on their plates. He nodded, unwilling to be the odd one out.

The texture of the meat was quite unlike anything he had tasted before. It was quite tough, between a raw carrot and an aubergine, but it had a softness about it too, once you started to chew it, and a quite distinctive flavour. It was not unlike army chewing-gum, apart from the fact that you could eventually break it down in your mouth into smaller pieces. Was this something available at every table in Populite circles? He had not heard Provlyn speak about it before.

"Effing good," Pridge said, chewing enthusiastically. He had clearly been won over, judging by the smouldering stump of his quarter-smoked cigarette, now two and a half inches of ash.

"Where did you work before you came to *Palby's*?" Rocassa asked. It was an unexpected question.

"Didn't you see my papers before I came here?"

"Recruitment is dealt with by the Administration Office. They seemed quite happy with you."

"This is my first regular job for nine years. I'm a war veteran," he said. "Well, sort of. I was shot in the foot in the last war. I'd show you the wound, but you're still eating."

She laughed, but the rest of the table grew quiet. He knew immediately that it was wrong to indulge in this kind of banter with a manager. Even Pridge's face had grown a perceptible frown.

"It's something we may see more of one day," she said to one of the men on her right, who was experiencing some difficulty with the meat. He nodded, but was not to be drawn into conversation.

The rest of the meal was conducted in virtual silence. Morda refused another glass of champagne in line with the response of the rest of the table. When the dessert was finished, the Chief Sales Accountant took her hat and shawl and left the table without a word. Within a few minutes, the conversation had returned.

"It's a cheap ploy," Pridge was saying. "They think they can buy you by a bit of friendliness every year, but it'll take a little more than a bit of posh food to break down the differences between us and them. I'm surprised you talked to her," he said, turning to Morda.

"She asked me a question, didn't she? What am I supposed to do, pretend I've got a couple of vegetables in my ear? I've certainly got enough of them sitting round me."

He poured himself a glass of champagne from the half-full bottle on his right. If the table had been silent before, it was now developing the atmosphere of a morgue on a summer break.

"You ought to hold your tongue, new boy," the green-suited clerk said, having appeared behind him from somewhere. "It isn't wise to get excited at the company meal. People rarely forget those kind of indiscretions."

Morda moved his chair back over one of the elderly clerk's featureless shoes and leant back with all his weight.

"You can obviously keep your mouth shut when you need to," he said, as he got up. He left the injured man holding his foot in some discomfort, and moved towards the door. The cool night air was the kind of fifth course he most needed to round off the evening. He let go of the door forcefully behind him as he left, but it slid quietly shut on discreet hinges.

"Why didn't you tell me about it before?"

"Because I knew you'd react the way you're reacting now."

"If you're being harassed at work, then you should tell Lady Challis. She'd have the man sacked as soon as you told her." Morda looked up at the tram conductor.

"Two to Barnet, please. Nuneaton House, if you could tell us when that is." The conductor nodded.

"I suppose it's your first one," he said, looking over at Provlyn. "I sired two at Harrow, up near the ladies' school. They'd both be siring themselves now, I suppose. Got killed in the war at Manchester in 1917." His expression changed at the memory. He handed them the change and went upstairs.

Provlyn had not been in to work for seven days, and, what was worse, he had not phoned in sick for the last three of them. He had only told Morda the periphery of events involving Dorjess, but the reaction had been no less hostile.

"It has taken me nearly nine months to build up the kind of reputation at Parkside that makes them feel they can trust me. How can I prove what Dorjess has done without destroying all of that? He's been there for ten years."

"What use is your reputation if you're never going to be able to use it?"

Morda watched the city thinning out as they reached Hendon.

Although the electric tram wires dangled on each side of the road overhead, the pavements were deserted. The flat expanse behind each side of the road was quite marked in contrast to the busy housing estates that they had passed just a few minutes earlier. The tram gathered speed, passing several unattended stops in the High Street.

"I only told you because I thought you might want to help me. You don't really understand what being in service involves. It's about discretion, about not being seen..."

"Don't you think you've taken that part of it a bit literally?"

"Let's not talk about it until we've been to the Trial. I can ring them later tonight and work something out then."

Nuneaton House was, in fact, a group of buildings in the centre of Barnet, surrounded by a few shops selling essential foodstuffs. The tram took them right into the centre of the complex, and dropped them off along with two slightly older looking couples who went on ahead, with the confidence of what was clearly their second or third visit. If couples wanted to sire more than two children, they were subjected to a lengthy bureaucratic vetting, which involved signing a commitment to a relationship with their partners for life; anyone who signed that kind of commitment usually deserved what they got.

Morda and Provlyn soon found their way to Block Three, a smaller building than its counterparts, not unlike a hospital. The sound of children playing could be heard, coming from behind the many walkway walls they passed. Morda wondered how many couples had made the journey to his Siring School; how many had held his filesheet before handing it back to the official for another choice.

He had only learned of the siring process at his Boarding School through its grapevine. Rumours abounded that they were all there because after eighteen months they were still not properly potty-trained. Some said they all had blood diseases that would kill them before they were twenty; others that they were less intelligent than those who had been taken for siring. It was only in the last month of their programme of study, *The World Of Work,* that they had realised they were just the unlucky ones. *'You could say that the independence you've had is a kind of privilege,'* one teacher had said, but thirteen years of polite refusals and correcting people at interviews had suggested otherwise. If he had not been injured in the army or met Harvil, he might have ended up in service. Not the luxury of 47 Parkside, but in one of those appalling hotels in Baker Street or Piccadilly, neck cricked in a permanently fawning bow, feet shuffling silently up and down stairs, clearing out other people's filth.

A young female doctor met them at the Enquiries Desk, and, after clearance, gave them two security badges and led them off back out into the fading five o'clock sunlight.

"It's not really the best time to look round," she said, leading them under an archway into a small courtyard. The square of grass in front of them was immaculately kept, and looked as though it had been recently trimmed with a pair of nail scissors. It was not unlike a picture he had seen at school of one of the Women's University colleges. The complex itself was quite busy, even at the end of the working day, with women in white overcoats or dark suits moving officiously past them in all directions. It was the only occasion in his life when he had seen women outnumber men, other than at a republican demonstration he had attended with Harvil, when the police had gathered in some force.

"First of all, I'm going to take you to the Rearing Clinic Building, where they raise children up to sixteen months, until they are ready for siring."

They were taken past another reception desk, where the volume of children crying, laughing and making other odd noises blew out forcefully. Provlyn had taken Morda's arm and had gone rather quiet.

The open door of the first room they passed, gave them visual access to a female nurse, who was holding a baby of eight months up by its ankles, and slapping it forcefully across its behind. Below them on the carpet was the offending substance.

"Number eighty-seven b," the nurse said, looking at it angrily. "It's the third time today the beast has wet himself." She smiled at Morda and Provlyn. "You want to be glad you don't have to do this," she said. The doctor hurried them on their way. Up ahead, they were taken into the Analysis Room. Another doctor was seated at a small white table alongside shelves of jars and tubes filled with liquids and tiny shapes. When they entered she stood up to receive them.

"This is the room where we work on every kind of disease currently known, from the killers like tuberculosis, to mild infections which people can carry and not even be aware of. In the Other Age, people risked infection from millions of different viruses, most of them floating freely in the air, so if you were in the wrong place at the wrong time, you caught them. Today, there are only seventeen recognised diseases that can kill, thanks to a controlled population and the many diseases that finally died along with their sufferers nearly four hundred years ago. It's our job in the Analysis Department to inoculate the new sirelings against as many of these diseases as we can in the sixteen months they spend here with us. We still find prevention is more laudable than having to worry about a cure," she said, looking around the room. "Your child, for example, whoever you end up siring, will come with a full sixteen month inoculation record, and you'll be required to bring him back every six months for tests until he reaches school age.

"What happens to those who don't get sired?"

The doctor looked confused.

"Why should that be of any interest to you?"

There was an underlying tone of invective in her voice. Morda pointed to the name tag on his security badge.

"I see. Well, they are all sent to a Siring School in Crystal Palace with facilities for pre-five education, and, of course, they are still offered on a rolling programme of Infant Siring. But our rate is very good at the School. It was ninety-eight per cent, last year." She gave a wide, spurious smile, which Morda did not return. She pressed a button on her desk and the doctor who had brought them in returned.

"We inherited the largest National Sperm Bank in the world, from the Other Age," she continued, as they stepped out into the open air again. "It is the strongest link we have with those times, as far as I know. As I am sure you are aware, every girl at each Siring Institution feeder school undertakes a conscriptive pregnancy in her third year, and, if she's strong enough, one in the fourth year as well. With a hundred girls in each academic year, we can have up to one hundred and fifty potential sirelings in this building alone, every year. So we offer west London couples, such as yourselves, over a hundred different boys to choose from, each with their own personalised set of medical records. Each set of controlled pregnancies, anywhere in this country, is currently required by law to be 5% female, so we have a smaller operation here which produces females, in conjunction with the other London Siring Institutions, for the five Outer Borough Populite Academies."

"The Other Age," Morda said. "If they could only see us now."

"Yes," said the doctor. But she wasn't quite sure what he meant.

"It's much more sophisticated that I would have thought," Provlyn said. "It gives you a feeling of national confidence to know things are this well organised at the grass roots of our lives."

Morda looked at him in disbelief. It wasn't something that he would have been able to say with any confidence.

They finally entered a four-storey building, the tallest and largest in the Siring Complex. Mounting stairs to the first floor, they passed a series of wards, each given up to boys born up to within three months of each other. It wasn't particularly different from the picture their neighbour Lorkoz from the Mews had given them from his own visits four and a half years ago. He was still involved in a legal wrangle with the authorities for custody of his sireling, since the death of his partner, though he had only been the First Friend. He was also the only person Morda had known for ten years to have been run over by a car, and a Ford Model T at that!

"Here are the sixteen to eighteen monthers," the doctor said. "They all have badges on their jumpsuits to show which number they are, though you might want to see if you can guess which one's yours from a distance." She consulted her notebook. "According to my chart, I think you're after number 107." She made a gesture of invitation to the ward with an open palm. "I'll be back in about twenty minutes, but in the meantime feel free to browse!" She let herself out of the children's section of the ward by unfastening the four foot high wooden gate behind them. They were alone now in the pen with the children. Provlyn counted. There were around thirty of them, though he couldn't be completely sure because the majority were running round the room, twisting and changing direction every minute.

"There's twelve shillings a week Toll Tax subsidy for fathers and four and sixpence for First Friends," Morda said, reading the leaflet *Siring Into The Next Century.* Getting no response, he turned to see Provlyn on all fours, playing *dribble on my face* with one of the less mobile sirelings. It was a disturbingly powerful experience, Morda felt, being in a room with so many children, possibly because it triggered some subconscious remembrance. He was conscious of the situation being somehow incomplete.

"There's your young man," he said, pointing to the corner of the pen.

A tiny dark-haired child stood in the corner, steadied by the wooden rail he was clutching. Morda was pleased to see that he was alone, not joining in the various improvised games going on in the centre of the pen. He also thought he saw a damp patch on the lower half of his blue jumpsuit. His thoughts turned to the spanking nurse.

Provlyn walked over to the boy and picked him up. He watched Morda from his new vantage point. His eyes were a deep brown, his skin not quite as dark as it had looked on the filesheet. He was a little lighter than Provlyn.

"He's *our* young man," Provlyn said. This, then, their pledge of fidelity. Morda took the child in his arms. He fitted quite nicely.

"Will you mind not being the father?"

"Not really," Morda said. "It was just a moment of selfishness. Like I said, I want you to be happy. Be happy and feel safe. The boy might steady things for us, providing you can sort out the job."

"I spoke to Lorkoz. He said he could look after it during the day if there were any problems. I might take him up on that." He moved across and took the boy's hand. Bloated little matchstick fingers clutched tight into a fist. He drew open the palm by pushing his finger into the boy's fist. Out dropped a coin, rolling onto the wooden floor to a halt. It was half a crown.

"How did he get hold of that?" Morda picked up the coin. "Shows the boy's got an eye for money, even though he isn't yet two."

The doctor came back to the ward, carrying a set of forms on a Siring School clipboard. She seemed quite pleased with what she saw.

"Well, it looks as though you three are a comfortable little group. Sign here, please. You're allocated a two week period to make sure it's what you want, and then you can come and pick him up. You can have a look at his records," she said, moving to the cupboard behind the pen. They signed the sheet, the ink smudging slightly with the dribble Provlyn still had on the back of his hand.

"I've also got a more up-to-date photo of him that was taken last week."

Provlyn took the documents. The photograph was sepia, on a hard cardboard backing. The boy looked unhappy and restless in it, but it didn't seem to bother Morda. They shook hands with the doctor and let themselves out of the pen. Although the boy had not really minded being picked up, he was obviously relieved to be allowed back to his corner again. He wasted no time in scuttling back there.

"I think I'd like to call him Harvil," Provlyn suggested, once they were outside. "What do you think?"

"Maybe," Morda said. He was wondering if any of the children they had seen that day would miss out on being sired. The one who had wet himself, perhaps.

"Lady Challis will see you now, Mr. Ranshell." It was the first time Provlyn had heard his patronym used at *Parkside*, since his interview there. Perhaps that, in itself, was of some significance.

There was a sombre quiet about the house that morning, even though it was a Monday. Everywhere around the house there was order and the sense of recent attention, but there were no footmen or clerks to be seen.

"I've given them the day off," she explained. "Now when you telephoned late last Friday, I was, naturally, delighted to hear that you were well, and that you had recovered from your influenza, but we were a little concerned about the fact that you had not communicated with us for three days."

Who is this *we*, Provlyn was thinking. She is the sole owner of the house. He found his head bowed rather lower than was usual in the company of women.

"There is also the matter of your contract. Everybody else signed theirs over a week ago. Don't you like working here?"

"You've been very kind to me," he said. It was a line he seemed to have been using quite a lot recently.

"You live in Hammersmith, don't you?" she continued. "Dorjess was telling me last week when you were away. He said you weren't sure about your contract; something about not being able to commit yourself. *Do* you have any plans?"

Could he tell her about his plans to castrate Dorjess, to acupuncture each of his testicles until they looked like pin cushions? He would have told her everything; the first scene in the bedroom and how Dorjess had forced himself on him later that afternoon. How he had made himself late for his second Siring appointment - risked losing his son - so he could go home and wash the filth from his body. But the revelation of the merest detail would involve Morda. Even he did not know what Morda might have to hide from someone as powerful as Serboth Challis.

"I am happy to work for you at the lower rate of salary," he said.

"I value your work, Provlyn. In the time you've been here you've proved yourself reliable, invariably punctual and well-presented. Many of my visitors have commented on how difficult they have found getting reliable service staff, such as yourself. Now was there any truth in what Dorjess told me?"

"I would never presume, on a working day here, to air any doubts I may have about my future, and with the greatest of respect to you, any conversations I may be forced to have with Dorjess will be restricted to whatever he feels he needs to ask me."

"He was concerned about your illness last week. We all were."

"I can assure you that it will not be repeated in the rest of my time here. I won't let something like that keep me away from work again," he said.

"Very well. Perhaps you'll let my doctor see you here next time. And please be ready to discuss anything that might affect your employment here as soon as it occurs. I might be able to help you." She shook his hand and handed him a small envelope. "From last week," she added.

He opened the packet in the cloakroom downstairs. *Three pounds!* They had given him the rise due for all those who had signed contracts. It could have been a mistake, it could even be blackmail to be exercised in weeks to come when the 'mistake' was realised and he was not in a position to pay it all back. He discounted both theories fairly swiftly. Serboth Challis was a little imperious with the staff on occasions, but had always been kind to him, introducing him to all the new political faces appearing at *Parkside* as well as making sure he took home a sizeable quantity of whatever surplus food there was in the house. Morda had often accused him of viewing everyone through tinted glasses, but he felt a confidence about the sincerity of her kindness. He needed to feel equally adamant about letting Dorjess know, at the first opportunity, that he no longer feared him. It was unfortunate that he would have to wait another day to see how well he would rise to this self-imposed challenge.

The isolation involved in the accurate accountancy *Palby's* required from their employees had been, in the last few days, a welcome relief to Morda. It was only at lunch-time and on the two occasions he left his office for the washroom that he was allowed to focus on the change of attitude his colleagues were now showing him. The Bloomsbury café, with its small turnover of visiting city workers, must have felt the drop in sales from Palby House. The sandwich man had cut the number of his display items by half, aware now that the majority were destined for the six o'clock dustbin.

Pridge was the only one who was still prepared to greet him in the morning, if their paths crossed, but even he would turn his head if there were others on the corridor. The most fascinating aspect of their 'blanking' him, as far as Morda was concerned, was how they had ever found the time to meet each other to arrange it! He enjoyed his new status of *rebel clerk*, sure that he would soon use it to the detriment of the company workforce.

He sat in his office, completing his Toll Tax return form. He had completed the summer debenture inventory at half past three, so a little time spent on his own administration was not unjustified. The form was proving as unpopular with those he'd discussed it with, as the tax itself. Once completed, it would provide whoever had access to it with the best part of your life's circumstances: your siring history, medical records file number, the number of sexual partners you'd lived with in the last ten years *(What use could that be?)*, your salary and the number of contracts you were bound by. It was quite fashionable to sign all manner of agreements about your home, partner, politics or whatever, to secure more pay or better living conditions. Some of the more unofficial organisations offered handsome payments in return for what amounted to offering your body as a receptacle for foreign diplomats' semen. He remembered two of Harvil's friends who had apparently signed it. He would have to list the siring registration forms they had signed. It might provide someone with a hold to exercise over him. He signed the base of the form and put it carefully inside his pocket. He would be leaving earlier than was usual, but he had completed all of the work he had been set. There was nothing else to do.

As the Metropolitan line train drew into Wood Lane station, Morda looked behind him over the bridge. It must have happened during the weekend. The Caricott Building was gone. He alighted from the train, though he was still one stop from home, and left the station. Outside, the change was not readily detectable, but he decided to walk to the green to take a closer look.

It was still quite early, and few people were about. He walked to the top of Wood Lane and turned into the Uxbridge Road. Shepherds Bush Green itself looked a lot larger than it had when he had last been there. A section of flats on the far side towards Hammersmith must have been pulled down. No turf had been laid yet, but several carriages were parked where the road had been.

He continued until he reached the Central line station. And next to it...? It was the first time he had witnessed such a dramatic change to an area over such a short time. The building was gone, and in its place, a small section of concrete had been laid, with a cobble-stoned courtyard. Two local shops, a newsagent's and a greengrocer's had already been erected where the front of the building had been. All those rooms - all that space - and now, just two shops. He crossed the road to the courtyard and listened. A distant train. Towards the wall of the old motorway, a large section of rubble and concrete lay, half broken-up, some of it proving to be the lower section of one of the pillars of the building. Unaccountably drawn to it, he began to examine the broken stone, kicking at its knobbled edges with his foot. It had probably been laid four hundred years ago when lorries of concrete were arriving to provide the foundations for the Caricott Building. The Other Age. Before. And now no purpose could be found for them.

He climbed over the first section of stone, crossing to something he had seen by the motorway wall. Peeping out from a large piece of broken concrete, was a tiny piece of denim fabric, pinched into a corner of blue, that had caught his eye. He pulled at it, but whatever it was attached to was set within this huge misshapen lump of stone. He stood still for a moment, looking towards a carriage set up on bricks a few hundred yards across the new courtyard. He climbed back over the wall and approached it slowly. He knocked at the rear, but there was no response. He tried the handle gently before kicking at the base of the flimsy door. The handle and lock came away in his hand, like balsa wood. Pleased at his success, he moved inside. As he had hoped, there were many demolition instruments within; a range of stone mallets, three large mattocks and several rock breakers, none of which he could lift. He satisfied himself with the middle mattock and left the carriage, pushing the door to as best he could.

He had to throw the mattock over the wall before he could climb over successfully, but he soon found his way back to the broken stone. As he pushed at it with the mattock, he wondered for a moment.

What did he hope to find there? An old pair of jeans? He looked over the motorway wall towards the city, through the dust he had raised, climbing amongst the broken concrete. Taking the handle of the mattock in his hands he swung it high behind him, and brought the head down a foot or so away from the lip of denim. Again and again he did this, but the only result was a tired arm and a few loose crumbs of flaking, dusty concrete. He looked round at the temporary wall of concrete behind him. If he could push the stone round and over the wall, it might break up on the concrete below. He would only have one chance. If it remained whole after the fall, he would never lift it back up. Putting the mattock down, he crouched behind the stone, raising himself in one movement to throw all his weight at it. It budged gently at the first few pushes, but he could feel a moment of give ahead. Standing back, he threw himself at it once more, and leaning forward, it lopped at the edge of the wall and dropped, bouncing slightly before it came to rest a few feet away. He climbed anxiously over, wiping the dust from his eyes as he landed.

At first it seemed as though the stone had survived the fall, but when he moved up behind it, he saw the front end had broken away, revealing the denim to be part of a large school satchel. After making its exit slightly larger with a few solid blows, he pulled the bag out. The flap of the satchel was covered by a section of floral material, all hand-stitched, the elegance of which could still be seen under its grubby appearance. He could feel his heart race as he pulled at the flap. The inner section was filled with ring-binders, different-sized boxes and all manner of odd paraphernalia. But he couldn't look at it here; he would have to get it home somehow. He must take it home through the back streets. Becoming aware of his surroundings again, he noticed how wet he was from his efforts. His suit was still dirty, in spite of his attempts to dust himself down. He pulled the heavy satchel over his arm and moved swiftly round the front of the shops to the Green. As he crossed the road, something fell from the bundle he was carrying. He moved back to pick it up and crossing hurriedly to the other side of the road, broke into a run. Had he been seen?

He turned into the first back street he came to and looked down at whatever it was that he had dropped. It looked like the front section of the binder in the satchel, and he observed, with growing interest, the inscription on it.

Dovedale Secondary School, Domesday Project, 1980.

International Women's Day

Provlyn lay awake, as he had done for most of the night. Morda had always been a little furtive, but it was usually attributable to a recent or forthcoming event. Now it was just baffling, and the presence of Lorkoz downstairs had made him even more withdrawn.

They had invited him for a meal to discuss what arrangements for care they could make after they had collected the boy from the Siring School next Friday, but judging by his expression when he returned, Morda had obviously forgotten. He had been covered in a thin powdery dust, *'I went to look at some rebuilding they've been doing in the City'*, his only genuine suit, the one that had cost him almost a month's wages, caked with concrete powder. And half an hour cleaning it - *in the cellar?*

Once they had put the six year old, Hadanna, to bed in the spare room, Lorkoz had revealed the true extent of his own problems. Five months after the death of his partner, he had finally been forced to give up his job with a demolition company, even though his son was now going to a local school, because they were not prepared to give him shorter hours. Provlyn had declared himself quite happy to give him thirty shillings a week, half of the higher wages he was now getting, in return for looking after their sireling. By the time the evening was over it was past Curfew, and Lorkoz was still there. The arrangement had not pleased Morda at all, though he had kept his feelings from Lorkoz. They had not even been able to discuss it because of the risk of waking Hadanna.

At least Morda could sleep. His suit hung in the bedroom doorway, stained patches of wetness in evidence around the arm and pocket areas. Provlyn knew that in a month's time they would have been together for exactly five years. A few weeks beyond this would signal Morda's entry into uncharted waters - he had made quite an issue of his relationship with Harvil lasting five years and three days. *'He told me he'd just wanted to see us properly through the full five years'.* Perhaps that was where Provlyn had got the superstition from.

International Women's Day! The headline covered three-quarters of the Saturday front page of The Informer. Morda crunched his way through a piece of burnt toast. The paper had compiled its own list of *'Women Of The Year'*, with the sub-header So Far. They were all there: Queen Edwina VII, Herben Asquith, Ethel Smyth - who had written some opera, Andrea Carnegie - a campaigner for world peace (World communication would have been more ambitious) and several others, including Serboth Challis.

"It could be worse," Lorkoz said. He was cleaning his son's face, spitting gobbets onto a grey-looking handkerchief and fingering away corners of grubbiness with pokes of his cottoned finger. Provlyn was trying to hurry him up so they could all leave together, but Morda was decidedly sluggish, sipping at his tea as if through ulcer-lined lips. He was resigned, eventually, to a solitary departure, leaving the house at a quarter to seven. Within five minutes, Morda was fully dressed and at the door.

"Let yourself out when you're ready," he told them. "There's no rush."

He closed the door behind him and marched off swiftly to the station. Tucked in his inside pocket were a bundle of papers that he had grabbed from the denim satchel after Provlyn had gone. The need for the irritating subterfuge had at least given him the chance to look at some of the documents alone before he got into work. He might yet decide that no-one else should see them, and he would then have to make sure he was back first that evening. The fact that he was not free in the afternoon was another irritating aspect of *International Women's Day* - men were asked to work a full day to free their bosses or seniors, who were usually busy taking stock of the week's activities, for celebrations. Even time and a half failed to soothe the sting Morda always felt from this annual tradition.

The early morning wind whipped up the Grove through the trees, causing Morda to button his jacket. Most of yesterday's dust stains seemed to be fading. He began pondering just how a seventy-one year old school project could have become embedded in a piece of concrete nearly four hundred years old. They might have built an extension to the Caricott Building then, or set something new in stone, highly unlikely though the possibilities were.

As he reached the top of the road he studied the government hoarding 'A paid Toll Tax return gives you your free democratic rights', under which someone had scribbled 'Fight for your democratic right to pay Fuck All', though a hose-wielding council worker was already jetting out the offensive addendum with some high-powered chemical solution.

He decided to sit in one of the Populite carriages, an act permissible only in the rush hour when the other carriages were full, but the rule was still new enough to excuse a liberal interpretation, if he were questioned.

The train stood in the station for some time, and it was only when Morda got up to see what was causing the delay that it began to move off. He sat down again with his back to the door leading to the carriage behind, and finally unbuttoned his jacket. The surrounding folder was of a light blue card, with a child's crayoned drawing of a group of his classmates, headed *Domesday 1980*. On the inside cover, his name, Sharon Lewis. Morda read the introduction.

'Hello from all of us at Dovedale Secondary School in 1980. You are from the future, which means someone must be knocking down the Caricott Building, because that is where we're going to be putting this when we finish it. Lots of schools in our country are writing one of these, so our teacher Mr.Evans thought we should do one.' Morda looked over his shoulder. A few bored looking people in the next carriage. No-one was interested. They probably wouldn't even care if they knew what he was reading.

'We hope you can understand what we're writing. You might speak and spell differently. We are all thirteen and fourteen, apart from Mr.Evans who is thirty-one! We hope we have put the kind of things in here that will interest you, but again, things might change a bit, and we don't know how.' He went to turn the page and a coloured photograph fell out. Like the paper, it was yellowing slightly, but it was the first tangible set of differences he had noticed. The children were all Caucasians, like himself. But more unusual, and a little unbelievable - he had to hold

the picture steady - some of them were young women... some of them were girls!

He instinctively thrust the photograph back into the folder and inside his jacket. *What on earth had he got hold of?*

He stood up and moved to one side of the carriage doors, his head pounding. Twenty past seven. He hadn't enough time to go back - he would have to take it into work - carry it round with him all day, he couldn't leave it anywhere. It would make an activist pamphlet look like a children's fairy story. The train drew into a station. Portland Road. His mind was racing. Was this some radical school run in the early twentieth century, or was this a *different* 1980? If the Caricott Building had been built in the Other Age, it was at least four-hundred years old. That would mean it had been built around 2309, so what was all this *1980* business?

His attention was drawn to a notice in the carriage; it was one he had not seen before, but it bore the standard Government bold black lettering, printed on a gold background, like the one he'd seen in The Grove. This one read, *'Warning - All Toll Tax forms should be returned by April 30th. From May 30th 1909 in the United Kingdom it will be mandatory to carry evidence of your Toll Tax Number with you at all times. Failure to do so could result in a fine of up to £50.'* He should have seen such a notice before, but he hadn't. Only now, by chance in a Populite carriage, had it come to his attention. He had already submitted the forms over a week ago, but they had as yet received no reply. He looked at the notice again to see if he had misread it, but the words seemed to harden, their significance lying within their businesslike appearance like a venus fly-trap.

The journey was taking on an unreal quality. The insecurity he had eschewed through a lifetime of gentle conforming and hard faith was returning as the train gathered speed. He looked around; no-one. So much was changing and yet there were so few people watching. No-one could ever be safe from potential harassment on the streets when this new clause became law. Anyone could be stopped, their number demanded, and, consequently, their details. It wasn't an aspect of the new Tax Law that Morda had ever been aware of during its media inception. And how many other people were still unaware of the consequences of this new power vested in the authorities? He gritted his teeth and took a firm hold of the package he held under the front of his jacket.

It was now two weeks since the beginning of his 'illness', but Provlyn was still being careful in his movements around *Parkside*. He hadn't anticipated any need to sort the problem out yet. Lady Challis had another At-home, and the house would be very busy in the next few hours.

He had remained downstairs after an overly-swift cleaning of the clerk's rooms. He later helped the greengrocer unload the week's produce in the yard at the side of the house, before helping Chatwick unfurl the *Venus* flag from the pulley in the loft. A newspaper photographer turned up just before lunch to take a picture of the women, almost certainly destined for one of the following morning's front pages. He wasn't as keen as Morda to question the significance of an International Women's Day, nor did it matter to him that there didn't seem to be an International Day for men. He was happy to live in a free country that, now the problem with looking after his son had been sorted out, paid him enough money and gave him enough free time to enjoy his life. He would, however, have to wait until the end of the week to find out whether or not his last week's pay packet had been a one-off bonus incentive or a genuinely unexpected increase.

Amongst Lady Challis's guests that morning were some of the more successful businesswomen of the year, including two teams of four from the top new financial houses, *Bannister's* and *Palby's*, something that would no doubt interest Morda. He would make a note of their names from the dining plan later in the afternoon when they'd gone.

Just before lunch he was given the task of sorting out the wine in the second larder and the cellar into years and makes and copying them up into a new black plastic copybook that Chatwick had bought the previous weekend. A trip down to the cellar with what he was told was the only key and one back to the second larder made it clear this was a job that would take a good two hours, so he decided in favour of a late lunch.

There were Rosés and Medocs, Clarets and Burgundies, Hocks and Moselles, Bordeaux and Beaujolais; some that should have been consumed thirty years ago, some that were still at their best. Not that any expertise was expected of Provlyn. He had merely been asked to list the stock and ensure before he finished that everything was put in the cellar, the whites in the lower racks, the reds in the uppers. It was one of those once-a-year jobs in the House that carried an in-built pleasure because of their novelty. He had been invited to take two bottles home but not to drink anything until he had checked it with Chatwick, who knew about wine. Provlyn was fairly sure that his relationship with it fell short of Dorjess' expertise. At falling foul of it, in any case.

As he began listing the headings under which the different wines would be divided, he thought about the boy, and about becoming a father so young. He could never replace his own father, but by becoming a father himself he would somehow renew the cycle, replenish the turning where it had stopped. His father would have been pleased he had a job and was earning money. Part of the reason he was determined to work so hard at keeping the job was because he knew how his father would have felt. It encouraged him. It inspired him.

He had left his home town as a fifteen year old after his father's death. He had left it to go and live with a twenty-four year old man in London. What would his father have made of that?

As a boy, he and his father had lived in a small flat in Manchester for all the early years he could remember, before that day at school when his House Tutor had told him the news. His father dead. Not even forty. Killed on an exercise; not even killed by an enemy. A stupid way to go. Almost as stupid and quick as the way he had gone three evenings later at the Peacetime Dance. Just a few weeks after his father's warning about the lure of the city and what older men might promise him; *'A standing prick has no conscience, Provlyn - you'll only make promises you can't keep, or you'll keep them and be sorry.'* But was this sorrow?

There was a creak on the cellar stairs behind him, and he looked up.

"Looks like paradise," the voice said, at the top of the stairs. "I've wanted the key to this place for many years. I thought they might have thrown it away, but they obviously haven't." The voice moved down into the dim light of the cellar.

"Chatwick! I thought you'd gone to lunch."

"I was going to, but Lady Challis told me you were working down in the cellar, so I thought I'd join you." He took out a small tin of lettuce and tomato sandwiches and a few savoury biscuits.

If Provlyn had been capable of suspicion, he might have hunted for an excuse to take lunch elsewhere. As it was, he continued looking through the rack of bottles behind him.

"This one looks reasonably new."

"A french claret... *1911*. Yes, that will do nicely."

Two bottles and eight sandwiches later, the conversation was ripening.

"I signed my contract last Monday," Chatwick said. "It's made a pleasant enough difference to my pay packet. I went to the theatre last weekend. The first time for nearly five years. You ought to get round to it, you know."

"I don't like the theatre."

"I meant your contract."

Provlyn looked at him wistfully. It seemed a genuine enough piece of advice.

"I can't sign, Chatwick. He'd be ten before I could get out of it. Can't you see how terrible it would be if I suddenly changed my mind?"

"Who would be ten?"

Provlyn felt light-headed, stripped of the self-imposed restraint he wore as part of his uniform at *Parkside*.

"My friend and I went to a Siring Trial last week." The child's podgy face stared suspiciously at him again from the corner of the pen. "He is sixteen and a half months old. Black hair, dark skin, with this evil stare - you would have signed for him if you had been there."

Provlyn leaned back and knocked over the bottle of wine behind him. Chatwick moved round him swiftly, mopping up the spillage with a cloth he carried under his jacket. His glass of wine had barely been touched.

"You never told me about your friend," Chatwick said.

"He signed our contract," Provlyn said. "That's why I can't sign this one. I've spoken to Lady Challis about it and she understands. She's been as kind to me as you have. I'm very grateful for that."

He turned back to the first rack on his hands and knees, looking for the pencil he had been writing with. When he had written *Claret* on a new page, he turned round. The wall was starting to slide; he steadied himself. Where Chatwick had been, there was an empty tin, and when he looked up the stairs, it was a very different face that looked back down at him, smiling this time, the hand steadily holding a full glass of claret.

Morda had waited two frustrating hours, visiting the washrooms twice before satisfying himself that the two offices next to his, housing clerks thirteen and fourteen, were going to be to the best of his knowledge empty for the day. Not everyone, apparently, had to work today. Fighting through the morning's paperwork, the financial accounting behind the destruction of four major office blocks in Knightsbridge, he had cleared a half hour gap before lunch, two debenture books balanced on an elaborate high rise stand of empty inkwells he had found in his cupboard. Under these he had arranged a spread of the next few sheets from the blue folder. He had turned the photograph face down, unable to look again at the mixed gathering of innocent faces. The sheets on his desk carried the three titles: *What I do at the Weekend*, *Where we Live* and *What's Happening In 1980*.

Working through the first, he began to think the package might not be so sinister after all. The author of the extract did a paper round, watched television, played football at the park and went down to Hammersmith with his friends. It wasn't any different from what boys his age had probably done seventy-one years ago. Even today, the only difference was the television. Once the authorities had stopped broadcasting in 1949, people had soon realised that no matter how much electricity they pumped into them, they would never again show a picture. Harvil had once said that they were still broadcasting programmes, but on a frequency out of the reach of ordinary televisions. It was an interesting rumour, but had probably only survived as long as it had because no-one was in a position to prove or disprove it. The boy writing the extract had, it seemed, spent most of his life watching television. Had he lived in 1909, he would have probably been an avid reader of *The Informer*.

Hammersmith hadn't changed a great deal either according to the coloured map two of the children had put together. The Palais was still the central dancing venue in the area, Ravenscourt Park was in the same position, if a little smaller, and the tube lines ran to the same stations. Why were there girls in that picture? He turned it over slowly. Could the activists have organised such a school? The Republican activists weren't formed until the first Order Controls in the forties. Civil strife only occurred in the declining years of the technological era. It was a picture out of time. Genuinely innocent smiles. He looked at the last sheet in front of him. *What's Happening in 1980*. It was evident that this was not a project cobbled together over a few weeks: each sheet looked as though it had been redrafted several times, and the sheets themselves all had the authentic smell and appearance of historical documents. He remembered the tacky souvenirs bought from France that he had in his dormitory at school, a mock ancient version of *La Populite*, the historical agreement signed in Paris in 2300 by the Fifteen Nations, supposedly the document that had instituted Western Civilisation. These simple sheets of school lined paper had the same tinted edges, the difference being that they were flaking at each edge; if he rubbed the corners between his thumb and forefinger, he could eventually wear them down to a light yellow powder.

The Conservative Party were in power - more likely than not. *John Lennon shot dead;* he was a *Beatle?* A strange name to give an opposition party. The top film was *Flash Gordon;* the margin illustration a graphic portrayal of a muscular blond man. The rest of it was just more names and events. Under a sub-heading, *Our Fear*, the extract became suddenly arresting.

'We have been told recently about our government's decision to invest £5000 million on a new nuclear weapon, the Trident missile, which will replace the Polaris system in our country in ten years. We know our government is spending billions of pounds on Defence, to arm itself against attack by countries from the East. It is a frightening time for all of us, to know that people might use these weapons in our lifetime. We only hope that they never will.'

Morda held his hand over his mouth. It was from the Other World, the previous world. Before the Great Rains, the Death Age, the Corbic Revolution... it had to be over *four hundred years old*. His first feelings had been correct.

He took the photograph in his hand and screwed it up, the cardboard backing crumbling in his hands; he tore it and ground it to a pile of dust, tears in his eyes. He tried to keep the thoughts away from his head, but they crept up on him like all the killer diseases the world had ever known.

What? Who? Why? When? How?

He took his handkerchief to his eyes. More than anything he felt fear. What information would he find in the rest of the folder? How would the finding of it come to affect his life? He swept the dust from the photograph onto a piece of card and put it in a small envelope which he put away in his jacket pocket. He combed his hair in the mirror he kept in the top drawer of the filing cabinet, and returned the inkwells to his stationery tray. He looked at his watch; there were only twenty minutes left of his lunch hour, but if he moved quickly to the café, he could dispose of the evidence. He would have to. All of it. Down the lavatory. He might as well go home on the train carrying a sub-machine gun in a plastic bag as have those sheets on him. As he moved his chair back to get up, he heard footsteps coming towards his end of the corridor. It was a dead end, and the other two clerks were out. Whoever it was could only be in the building to visit him. He busied himself in one of the Accounts books.

"Hello," a voice said. "Bit over-zealous aren't you, working during the lunch hour?"

He was ill-prepared for another shock, but it came, along with a paralysing speechlessness. The voice went on.

"I had been meaning to come in last week, but I thought I'd do it today, once I knew I could get a few of the more reactionary of the staff out. I wanted to apologise to you for the embarrassment you must have suffered at the meal the other night."

He could feel the grains of the photograph dust in the sweat of his closed palms. It was like sand.

"I was part of the committee that thought up the idea of a little business integration for a change; I don't think any of us were aware of the friction it would cause."

"I can sympathise," he said. "With the men, that is. The only time most of them see a woman is when she is in the building to check that they're doing their job properly; in the newspaper justifying some new radical political measure; in a black and silver uniform ready to arrest them for breaking Curfew, or in some Law or Employment Office showing them what forms they have to fill out. I suppose they might have felt it was a little hypocritical for them to suddenly want to show a bit of solidarity."

He wiped his hands on his thighs. Rocassa Milo nodded; she was still standing in front of the filing cabinet opposite him; it looked as though she was taking stock of the surroundings to convey the feel later to an Estate Agent. She pulled the top drawer out, and then pushed it back in.

"Do you know what day it is today, Morda?"

"International Women's Day, I believe," he said, guardedly. It was increasingly unsettling, having her wander round the office, not knowing why she was there. Added to which the bundle of sheets in the folder was slowly making him feel like he was carrying an anvil in his inside pocket.

"I have a ticket for Diaghilev's *Ballets Russes* at the Royal Opera House in Covent Garden this evening, and you struck me as the sort of person who might enjoy a cultural night out." She took a blue-edged ticket from her bag and placed it on the corner of his desk.

The only knowledge Morda had acquired about Opera Houses

was a suspicion that it had been Harvil's branch of the Republican Activists who had bombed the Kensington Opera Palace in 1915, though he had denied it at the time. Like all other types of music, if you could get around to seeing a concert or going to a dance, you'd have some music. If not, you wouldn't.

"I'll offer it to Pridge if you're not interested."

"Leave me the ticket," Morda said. "What time does it finish?"

"Ten forty-five. You can get a Curfew pass from the Box Office before the performance if you show the ticket."

She left, and then put her head back round the door. "I meant to add. It's a Royal Performance, especially for International Women's Day. The Queen will be there." She shut the door, her clicking steps moving to the stairs and then disappearing into carpet.

Morda coughed and cleared his throat, spitting the residue into his handkerchief. It was the only substance her appearance had seemed likely to prompt from him that afternoon. All his feelings seemed to have numbed and then hardened. What was he going to do with a ticket for the Ballet? He almost felt like telling Pridge. It might go some way to settling their recent differences.

"Here, let me help you up," Chatwick was saying, but the room was still spinning. He clutched at the table, forcing himself round to the chair. As he lowered himself down, he had the sensation that he was bleeding; he could feel a warm stickiness around his inner thighs. Chatwick passed him a cigarette which he parked on the edge of his lower lip.

"You must have fallen quite badly." A cold cloth was pressed to his temple. Something awful had happened to him, something unspeakable. It had something to do with the taste in his mouth, the bitter aftertaste. He sat up in the chair and tried to speak, but a horrible chewing sound came from his lips. He picked the cigarette up from the table. The clock. *Seven o'clock.* He had to get back. He tried to stand, but strong hands held him down.

"You mustn't move until we let the doctor have a look at you. You must have hit your chin on one of the steps." He could hear

Chatwick moving round the room, the sounds of drawers being opened and closed. What had they done to him? Through a blur in front of his eyes he saw someone looking into his face.

"He'll be alright, but it must have been quite a fall. Can you get that green bottle from my case? Thank you."

A swab of some kind was dabbed over his eyes and across his chin. He tried to free himself from the sting, but found the swab pressed further into his face. He stubbed out the useless cigarette. Try as he might, he could not see much beyond the pain to remember what had happened. He saw the book he had been writing the wine lists in, closed on the table. It was bloodstained. He expected any moment to have someone force a contract under his nose to be signed. His logic had to be failing him because he could only hear soothing voices enquiring after his health, dabbing things at him, faces looking on.

The pain around his face soon became subsumed under a new pain below his back. It felt as if someone had taken a knife to his backside and attempted to tear out his innards; he retched as the pain increased. This time he was propped over an enamel bowl, a towel between its edge and his chin. He would have to get home soon. He would have to get away from this place the moment he felt the strength returning to his legs.

Morda slipped quietly in at the front door, pushing it to with an almost inaudible click. The house felt empty, but it was almost seven. His shopping idea had made him late; a vacuum bag for keeping drinks cold. The shop assistants he had spoken to, on a cold Saturday evening, had given him some serious stares. He had found an alternative function for it. The paper bag it was in rustled noisily in the hush of the house. Provlyn could be upstairs, having a wash... but he would have heard him. There was one place in the house where sound didn't travel too well... He moved round desperately to the cellar entrance, but the catch was down. He lifted it up and lowered the vacuum bag over the back of the door before closing it.

"Provlyn!"

There was a note from Lorkoz on the table. Thanks for the meal.

You're welcome. But Provlyn had not been back; his two ounce packet of tobacco lay untouched on the old radiogram. A few letters were couched in the letter rack; a phone bill, a pension scheme application from *Palby's* and an official brown envelope. Their Toll Tax numbers sinisterly moulded on two white plastic cards. He poured himself a glass of soya milk from the larder. It was totally untypical for Provlyn to be late, he thought, as he fingered the crisp white card bearing his name. He reflected plaintively that he had been less than kind to him in the past weeks. He hadn't given him much support over the sireling; he had been sleeping alone, too. And he had let him convince him that he would be able to deal with this Dorjess man. If it had happened last year, he would have phoned the house and told that Challis woman about it, had him dismissed. But since the beginning of the year, a curtain of wariness had often blown in the face of Morda, occasionally checking his impulsive nature. It had first held him back behind the police van with Harvil in it. It was keeping him more and more from telling Provlyn his thoughts, his fears. He wanted to feel that he was protecting him from acquiring a radical state of mind, consolidating the idealistic innocence of his youth. But this was bilge.

He came up from the cellar with the denim satchel and flicked through its contents. He tried to spurn the sense of nervous lunacy that had made him turn those three sheets and the photograph to powder. There was not nearly as much in there as his time away from the bag had made him think, but there were a few more photos, and articles written in the same coloured ink by different hands. He folded it carefully into the satchel and pushed it all into the vacuum bag, sealing it with the airtight zip. Handling it had the same feel as rifling through the jacket of someone you had just killed; your heart spun out a dancebeat of decibels, the ends of your fingers went clammy.

He breathed in deeply as he threw away the paper bag that had housed his purchase, the vacuum bag now safe behind one of the joists in the loft. Provlyn's height was one factor in the relocation, the other being the wariness of the satchel's contents. He knew that they would tell him many things that he was not ready to find out; there would be more questions that he could not answer. He would need time and a clear mind before he looked at them again.

In any other circumstances he would have spent the whole of the afternoon thinking about the ticket to the Ballet, but it was only now that he took it out of his wallet. *'Complimentary'* it had printed across it length and breadthways, making the œ5 stamp almost illegible. It would have taken him three weeks to earn enough to buy the ticket, but there it was. Box 25. He scribbled a short note to Provlyn on the back of Lorkov's note, took his jacket and left the house.

As he came out of Covent Garden station, Morda was swamped by crowds of women in expensive coats and more of that peculiar face paint. Across the streets, gold banners threw out the message everywhere - it's *International Women's Day* - as if you didn't know. He slid uncomfortably through the crowd, a few heads turning to look at him, most too busy with their own conversation. He had at first thought someone might be giving him a chance to prove how brave he was, that it was a test of nerve as part of his apprenticeship. But it would be pointless; there were much simpler ways of putting him under pressure. In the note, he had told Provlyn he was going to the theatre; although it had sounded a lot less suspicious, it wouldn't help him much if anything happened to him.

An official in a top hat was directing people along the street. He could see the Opera House as he turned the corner. A building with that mysterious quality of history, one of those in no danger of being demolished. He was relieved to see a few male faces, although they looked destined for the cheaper seats, their excited expressions signalling a once-in-a-lifetime excursion. After taking a Curfew Pass and having his ticket stamped at the Ticket Office, he moved to the entrance labelled *Boxes and Upper Circle*. Three different ushers checked his ticket on his way to the stairs, the last one stopping a tall woman in an evening dress to confirm, presumably, that she was prepared to let men into this section of the theatre. But he got past them and made his way to the Upper Circle Bar. The smell of cigar smoke and the clink of glasses reminded him, oddly, of the Hammersmith Palais. There were over a thousand people there, but as he stood at the railings of the bar, looking down at the crowds below he felt alone. This was the point, was it, to show him how important he really was? He looked across the sea of drinking female faces at his reflection in the gold rimmed mirror at the side of the bar. He looked quite smart in his suit, the powder stains having gone, and he smiled weakly at himself.

"Can I see your ticket please, sir?" A voice said, alongside him. He noticed in the reflection, before he looked round, that it was one of the policewomen he had seen at the house the night Harvil was killed. Even though she was wearing an evening dress herself, she was obviously on duty. He handed his ticket to her without turning round. He watched her examining it out of the corner of his eye, his attention drawn to the hip section of her dress. Was it a gun, a cosh or a face-paint bag?

"Thank you," she said, returning the ticket. He watched her disappear into the crowd. It would be a good time to leave, if the events so far were anything to go by. As he moved towards the stairs, a bell sounded.

"The performance of Diaghilev's *Ballets Russes* begins in five minutes. Would you please finish your drinks and make your way to your seats." A crowd of elderly women moved up the stairs towards him. He turned and went the other way, the crowd driving him up a further set of stairs. He eventually broke free and found an empty corridor with a distant Exit sign. As he moved towards it he saw the policewoman. He turned round again. He was facing another usher.

"May I have your ticket, sir?"

"Yes, but I..."

"Box 25? Through the door on the left, up the stairs and it's at the end of the corridor." Catching the last words behind him as he took off, Morda moved in the direction of the Box. He soon had mastered the directions sufficiently to find himself at the curtains of Box 25. A passing usher gave him a small silver key after examining his ticket, and he let himself into the box.

Pushing past the red velvet curtains he found a tiny vestibule with a hat rack and coat stand. Then, a further set of curtains, which he pulled back. The audience was down there before him, jewellery and trinkets glinting in the light from the theatre chandeliers. It was a grand platform for a spectacular suicide. You would have to think of something suitable to scream as you went down, though.

He drew up his chair and sat down. There were, a little disconcertingly, three other chairs in the box, but with only a minute until the performance... He moved back through the curtains to the door and turned the lock. Back in his seat, the lights went down, and then one waving spotlight came shooting up past the Upper Gallery to the boxes, just missing Box 25. Moving round to the right, it found it's target and stopped. There was a shuffling as the audience stood.

"Her Royal Highness, Queen Edwina VII," a voice said, over the intercom. A light rose on the orchestra below, and the National Anthem was played. Morda considered the repetition of the words, 'Save Us The Queen'; had there always been a Royal Family? Had there been one in the Other World?

The music stopped, amidst rapturous applause. Leaning out, Morda could just see a little withered arm waving mechanically. He looked round. It was now obvious why the security was so tight here, and there he was, just a few Boxes along, his white Toll Tax card in his top pocket; they would search him, they would find the card, check the records; Provlyn, the sireling, *Parkside*. It would all be over. He would have to leave during the first interval. On the ledge of the box there was a complimentary spread of programmes. According to the programme for tonight, the first part was an hour and a half long.

The lights were now out, and the orchestra stirred to perform a rousing opening. The curtains flew back and dancers poured onto the stage. It was only when the opening chorus of instruments subsided that Morda heard the scraping behind him. Someone was trying to get into the box. Genuine guests? The officials would have spare keys. He moved to one side of the curtain, holding his breath. The scraping became a gentle knocking. If a scene was created, the police might be called. He would have to open the door. He got up, the music having risen in volume again, drowning his steps to the door and turning of the key. The door was opened swiftly, the key taken from him and turned once more in the lock. He looked up at Rocassa Milo, her back to the door. She looked angry.

"Why did you lock the door?"

"You didn't tell me anyone else was coming!"

She looked at him speculatively.

"I said I had a ticket for the Ballet; you took it. I didn't say anything about whether or not other people would be there. Now sit down, will you? You're making me nervous."

He did as he was told, and remained there for the next hour, drawn to the dancers on the stage. The programme explained that Diaghilev had been responsible for bringing a whole new Ballet experience to the West, and that this was the last performance of the tour before the company returned to Russia.

It was an experience that Morda was unaware of; it was an entertainment form reserved, almost exclusively, for members of the Populite. Eventually the dancers came to a bowing halt at the front of the stage, the houselights rose, and Morda looked quizzically at the other occupant of the box. She watched him closely as he formulated his words.

"Alright, it's a Royal Ballet Performance. I'm quite interested. But what was the real reason for bringing me here?"

"I thought you might like it. Perhaps you don't."

"I've only been working at *Palby's* for three months; I'm still an apprentice until October. You hardly know me. Can you blame me for being suspicious?"

"I can't blame you, no. But you seem different from when I spoke to you during the meal at *Palby's*."

"The ticket for that evening came to me through the internal mail."

She laughed. He found it difficult to look away from her. Women generally wore their hair tucked into their hats or scarves. She had let hers down; it fell comfortably over her shoulders. It would be so easy to tell her that he wanted her; that he wanted her to find somewhere where they could be truly alone, where he could look at her. It would have been enough.

"I got my Curfew pass at the desk," he said. "But I still have to be back before midnight." He wanted her to take command of the situation; to declare her reasons, her desires, even if she had to tell him it wasn't a good idea after all.

"You must be back by midnight," she said, with a little irony. It was as if she knew what he was going back to; a tiny house in Hammersmith. A twenty year old lover he was about to sell himself to for fifteen years. These were not security expenses she was likely to incur as a member of the Populite. He finally looked away from her. He dropped the theatre programme to his left to create the diversion necessary to adjust his dress. To say he was wearing his heart on his sleeve went only halfway towards capturing the problems men had with the expression of sexual feeling. He looked back at her and smiled. Perhaps he should tell her about Provlyn. If she didn't know.

While he was making up his mind, the lights began to die down and the second half of the performance began. Although it seemed the most natural thing in the world to lean across and take her hand, he did not. However, as the ballet continued and the palms of his hands grew wet, he decided that no matter how long it took, no matter what personal sacrifices he had to make, he would see her again.

As he approached the house, he was surprised to see all of the lights out. It was five to ten; Morda would not be in bed yet, if he was there. He went down the alleyway and looked up at the back of the house, but still no lights. He remembered the day after the killings at the house in Whitechapel. He raised his hand to his jaw and pressed it a few times, still fascinated at the stabbing pain it produced.

In the dark hallway he took off his coat. *'I'm at the Theatre,'* the note read. *'I'll be late back.'* He was so stupid to be out after Curfew, running the risk of being taken in. He could be recognised; as a Caucasian, he was in the minority. He picked up the white plastic card on the table; *Provlyn Ranshell. A3705112.* He looked at himself in the Hall mirror. What would Morda say when he got back? He wouldn't react calmly now. He would be angry.

Morda had once punched the wall; he could remember the act but not the reason. It must have been something he had said about activists; it must have been before he had told him about Harvil. Last year? The year before? Sometime in those four years before he had been told. But hitting that wall. What had he said? He could not remember. He went upstairs.

He would have to write it all down, because of Monday. On Monday he would have to tell Lady Challis. He had to. He closed the curtains and took off his trousers. His underpants were dark with dried blood. He began to weep. He had tried to tell the Doctor, but he had been too ashamed. And to think he had gone into work that day, promising himself he would do something if it happened again.

'I can only relate what happened to me today this way,' he wrote. *'I did not have a fall this afternoon, though I am aware that this will be what you are told. I have been the victim of my own misplaced trust in the others in service at Parkside. This afternoon I was...'* He thought for a moment. What was the word? Was there no word for what had happened to him? *'Taken by force'* did not convey the full horror of his experience. He put a few asterisks and added an -ed. She would have to understand.

He wrote for another hour, and sealed the letter in an envelope, putting it in his work bag. On Monday he would go into work, deliver the letter with a note instructing her to phone him, and return home. He was sure she would not involve the police - it would look bad for a politician not to be able to judge the reliability of her own staff. She would perhaps find him another job somewhere else, maybe offer him some compensation. If she was sympathetic. It didn't bear thinking about what might happen if she didn't believe him, but at least he wouldn't have to go back. And what was he thinking at this moment - the man whose name he could not even bring himself to write - he had just put down the letter *D*. He must have realised that he had done something horribly wrong, something criminal.

He went upstairs to wash out the stains from his clothes. He took off the dressing from his chin in the bathroom. It was quite badly bruised, but he would use the story of the fall, at least until he knew what was going to be done. He would still sort this out alone; he must not involve Morda.

When the key turned nervously in the lock an hour later, he was asleep.

May

Provlyn sat with his feet up, reading *The Informer*. The Monday headline feature dealt with the important steps the government had taken with regard to individual liberty. The introduction of the Toll Tax card would safeguard everyone from fraud as well as ensuring each member of the community their own value in society. His value was A3705112. Within the paper, the Leader column welcomed the new cards, declaring how important it was that every citizen carried hers or his at all times, being ready to assist the authorities in the first few weeks of their implementation.

It was half past ten, but there had still been no phone call. It was fortunate that Morda had spent most of Sunday in bed, unwilling to make conversation, more interested in organising a spring clean of the house. He had seemed preoccupied. So much so that he had not seen the bruises - hadn't commented on them in any case. He had just spent most of the time declaring how glad he was that *International Women's Day* was over.

The pain was greatly reduced, and he was no longer bleeding. It had been pleasant that morning to be making the journey back to Hammersmith when everyone else was going to work. He had dropped the letter in Serboth Challis' personal letterbox, even though he knew the mail was always collected by Chatwick. He had gone to great pains the previous evening, after Morda had gone to sleep, to make the writing on the envelope look important, rounding the letters with a quill pen he had found in the bureau drawer. Leaving a little earlier, he had still been unable to get to the house much before ten past seven, so there was was no guarantee that he hadn't been seen delivering the letter. It was a chance he had decided to take. It would all be worth it if the phone would only ring!

Morda sat at his desk at work, his bent elbow propping up a sagging head. After spending most of the previous afternoon thinking up an excuse to steal quarter of an hour in the loft, but had finally decided against returning to the ice bag; his thoughts were marching soldiers, leading off in different directions towards alternative modes of action. But however he looked at the coming months, one fact was establishing itself more and more clearly each day. There was no place in his life for Provlyn any more. Whenever he thought about him, it would be through a range of pitying focuses; any memory he dwelt upon was always offset with the tag - *poor Provlyn; how badly he had treated him.* He focused on this thought as he trailed his pen down a line of debited demolition costings.

The noble act, if he had been capable of performing one, would have been to have said it straight out. To have declared it openly, the moment he realised it. But, unable perhaps to admit it to himself, he had fought his way down the circuitous road of suggesting a permanent lodging at *Parkside,* taking up a job to make himself more independent, giving in too easily over fathering. He had even held back when Provlyn had been bullied at work. But he had signed the fifteen year siring agreement; fuck and bitch to that. He only had a week left before they would have to register the boy as their sireling; next Friday. There still might be a way out, but he would have to somehow precipitate events. The coldness of his reasoning was the biggest surprise. He knew how much the boy meant to Provlyn and how much Provlyn doted on him; perhaps that was just as much part of the problem. It was sometimes just a matter of finding the courage to be alone. He had done it before.

The firm knock on the door made Provlyn jump. Just one single, forceful knock. As he rose to answer it, he caught sight through the curtains of a small police van, which must have been there for some time, or had arrived extremely quietly.

"I'm sorry to disturb you sir," the dark-haired policewoman said, "but I'm looking for a Provlyn Ranshell."

"That's me," he said. Her expression immediately changed.

"I would like to ask you a few questions. May I come in?" She was already in the hallway, a taller policewoman following behind. He knew he had done nothing wrong, but it wasn't a profound insight to conclude that he might be the only person in the room of that opinion.

"You're not at work today," the other one said.

"No," Ranshell replied.

"Are you ill?"

"I'm waiting for a phone call from my employer," he said.

"She wouldn't be the Right Honourable Serboth Challis, M.P., would she?"

Provlyn was trying to be two or three steps ahead of what was happening, but he couldn't reason very far in any direction. If Chatwick had read the letter he would have thrown it away, or hidden it somewhere, the same as Dorjess. If it had got to Lady Challis she would have telephoned. He could not make either happening reach the conclusion before him, no matter how he reasoned it through.

"I work at 47 Parkside," he said. "I am the Junior Footman, and have been working there for nearly a year."

"Haven't you telephoned your employer yet to tell her you won't be in today?" The police officers looked at each other ironically.

"She knows I'm not in today. I have written her a note."

"Did you have any other reason for explaining your absence with a personally delivered note?"

Thank the Queen that Morda was at work, he thought.

"I wrote to her about an incident that happened yesterday at work. The incident is the reason why I couldn't go in there today."

The dark-haired officer stepped forwards again. It was a well-rehearsed routine if nothing else.

"Are you aware that it is a criminal offence to attempt to blackmail a member of Her Majesty's Government?" He could see that she had taken his letter out of her pocket. She read it back to him. It hadn't required a significant angle of intonation to make it sound threatening. But why hadn't Serboth Challis telephoned him? Didn't she trust him? She had automatically concluded that he was ready to blackmail her. Why? There had to be another factor.

"You live here alone, do you?" the blonde one said. She had moved to the radiogram, on which there was his favourite photograph of Morda, in his army uniform, taken in Liverpool in 1917. "Good-looking boy," she continued. "Does he live here?"

"It's not just that," Pridge was saying. "It's a matter of pride. It's obvious what they're up to. If they can convince the Populace that this is the best system for the country, then the country will swallow it. They don't exactly have to convince the Populite now, do they?" He crammed the last piece of currant cake into his mouth, laughing as he ate. A raft of crumbs hung loosely on the side of his mouth.

"I suppose you think I'm naive?" Morda said.

"A bit. But there's no harm done. They all got the hump because it was the yearly meal. They're always like that."

It was significant that Pridge had managed to extricate himself from the membership of 'them'. Morda had been surprised to see him in the café at lunch-time but had beckoned him over, and had made it clear that the previous week's isolation period was over. He should have walked away on principal, but he wanted to talk. Talk could often consolidate a mood, harden your personal convictions, even if you were doing most of the listening.

"Do you ever wonder about the women in this country?" Morda asked.

"Well I'm not a hetero, if that's what you're getting at."

"That wasn't what I meant. It's just that you don't ever see them pushing paper around in stuffy offices at *Palby's,* for example. You never see them involved in demolition on the actual building site or bringing tea in on a tray for a group of men at a business meeting."

"And you never will. Those kind of things don't change. They've been with us since the beginning of time."

"And when was that?"

Pridge waved his hands in the air. "How do I know? At the start of the Other Age, I suppose. Nobody knows that. Those bombs destroyed our history, all the records and things."

"Why does it follow that things have always been like they are now, if all the history and records were destroyed?"

"Things don't change," Pridge continued, unimpressed. "They tried it, didn't they, in the war. They didn't get anywhere. Things don't change."

A middle-aged police sergeant ruffled back her hair impatiently. For the past hour she had gathered together the evidence in front of her to try to reach a conclusion, necessary if they were going to be able to press charges. The boy had written a letter which alleged he had been a victim of unconsented sex (whilst unconscious) with one of the senior employees at the establishment, who was also accused of subjecting him to the beating which led to his unconscious state. Another senior employee had also been implicated. Whilst he carried bruising to his face consistent with such a physical attack, they did not have the means, and therefore the evidence, to prove that the sexual part of the attack had occurred. The two officers who had first interviewed the man were convinced, due to the involvement of a high profile politician, that the facial injuries had been sustained elsewhere, and that the allegations were bogus, drawn up in the first part of a plot to blackmail the politician. It was odd to have written such a letter, hardly justified by the boy's comment that Lady Challis had told him to always bring his problems to her. His account had only been taken seriously because of Lady Challis, who had merely involved the police to consult them on how to deal with the Dorjess man. It had been on the advice of the Investigating Officer that she had let the police question Ranshell.

"Put yourself in my position," the sergeant said, lighting a cigarette. "A man is brought to you who has made these allegations in a letter. His character is sound, he has shown himself to be reliable and trustworthy. But he has made allegations about two of his colleagues who share quality reputations gained over decades. What would you do?"

"Interview the other two men. See if they could account satisfactorily for what happened yesterday," Provlyn said.

"Even if we did, they would have had virtually the whole day to mutually concoct a satisfactory version of events."

"What you're saying is that it's my innocence you're concerned about, not their guilt."

He exhaled deeply. He had so far managed not to directly

involve Morda, but he couldn't hope to keep him out of the whole process for much longer. Whatever he said when the police finally interviewed him would sound suspicious. He wouldn't know about the sexual attack, for example. What kind of a relationship could last five years and preclude those kind of details? He was able to put himself in the position of inquisitor effectively enough to predict the question, though the answer was not nearly as obvious.

He drew further inked rings around the Friday date. If it wasn't for the siring, he would have had more time to plan things, to work round the issues. He found himself looking at Provlyn like a corrupt statistic, something that had been forced upon him against his will. The coy fifteen year old in those dance shorts, that crazed fashion that thrust everything out on show like a greengrocer. Sex with Harvil had been more than satiating - the touching, the teasing, and then the moment, held back for as long as you dared. The only irritation was that unarticulated need that was always there for things to be precise, measured, just so. It would never do to share a moment spontaneously; the evenings were always planned. *'It's Friday'* or *'We're staying in tonight, remember?'* But that was Harvil; the planner. It was part of his plan that he would not talk about where he sometimes went. *'Business.'* He would deny involvement in the headlines that followed; he had not once relented from that devotion to *the cause*.

With Provlyn he had been able to take, to have, whenever it felt right. *'I want you now,'* and the boy would understand, moving down across his chest. At first it had been so, so good. He had come like liquid fire, holding the vessel steady as he stretched the moment out as long as he could, pushing, releasing, stretching down to the muscles in the balls of his feet.

Things only happened now when Provlyn initiated them. They still happened, and happened well, but he had become passive, only able to react. And afterwards he would still say things, make promises, talk about the future, but by then, like his loins, his words were spent.

So to the Friday date. He could see himself holding the child, smiling, going through the whole sham just to avoid the harder moments of silence and chosen words, the need for justification and denials. He rolled the corner of the diary page around the stem of his pen, curling and straightening it, creating an interplay between the two Friday dates. He eventually released the pen from the tedious pursuit, noticing, as the corner folded further back that something was written on the opposite side of the page. The diary contained a few circled days and completed lists of accounts projects he had finished, but other than that it was just a desk paperweight for any floating bits of paper. *'Down Street Station, 8.00 p.m.'* he read, although the p looked a little like an r. Why should anyone write in his work diary? More to the point, what would he be doing around Down Street Station in the day, let alone the evening? It was the station that served the immediate area around Mayfair, but it was rarely used, because Mayfair was almost exclusively a Populite area. Morda had often passed through in a taxi, trams having been withdrawn from the area. Though the houses there occupied the same space as those on the outskirts of London, it had become a desired place to reside, and in consequence raised prices on its property that only the Populite could afford.

He looked again at the *p.m.*, or *r.m.*. He tried furiously to find other reasons for the jotted instruction, but to no effect. It could only be her. *Rocassa Milo.* A clever message that she could easily deny having written if he was to show it to anyone. He drew his hand to himself in surprise; another chance - this soon?

He had shaken her hand at the Opera House door at twenty past eleven. The latest he had been on the streets after Curfew since the night at the hospital. The hand had been soft and a little damp. He had then thought it a little ironic that someone with so much power in such a big company, someone who was prepared and able alone to take steps to try to integrate managers and workforce, Populite and Populace; that this someone should have such a gentle hand.

He looked back at the writing on the page. There was something decadent about it; decadent, but at the same time authoritative. And she was inviting him to visit a Populite area this Thursday? She had to be a lunatic. It had been awkward enough at the Ballet, but he couldn't possibly be seen round the streets of Mayfair without being questioned. Strange how those words, a few black scratchings on a piece of paper, could make his heart beat so fast. And it wasn't the only part of his body blood was pumping round. But wasn't it disgusting, he kept telling himself. To be a hetero, to have those kind of thoughts. And if anyone ever found out... the shame and the punishment could never be faced. You would find a way to destroy yourself before anyone else did. It was still unclear what she wanted, however. They had only talked at the Opera House. But he eventually tore the page out of his diary and put it back on the corner of his desk. Then, tucking the torn page into his jacket pocket, he left his office heading for the direction of the washroom.

It was now nearly six o'clock. Provlyn sat in the small white room with the chair. At least they had listened to him; at least they were interviewing Dorjess. He could picture the silhouette of Dorjess, pontificating confidently in the interview room, defending his honour, making the charges seem absurd.

He was relying, he knew, on the police sergeant's intuition; he knew the evidence wouldn't be singling out Dorjess in any way. The questioning would have to be inspired. Dorjess would have to make mistakes.

The established atmosphere of safety and unified purpose he had basked in at *Parkside* had crumbled to dust; his admiration and love for Chatwick; underneath all that kindness and fatherly advice, he, too, was motivated by other forces. It was not enough for people to acquire positions in society and honour them, Provlyn reflected. There were other forces dragging them beyond the immediate tasks in their life. Dorjess was wound up in some way sexually; at least his motivation was explicable in the terms of what he did, appalling though it was. Chatwick was drawn by a more sophisticated force; he didn't seem in a position to cherish personal gain; he could hardly achieve a higher position at the house - he was as successful as most men could ever hope to be in their lives for what he did. So what was it that motivated him?

The key turned in the lock and the sergeant came in, an officer waiting behind her in the doorway. He immediately noticed the change in her demeanour. It did not suggest a theorising or questioning approach any more; it seemed resolved. The officer pulled the door to.

"I've interviewed both of the men and certain facts have come to light that I was not aware of this morning." Her voice, in its new businesslike tone, had the same effect on the silence surrounding it as the toll of an old bell at a public execution. "It would appear that you were not intending to work at the house for much longer, and that, I imagine, was why you had no intention of signing your contract." She moved to the other side of the room and leaned on the wall, watching him. Watching him with interest, expecting him to say something, but he merely looked back, mute. "It wasn't your idea," she said, eventually. "You're just a bloody victim; you're the bait put out for someone else's ideas."

It was remarkable just how complete the change was - from defence to attack; voice, expression, pose - all changed.

"Not a particularly clever idea, either, blackmail. You see none of you people really understand just how closely we work together. Blackmail can only work where there is friction and difference - where people have a lot to gain by tripping up those in the public eye. These people aren't just elected, they are bred to take these roles, from an early age. Should anything threaten them, which it rarely does, then the ranks close. You can't imagine that your fate is likely to trouble many people here, can you? It doesn't even seem like your partner has much respect for you, setting you up for this."

"Morda doesn't even know about the attack," he said, impetuously.

"Doesn't he." She removed a sheet of print-out paper from her pocket and read in the same toneless voice. *"Born January 20th 1938, unsired. Caucasian. Manor House Siring School. Army service 1916, Kirby, Liverpool. Middlesex First Battalion. Gunshot wounds to foot and chest, 16th July 1915, Manchester Barracks. Discharged 9th September,* same year. Amongst other things, it says here that he recently took up a full time position at the Finance Investment House, *Palby's.*"

"Morda doesn't know about the attack," Provlyn repeated. The sergeant looked at her watch.

"In fact, he's probably on his way home this very minute."

"It's got nothing to do with him!" Provlyn shouted. The officer looked round the door at the noise, but the sergeant waved her away. He fixed his eyes firmly at the ground, still hearing his own shout, like an echo, in his head. If nothing else, it seemed to have stopped her from talking. He sat there, face down, focusing on his shoes, focusing on a fog of nothing. Soon he could hear the ticking of the sergeant's watch.

She walked across to him, crouching level with his down-turned face. Eventually he looked up, eyes parallel with hers. For a moment it was like she was trying to read his mind, but he did not budge. He was screaming his innocence behind his silent stare, but he knew the eyes watching him had turned deaf. But he did not blink.

"What's worse about this is that I half believed you when you came in," she said. "Anyone who makes me look a fool usually regrets it." She pinched the bruised side of Provlyn's face, sending waves of pain to the back of his head. He fell off his chair, couching his right cheek in his hands, fascinated at the extent of the pain. He lay there some time before the sergeant spoke again.

"Anything to tell me about your *friend* before I find it out?"

There was no response.

The sergeant left the room.

He closed the door of the telephone kiosk and dialled the house. The phone rang several times before he replaced the receiver. He had waited for Provlyn at the station for the best part of an hour, but as the rush hour crowd had thinned to nothing, the fear of mishap had grown. He was not at home. Was he at work - he had worked late on Saturday.

He had wanted to meet him coming home from work so he could find a different backdrop to discuss the thoughts he had been having earlier in the day. It had been awkward enough waiting nervously to implement the first moves towards his independence, without having Provlyn disappear on him. If Provlyn came home late, it would be another evening gone; only two left before the Friday siring, if he intended going to Mayfair on Thursday. The fifteen year agreement could not be deemed legally binding if they had not collected the child, but how legally binding were the forms they had signed at each of the Siring interviews? There had been several. The whole procedure seemed to be enveloping him slowly, like a winding sheet of wire mesh.

He went to the ticket barrier again and waited for the arrival of two more Westbound trains. Nobody came through the barrier at all. Little wonder that they were considering disbanding the service sometime in the next century. He left the station; he would go home and change, see if he had left him a note. He marched down the Grove, cutting round the back of Trussley Road to the Mews. As he approached the house he realised he could use this time to go up into the loft and have a look through the icebag. Captivated by the idea, he increased his pace, closing the door just as the police carriage pulled into the mews.

He walked into the hall, throwing off his jacket and loosening his tie. There was a handwritten letter, addressed to Provlyn, on the mat. Morda took it with his jacket and tie upstairs to the bedroom. He watched the police carriage with interest, from the window. It had parked a few houses on up the street.

Changed into his easy clothes, he put his suit away in the wardrobe and sat down on the bed to read the note.

'Provlyn - some police officers were round here this afternoon asking questions about you and Morda. I'm not sure which of you they were more interested in. Perhaps you ought to phone the police station to find out what it's about - L.'

Lorkoz! He lived several houses down the road from them; what would they go all the way down there to find out? His eyes caught the bag in the corner of the room. *Provlyn's work bag.* He couldn't have gone in to work. If he had, he'd have been back by now. Why hadn't he read the note? In the few seconds of mental agility in the silent room, Morda had turned, was already moving towards the loft. He pushed back the hatch and pulled himself up.

It was still there. They could not have known about it. He moved to let himself down, when he heard a key turn in the lock. Provlyn? He leaned back against the joist and slid the loft hatch back into position with his foot.

"Morda!" he heard a woman shout. "You had better come out. We have a warrant for your arrest." Morda closed his eyes. What had he left in the bedroom? He tried to create the picture of his last glance in there. *The note!*

"Up here!" a voice called from under his feet. "It's a note from one of the neighbours. If he's read this, he won't be here." He held his breath until he thought his chest would burst. Their voices were now directly underneath.

"The fact that he's gone proves he knows we're on to him."

"Where would he go?"

"That's not our problem."

"Even so, I'll get back to the Unit. They might have some ideas. Put someone on behind the house and cover the front. Discreetly, mind. Just in case he comes back." There was a lengthy silence. Morda waited for the loft hatch to rise. Another silence. Followed, finally, by the closing of the front door. Then a further stillness. What the fuck was going on? And why was Provlyn involved?

He waited a further fifteen minutes, leaning against the joist in the dark. The loft was dusty and chokingly stuffy, his throat felt like someone was lowering a thin reed into it, brushing it backwards and forwards. He lifted the loft hatch with his foot, the carpet below coming into view. He crouched gently, and lowered himself back down. As an afterthought, he reached up again and grabbed the icebag. He moved silently to the bedroom, his mind racing. At the back of the top drawer he found a small cudgel. It had been there when he had first moved into the house. There was no need to question the history of its use. He slipped it into his back pocket. He went downstairs, his ears and eyes alert. Looking through the kitchen curtains he could see no-one outside. Through the back window of the lounge though, he could see a tall policewoman, her back to the house, behind the rear gate. He moved back to the upstairs front room. He could now see the policewoman; she was waiting at the side of the hedge separating the two houses.

He went back to the bedroom and put the icebag into Provlyn's work bag. He put on his grey jacket and left the bag beside the front door before returning to the window. He took a small china ornament, a white statuette of a muscular young man he had bought for Provlyn on one of their first meetings. He eased one of the windows gently open, and held the statuette out above the path below. It made a significant crash as he dropped it, alerting the policewoman. She looked up at the open window; Morda could see her from behind the net curtain. She moved stealthily towards the door. He had hoped she would alert the other policewoman so he could exit from the back, but she moved in alone, carefully, with no sign to anyone.

Morda sped down the stairs on light steps, raising himself behind the door. The key was put into the lock, but not turned. He stood on tiptoe, holding his breath. He could hear sounds from the back of the house that made his heart stop. But he had no further time to reflect as the front door swung open. He threw himself on the woman, kicking the door shut with his feet. Although she was much lighter than Morda as he wrestled behind her, she was tall and lithe, pulling herself free from his grasp, her hand moving towards her bag. He hit her a crisp blow across the back of her hand causing her to cry out, and her bag fell from her reach. Inspired beyond hope, Morda moved to the telephone table sighting the bunch of keys above it. He was able to grab them, but she struck him on the face as he turned, blood dribbling at the edge of his mouth almost immediately. As he fell back from the blow, he caught the lounge door by the handle and swung it back at her, catching her in the face with its weight as she moved towards him once more. With clumsy fingers he fumbled with the keys. There would only be one chance. He twisted the iron in the lock and, mercifully, it held. He could hear the lounge window break from behind the door. It would not take two of them long to kick it down. He grabbed the work bag and went out of the front door, bolting the mortice as he went.

Once on the mews, he wiped his mouth with his handkerchief and broke into a slow run, heading towards the Grove. The sky was growing dark and the lightman was already at the other end of the street in his battery carriage, ready to start lighting the lamps with the iron taper couched at the side of his vehicle.

"I don't believe you. You've already shown me how little you know about him by accusing him of all this. If he knew I was here, you wouldn't have to look for him."

"I think you're the one who doesn't seem to know anything about him," the officer said, handing him a glass of water. "The moment he finds out you're in trouble and that the police are looking for him - he's off. This is a bloke you've lived with for five years, is it? Someone you can trust? Bollocks to all that. He's taken you for a ride. Knows he can't get any further with that letter and is off into the night."

"You're lying," Provlyn said. "He wouldn't attack a police officer. He has respect for authority." He sat back on the bed in the cell, watching the occasional feet in the darkness outside pass over the murky glass sections of the ceiling above him.

"Strikes me as a bit of a victim," the sergeant was saying in the Investigation Room. "He's too bloody naïve to keep up an act this long. Something may well have happened to him at that place, but I can't imagine he's the one behind some kind of elaborate blackmail plot. His friend might be, though."

"Morda," the officer in front of him said. She sat on the side of the bench at the back of the room. She had a piece of gauze bandaged to the side of her face where the door had hit it, and a bandaged right hand.

"He may have just panicked."

"He had no intention of us stopping him. I didn't get a good look at his face, but this guy was violent, sergeant. I have no doubt."

The sergeant fed in more information into the keyboard in front of her, but the computer was not able to make any link between people and places. It did not help that the Central Records Office computer was only available for one hour a day. Another case of the government sacrificing the efficiency of the police in the name of energy conservation. She shook her head and pressed *Exit*. Some of these bright young men on the streets with tedious jobs; their minds eventually turned to crime, just out of boredom. Spent most of their leisure time not down at the football match or snooker hall. They would be packed into those tiny public houses in the East End, whiling away their time hatching plans to make money or disrupt some Populite activity. Money was becoming less important though, now the big shops were closing. There was nothing that you could buy, particularly, to set yourself apart from others. Only food and clothes. There were not many new houses being built either, just those factories and extensions to the parks. As a senior policewoman, she felt she had a clearer view of what was happening in London, but these reforms were not always changes she would have wanted to justify. Too much change too quickly and the working people would become unsettled. She looked at the wounded officer. If they had the old police vans they would have been at the house when he got home and spared her that swelling face. Poor kid.

Whitechapel had seemed the place he should head for, to look out for those who might have known Harvil, the ones that he had promised would find him. They were still dark unknown faces in unfriendly crowds. He needed someone to trust, perhaps it was something he had always needed. But having boarded the train, he had reconsidered. If they knew his history, they might be waiting for him, might somehow have intuited his moves. He had got off the train at Edgware Road, the streets now in darkness, and was on a tram bound for Hendon.

He got off at the Hendon Central terminus, the last passenger having left the tram at Kilburn, some five miles back. The journey on the upper deck had been uneventful, the conductor preferring to stand at the entrance, filling in his chit for the day's work. There were two krat and lettuce sandwiches at the bottom of Provlyn's work bag, which had tempered his hunger, something that would be important in the next few days. He had eleven pounds on him, and had found another four pounds fifteen shillings in the bag. If it would make any difference, he was not short of money.

Hendon was, as he remembered it from the journey to Nuneaton House, a short parade of local shops and houses. A few dotted lights here and there in the houses he passed sign-posted life, but he walked on, away from the lights. After twenty minutes, he had seen the last light, and was crossing roads where houses had once been, now stockpiling centres for demolition. There were probably other such areas, too, where all the Clearance Act debris would come to rest. As he went further and further away from the town, his eyes became used to the darkness, and he was able to keep clear of some of the more dangerous piles of rubble. He was keeping level with the main road to Barnet - he followed it with reference to the tram pylons overhead to the right - but in order not to attract attention walking along the High Road at night in the middle of nowhere, he stuck to the older roads with their damaged buildings and piles of rubble.

He had walked for almost an hour when he noticed it had passed Curfew; did they try and enforce it round here? He laughed. The government were keen to centralise where people lived and worked, to exercise control over these areas. But even with half a million people in London, there would always be places in need of repair, where people didn't live or work. He was lucky that he'd passed this place recently; he would not have known where to look.

'You are entering Burnt Oak (Watling)' an old sign said, in front of him. Across the street he saw what looked like half a house, the side walls open and exposed, the top half broken away. With a stretch of the imagination it was possible to picture a whole row of these houses further off, the one in front of him being the last, in both senses of the word. He walked up the path and pushed the door. It was shut. Entering at the side, it was soon clear that the area must have been declared a war zone in one of the last wars. There were several empty ammunition crates, and sections of an old tank in the garden, casting thin pencil shapes against the moonlit sky.

The front room was the centre of operations. It still had a complete radio base, but the equipment was corroded, and in each room the musty smell of damp and rust cut into the air. It was impossible to calculate just how safe a place like this would prove to be, but at least he had got there, at least he had the icebag with him. It was ironic that in the short term he was now in a safe position to sift through the remainder of its contents in spite of the long term danger faced of possible capture. He left the work bag in the house and went out into the street again. He could hear no sound at all. Even the wind blew gently, soundlessly.

Like many others from the Middlesex battalion, he had been forced to live rough in Northampton. As an area it had been undeveloped since the Other Age, off limits during peace time, but a strategic area of refuge in the war, south of Leicester, after a wave of crippling battles where several men had died. He had come across the remains there of a whole town, some houses still intact, visited now only momentarily by government and republican soldiers. Much of his curiosity about the Other Age had stemmed from the week and a half he had spent in Northampton. After the devastation that had wiped out Old England, most buildings must have still stood, virtually untouched. Four hundred years on, Northampton had remained a picture of that devastation, a macabre museum of the destruction. In that town, he had found stagnant evidence of the lives people had led; mechanical instruments that could have been televisions or film boxes, further proof that it had been a society wantonly thriving on natural resources: burnt out cars, abandoned power stations. The only thing that he had not found was evidence of the actual life itself.

His days in the army, provided by the state, had armed him well with the mental resources to carefully plan the days ahead. In Northampton, they had carried bleepers, then; army signalling badges that helped the commanding officers locate their forces. They could also inform the wearer when he had to make a reconnaissance, the strength of the signal indicating the location of the battalion. Many inopportune bleeps had played their part in the deaths of soldiers drawn out from their hiding places. He had thrown his away in the end, preferring to calculate his moves unaided. Instinct was often more reliable than gadgetry and was, above all, silent.

Satisfied that he was safe, he moved with his bag to the back room of the house, folding up a piece of tarpaulin to create a makeshift bed. Once he had got himself comfortable, he dragged the bag towards him, intent on going through the contents, determined to try to read in the dark. The strain he felt in his chest, however, had become more acute as he lay down, and his foot throbbed painfully. He had no alternative but to lie still with the pain until it eased. When it did, he found himself drifting off through reflections on his plight into a narrow sleep, and subsequent uneasy dreams. Behind him, on the main road, the last tram rolled on into the night, back towards London.

Acorn House

'I am the youngest of the family. We have lived in Hammersmith since I was born. I have drawn a family tree to show how my family has changed. Thanks to my grandfather I have been able to trace right back to 1750, and, as you can see, we have always lived in England. Our names have had to change, though, and as the two eldest in the family are also girls, the next generation will have different names, too.'

He looked at the names. Atherby, Mornington, Jennings, Rogers and now Lewis. Not only did the women link up with men to have children, but they gave away their names, too. He followed the dates with interest. At that time, they must have logged their years forward, but 1980 years on from what was unclear. Today, Tuesday 4th May 1909, the world was 1909 years away from oblivion. A fact still too distant to be of overt bother to him, but a fact almost certainly unavailable to those in the world of 1980. To the few facts he knew about the Death Age, he could now add that it had produced conditions to hasten if not cause the destruction of the world, and that it had changed the way years were measured.

At that moment he longed for Rocassa to be there, sharing the discovery; he had learned more about women from this children's project than in the whole of his twenty-nine years on the earth. From the dates, counting forwards, most women had children between the ages of twenty and thirty-five. He could find no woman on the chart who had made a child at an age under nineteen. Conception here was a part of practical biology, part of growing up, an impersonal experience compared to what must have gone on then. The fathers were identifiably real people then, not a sample from an endless sperm bank. It was ironic that the real fathers of everybody born in the New World, if they could have identified them, came from the Other World, and had been dead for hundreds of years. The last real father in the world might have died over four hundred years ago. He stood up and folded the tarpaulin into the corner of the room, moving towards the front of the house.

It was a surprisingly warm morning for May; if they were lucky they had a few hot days in November, but, though the sun was lost somewhere in the clouds, he took his top off and moved to the front of the house. He had woken an hour ago, distant rumblings of demolition a few miles off stirring him from sleep. In his dream he had waited at Down Street station for her, past eight o'clock, on towards nine, alone in a swelling crowd of anonymous women. Each one, as she moved towards him, was Rocassa, with her orange hat and jacket, but as he reached out to draw her near, she looked at him, face changed, a different person. He had also the sensation that he was being continually watched, and eventually he saw them, a group of small children, male and female, pointing at him and laughing from the upper floor of the building opposite the station. It had been very real; he awoke in his own sweat, shaking, although he knew it to be a dream.

There was no water to be had from any of the taps he could find, all of them tightened up with age and lack of use. He ran his fingers across his stubbled chin; he had forgotten his razor. He felt uncomfortably unclean and unrested, but while he studied the folder it would be wise to be in a position to move quickly in case he had any visitors. He moved several hundred yards further down the road to a tree-lined avenue turning, the trees wild, branches loping over missing roofs, winding twigs and leaves pushing into long since-abandoned upstairs rooms. He stopped a few houses down at a doorless front and moved in. Climbing over some broken glass and part of a broken bannister, he moved into the front room, which had a carpet! Sitting in the corner, in a more comfortable position, he began to read.

'The Time In Which I Live - I am worried about all the muggings that go on in London, with old people getting beaten up for just five pounds. We have a new Prime Minister now who is the first woman Prime Minister in this country. My dad voted for her because he thinks she will make more laws to stop this kind of violence. I am a Christian and I don't believe in violence, but my sister says how can there be a God if so many terrible things happen in London.'

Morda wrote down an alphabetical list of the new words he had learnt, in a notebook he found in Provlyn's bag. *Animals, Christian, Church, God, Library, McDonalds, Mother, Mugging, Raping, Religion.* He had found some of the words on another map of Hammersmith which had fallen out of the back of the folder. He read through the other sections, circling the new words in pencil each time one appeared. Though he spent most of the morning doing this, there were words he could only guess the meanings of, and in spite of this monolithic find, there was immense frustration at the number of loose ends it produced each time he tried to concoct even the vaguest picture of what the Other World might have looked like.

He had been terrified when he found a photograph of a younger boy holding what looked like eyes and a set of teeth wrapped up in a brown carpet. The boy had been embracing it fondly in spite of its appearance, and had labelled the photograph *Me with my Dog, D'Artagnan.* Morda recalled the use of the word 'dog' from his army days, a term of abuse for unappealing males over forty with fat bellies. Looking at this thing in the photograph, its label was obviously a word that had paddled across the Great Rains into the New World, even if it had lost a little in translation on the way. As he read on, the *dog* was emerging as a founder member of the *animal* family (also called *'pets'*),which included all manner of different sized and shaped unintelligent creatures, at large all over the world. There was an unpleasant double function performed by these creatures, evident in the difference between one girl who kept a pet rabbit and a boy whose family often ate rabbit. Mercifully, there was no photograph of the animal concerned, cooked or otherwise.

He recalled the meal at *Palby's*, and his first introduction to meat. Now he knew that this was the substance taken from animals it was difficult to understand how it had not poisoned him. What part of them did it come from? He remembered the chewing and looked again at the picture of the dog. It had come from North America, Rocassa had said. A place where they might still keep animals. Most of them had obviously been killed, though, in the Death Age.

There was much raised by the folder to consider, not least why things had changed so dramatically. Even though it was still a set of sharded fragments, he could still calculate a few aspects of the old way of life by looking at what was *not* mentioned in the folder. The most obvious omission was women. Although half the children writing were female, they wrote almost exclusively about men. The first *man* on the moon, the first *man* to run a hundred metres in under ten seconds, jobs our *fathers* do; the pronoun 'he' came up four hundred and fifty-seven times, 'she' came up on just forty-three occasions; the children even spoke collectively of the world of *man*kind. Then, one day, *pow.* Many dead. A chance, perhaps, to change the world now it had less people. A chance to correct all the things that had been wrong. But even after four hundred years of change and path covering, they still had a government trying to reduce its problems by the introduction of new laws. Fragmentary, but it was a privileged historical perspective. It was a story that could have run for several months in *The Informer.* However enlightening the discovery had been to Morda, the value was limited. His response when he had first found it was to go out and proclaim the arrival of this *new knowledge,* but the difference in the change of lifestyle over a few hundred years would render all of this merely an imaginative (if ideologically unsound) piece of children's fiction. If he approached anyone in authority about it, they would simply confiscate it and make him look a fool, or do something worse. As it was, he was now not in a position to do anything with it other than carry it around in the icebag until it disintegrated or burn it. If it could have been found by someone with political power, someone who could and was prepared to use it as a weapon against the defenders of the country's system, be they the government or whoever, it might have changed things. It was, though, unlikely that he was the only one who knew. This knowledge could well have come into the hands of the activists from other sources. The oath Harvil had often spoken about could have been not to pass on the information to those outside the circle, of which he was one. He would have been better off without the knowledge; it was a gift he could not use.

The unlawful feelings he had for Rocassa; it was not enough to say that they were wrong. He knew now that many people had been heteros before the Death Age. But no longer; it was an institutionalised wrong, punishable by castration and, sometimes, death. It had been enough to stop most people for four hundred years, but it was not enough to stop him. He would have tried even without knowing about the Other Age. He looked at his watch which had stopped at nine o'clock. He would have to find some food, buy some if he could, hoping he hadn't been deemed important enough for any front page publicity mugshots.

"You understand you're not to leave the city for the next forty-eight hours," the sergeant called out after him. "I want that phone ringing tomorrow at half-past twelve, and you on the other end. Is that clear?"

Provlyn crossed the street, feeling his strength returning as his legs got into stride. Three days he had been there, tired and confused, ready to give up and find something to admit to in the hope of bringing the waiting to an end, but now he was out, and although he felt slightly dishevelled in his three day old clothes, there was somewhere he had to go to before he went home. He had no desire to ever return to the police station again. To arrive in the afternoon would be perfect.

"You had better tell her I am here, Chatwick."

"I am afraid she is busy with Lady Arkandale," Chatwick said, watching him nervously. He stood with his back to the hallway doors.

"I thought I could trust you. I even told you about myself, thinking you could help me. But you told Dorjess, didn't you?" Stung by Chatwick's play of innocence, Provlyn could feel himself being drawn. Chatwick seemed unable to look him in the face. As he pushed past and reached for the door, there was a creak on the stairs. Dorjess stood there, looking down at him haughtily. He looked back at Chatwick. He had not noticed it before in his innocence, but the likeness was quite stunning. While Chatwick had made the most of his features, a bastion of domestic service, Dorjess had failed. He was fatter, his lip curled downwards on one side; he gave the continual impression that he was about to spit. What a loathsome pairing. He opened the hall doors and moved towards Serboth Challis' room.

"It's alright," he said, raising his hand. "They let me out this afternoon." She moved her hand away from the open drawer and pushed it shut. He sat down in the chair in front of her.

"Chatwick said Lady Arkandale was here."

"She was, about half an hour ago." He looked round at the room; a room he had hardly ever studied very carefully before. It had been a means to the end of his job. The *end* of his job?

"I need to talk to you. I would have spoken to you on Monday, but I couldn't risk them getting to you first, or getting to me." He gestured towards the door with a movement of the head. "The fact that they let me through should say something of my innocence."

"Are you innocent?" she said.

"Yes," he said. "And so is my friend."

"Is that so?" She picked up one of the newspapers and handed it to him.

"It's not particularly well ironed," he said, smiling. His smile faded when he looked at the newspaper. Folded open at page seven, there was a two column photograph of Morda. Provlyn had seen it before, part of an old army photograph taken in Liverpool several years ago, with Morda looking a little gaunt. It was a suitably criminal pose for the article, headed *'Republican Activist On The Run From Police';* it listed his various *'crimes'* which included attempted murder, abduction and planning of anti-government activities from sieges to bomb campaigns. Provlyn looked at her and she shook her head.

"Before you waste your breath any further, it was discovered that he used to live with a known Republican Activist; he was identified by a policewoman at Whitechapel Police Station, after she saw the photograph, as someone who she remembered visiting the station in January. He had gone in there to ask about the activist - the same one, it turns out - who had been shot after police had broken up a local siege. He gave a name which proved to be false after the police had run checks on it. Interestingly enough the man he was claiming to be was found brutally murdered a few weeks later at his flat in Stepney."

Provlyn looked through the article again. None of this would have happened if he had not sent her the letter; it had gained momentum like some grotesque carousel, whirling up miserable circumstance into a rolling wall of apparent anti-government activity. And now Morda was somewhere, running for his life.

"He stopped living with that man because of his activities."

"After *five years*?"

"You used to trust me. You were good to me, but you said it was on account of my reliability." His look now had turned to despair.

"Part of your reliability, Provlyn, may be to do with your naiveté. I can't really commend you on account of that, much as I like you. You placed us in great danger by failing to tell me about Morda, and when I read your letter and made some enquiries, I quite naturally concluded that you were being used for blackmail. However, I am also aware that the likes of Dorjess should not be left within a twenty mile vicinity of a wine bottle, and after further interviews with all the staff, I accept that all you said in the letter was true. As a result of this, I am prepared to find you employment as a clerk at one of my offices in Baker Street, after all of this has blown over, naturally. In the meantime I will continue to pay your *Parkside* salary. I suggest you return home at once and stay there."

He might have left then, but to have done so would have indicted Morda. Instead, he looked mournfully into the fireplace, licking his top lip in search of an inspired idea. The last time he had placed himself at her mercy had almost sent him to prison, but even though his name had been more than cleared, he would have to ask her for more. He owed it to Morda.

"You have been very fair, but this is all worthless to me if I can't help Morda. We have lived together for five years. We were going to sire this Friday," he said, bowing his head. He could not let her see him cry. "In any case, I am ready to help you find him on the understanding that he is looked after. If he is taken to prison, I will wait for him."

"You mustn't think simply because I am the government Home Secretary that I have powers above the law. If a court find Morda guilty of treason, they can impose any sentence on him up to, and including, death." She took Provlyn's hand. "But if we find him soon, I am sure, at his trial, we can work on emphasising the love and commitment he has shown you." She shook his hand and stood up. As he turned for the door, she placed a small card in his hand, which he read once outside. Underneath the orange-printed heading *'Nuneaton House Siring Centre'* was the message *'Don't forget number 107. He'll be waiting for you to pick him up as arranged on Friday.'*

Pridge sat at his desk and cackled until he coughed. He had been leading most of the office speculations on what might have happened to the Disappearing Man. He had grown to quite like him, even if he didn't always choose his company very intelligently. He remembered showing him that story in the paper; he thought he hadn't laughed very much then. All those young men, though. They all thought because they had a bit of spunk in them that they had to go out and prove it by doing something outlandish. He had seen a few of them in his days at the shop, sacked for going over the top. Two they had caught having a quickie in the broom cupboard when they should have been in the Men's Department; then there had been Yolaf, the enormous Food Stores assistant who had brought a Menswear Mannequin down to the fruit display and created a display of his own with a banana and two pomegranates. After the Stores Manager, as then was, had put in her complaints, he had attempted to remove the banana, forgetting he had half-peeled it, and the contents had slipped out, so to speak, in genuine fashion. But this was the first clerk to go, and, well, he had just *gone*. Not even a farewell trick, apart from leaving a photo with the newspaper.

He put the file down and looked at the paper again. He looked a lot younger. And haggard. But that business about sieges and abductions: he hadn't been able to abduct a few pieces of precious meat on a dinner plate; why should he fare any better with human beings? He stuffed his newspaper in the drawer as the footsteps approached. He always left his door open. Why should he have anything to fear? He pushed at the corner of the newspaper that was still sticking out.

"Good morning, Pridge."

"Good morning, Chief Sales Accountant. Would you like to see last week's Sussex Account? It's been finished for twenty minutes."

"No thank you," she said. "I wonder if you might have any information for me about the disappearance of Clerk 15. I take it you've seen the newspaper articles."

"Yes," he said. "I only hope he has, that's all I can say." She stared at him. He busied himself about his desk. No sense of humour, these managers; if he wasn't so nervous he'd have dispensed with the cracks.

"He has only been with us for three months; we can't keep filling these places with all these men going in to service; we certainly can't hope to compete with the wages they pay them." She lifted up his jacket disdainfully between thumb and forefinger, rescuing it from where it had been thrown, over the open door of the cupboard, and put it on a hanger over the rail inside.

"He used to talk about women quite a bit," Pridge said suddenly. "I suppose it all fits in with this activist stuff in the paper. We were talking just the other day, last time I saw him, I think, about the jobs women get. How they, well, it was the old anti-Populite argument." Rocassa Milo looked unimpressed. She walked round the side of his desk and opened the drawer. The newspaper fell out, along with an old edition of *Men's Health,* a publication which, it was soon clear, featured impressive close-ups of the male anatomy, photographed in black and white.

"Did he seem nervous on Monday?" she asked, discreetly returning the items to the drawer.

"No," said Pridge. "Why are you interested? Did he take anything?" She turned herself from the proximity of his breath towards the front of his office.

"I would consider it unwise," she said, "to be frivolous about this man. I have been asked by the City of London police to find out as many details as I can about him. It is obviously in the interest of *Palby's* for me to ascertain with a high degree of certainty that he was not involved in anything remotely illicit during the time he spent working in this building. Now do you have anything useful to tell me about him?"

"No," said Pridge.

She left.

Provlyn looked out into the garden, through the new French windows. He had spent the last two days clearing up the house and the mud-stained carpets. It was the glazier who had suggested knocking out the broken frames and putting in French windows. With panel locks they were, as had been demonstrated, more secure than the previous window.

When he had first got back, the mess had been off-putting. Two chairs had been broken; there were pieces of glass trodden into the carpet throughout the downstairs back room. Across the back of the front door and the door to the lounge, smears of dried blood had decorated the panelling. But two days on and the house looked as neat and tidy as it had ever looked. There was something in the neatness, though, that expressed the lack of human conflict within. A house that was too neat had always said that to him. Nobody lived in tidy houses.

He sat on the bed upstairs, rolling a cigarette, wondering why Morda had taken his work bag. He had changed out of his suit into his black jumper and slacks. His grey coat was gone, too. He must have had some kind of warning before they arrived. He had thought Lorkoz might have noticed something, but there had been no answer from his house, no smell of food from inside the letter box. They had gone away. And the phone had gone mute. He had not spoken to anyone since he had left the house at *Parkside*. Tomorrow he had to be at Nuneaton House at four o'clock. Wherever Morda was, he hoped he would get to a phone by then, at least to tell him he was alright.

The three newspapers were laid out on the floor in front of him like a hand of large playing cards. A second photograph had been published that morning with more biographical details. He was, he discovered, a keen sportsman at his boarding school, representing them at cricket and rugby football. He had also been shot twice in the arm in the last war. Oddball. But it would do much to stir up local people to keep their eyes open for this *'dangerous activist'*.

He left the last of the carrots, which had gone a little pulpy, and finished off his improvised meal with a small pear. Walking to the fringes of Hendon on the first day there he had bought supplies to carry him through until today, but subsequent visits to the newsagents had proved extremely dangerous, buying newspapers in which he was beginning to feature so prominently. The old shopkeeper belonged to the unemployable belt of London's elderly generation. He had probably kept his shop going for three or four decades, but the recent lack of cigarettes and general provisions heralded an imminent departure from the retail world. He still sold newspapers though; at least he had certainly sold three in the last three days. Morda had never felt himself such a welcome customer anywhere. However, the offer of a cup of tea that morning had made him pleased he was leaving the area. Even the withered old newsagent would recognise him soon enough. He had enough time in his day to read through all of the papers.

Morda looked at himself in the tiny face mirror he had found in Provlyn's bag. It was fortunate that he had quite a heavy beard, as three days' growth gave it a pronounced dark edge. He had managed four circuits of his exercises each day and, after the tarpaulin, had slept well on the carpeted surface. He was grateful enough for Provlyn's habit of taking showers at *Parkside* because of its luxury shower room. His toiletries bag had contained a shampoo bottle, comb, small towel and several other effects. There had been no razor, but the beard was now his most important ally. They had become fashionable of late amongst the Populace, sported by many early evening revellers up and down the streets of London. With the bucket of water he had pilfered from the tap behind the newsagents, he had washed his hair and face. Even within the semi-shelter of the deserted house, the freezing water cut into his scalp and made his new beard stand out on his face like a bed of tiny needles. His clothes looked a little creased, but the icy water had made him feel fresh and alive. He took out the torn sheet from his wallet. *'Down Street station, 8.00 pm.'* He had rounded off the lower stem of the *p* to curb the ambiguity. On an evening train in London, he would curl up in a carriage corner, under Provlyn's cap, and then to Down Street. Now he had graduated to the front page of this morning's newspaper he again felt the two-sided edge of stirringly dangerous pleasure. Perhaps the same challenging pleasure had been felt by women in the Other World as they battled against whatever injustice had stood in their way. Because it had been changed, the New World was, in all its morbid bureaucratic misery, an unqualified improvement for women. He shook his head. It was difficult to imagine that it had really ever been other than it was now.

In the three days he had spent in Burnt Oak reading and thinking, he had been ready to change his mind about making the journey across London to Mayfair to honour what was still a dubious appointment. He had, though, found it was providing him with a focus for the withdrawn state of his life. He had lost the feeling of commitment to Provlyn and the child. He no longer wanted to do anything that would make him feel he was a part of this England; a place that had made him feel unclean for wanting to make love to somebody. His feelings for Rocassa had changed from rough, pokey imaginings of solo fleshy sex to wanting to touch her, wanting to see her, and wanting to be seen by her. She had risked giving him the ticket for the Ballet, the gesture that had killed off the last of his stubbornness. Over the three days he had recognised the development of his feelings, and he knew it was time for him to be prepared to take risks. He had little left to lose now. Nevertheless, at a lower level in his thoughts, the crawling fear that she might not want him, that she might reject him, grew too.

With his watch damaged, he was having to judge the time of day by the sun's position in the sky. From army days he knew that he could judge this to within half an hour either way; the newspaper kept the sun-setting times under the weather chart on the back page. It was a time of day that Harvil had often referred to as the first curfew.

He moved round to the back of the house, to the concrete garage at the end of the garden. It was one of many built at the back of the row of houses, leading to the private drive for residents of the estate. The door to the garage was gone, as was the car, if there had ever been one. The owner had nevertheless built an old chest of drawers into the front of the garage, which was oil-stained; full of nuts, bolts and garden tools. The lowest drawer contained strips of towelling, but had a large space at the back, where Morda pushed the icebag. He covered it with the towelling and closed the drawer. It was likely to be the last time he would ever see it, but it would be safe from a further discovery that might lead some poor well-meaning idealist into serious trouble with the authorities. The garden would soon be filled with debris and the house demolished, and that would be it.

He had made further notes in Provlyn's book, more words, some dates and some observations. It was dangerous information, but not as dangerous as carrying the source material. He went back out in front of the house. It had probably once been occupied by a *family*. A father, a mother and two children; a boy and a girl, maybe. People living their ordinary lives in the Other World. What had they been doing when the signal had come - when their World had ended?

His time was good when he got to Hendon Central. It was half-past six. He pulled up the lapel of his grey coat and boarded a waiting tram. He had planned the journey carefully. Few people lived out as far as Hendon, so he would be reasonably safe at the outset. He needed to catch a tram that would take him right into the centre of London, and then he would have only a short tube journey to Down Street. What happened when he got there, however, had to be left to the planning of Rocassa Milo. If she didn't turn up, and he would give her as long as he could, he would simply return to Hendon on the last tram and work his next move out from there.

He looked round as the tram pulled away. There was an old man at the back in a trilby hat, smoking a pipe. He squinted feebly at Morda through heavy lenses before returning to a contemplation of the outside gloom. A distant bell sounded somewhere. All that could be done now was to sit back and enjoy the journey.

The lights of London greeted the tram's turn at the Marble Arch roundabout; just a few stops to Piccadilly Circus. The tram had filled up after it had reached Kilburn, but no-one inside seemed worried about anything but themselves. It was one of the few rewarding elements about people's indifference, Morda thought. The tram stopped at the Circus itself, crammed now with people on their way to one of the brightly-lit theatres for their evening's entertainment. He left the tram and pushed into the crowds. It was twenty minutes to eight by one of the theatre clocks, but his tube journey was only two stops. He still had plenty of time. Once on the train he wondered if he should perhaps have been wearing the suit - he would have been under any other circumstances. It was a worry compounded by the hordes of suited clerks, some arm in arm, in search of early evening West End culture.

But now he was alone on Down Street station, as the train moved off. There was no-one to lag behind on the steps on the way out. He walked at a steady pace, looking at the advertisements above the handrail. *'Gyina - the professional coiffeuse, 42 Mayfair', 'The Businesswoman reads Business Journal' and 'International Travel? We still run. Contact Women In Europe. Ring MAY 4132'.* He passed another poster at the foot of the escalator warning about the Toll Tax. At the barrier, a young underground official in perfect uniform took his ticket.

"Good evening sir," he said.

"Er, good evening."

He looked hurriedly around the station concourse, but he could not see her. The station lights were very bright, but there was no-one else there apart from him and the ticket collector. He moved outside. The streets were a lot darker, and he felt a little more settled. It was three minutes to eight. And as he moved into the shadow of a shop doorway he saw her. She was wearing a long black coat and the light from the station fell on her face at a distance. It seemed artificially white, emphasised by the fact that she was wearing *face paint* on her lips. The reddest of face paint. Fuck the Queen, he thought, this is all for me. She's like this for *me*.

His heart was thumping as he drew back into the darkness. In comparison, he looked disappointingly shabby. There was a stain on his coat, and a foul taste in his mouth. He brushed his coat with his hand and sucked on his teeth. Across the streets, lights from the residential blocks came on slowly, one by one, as people came home or moved into dining-rooms to eat. Did any of the darkened windows belong to her?

He moved out of the shadows. Down Street was beautifully kept, more like one of the old-fashioned shops than an underground station; litter-free, sparkling with new ticket machines, unlike the grubby innards of Hammersmith. She saw him and moved to the opposite exit. He understood, stopping to tie up a shoelace before moving across to the other side of the station. She had begun walking down Mayfair, and he crossed to her side of the road. Although she was wearing high-heeled shoes, her height was still fascinating. Considerably less than his five feet ten inches. She stopped by the steps of the Country and Westminster Bank and did up her coat. Was he supposed to pass her? He slowed his walk.

"Meet me at the end of the street by Acorn House," she whispered urgently. He carried on walking. There didn't seem to be many people around, but he followed her instruction. She had not looked at him directly yet, but if he had been in any doubt about the unlawful nature of their meeting, the whispered instruction had dispelled it.

He stood in the forecourt of the building, surprised to find that it was a business complex, not a residential block. Nevertheless, it was in total darkness, so he felt safe by one of the rear pillars. He jumped a few minutes later when he saw her emerge from another side street further up. Someone was *with her!* It was another woman and they were both marching quite briskly towards Acorn House. His bowels turned. He moved across to the second rear pillar. He was within a hundred and fifty yards of the nearest side street. Doubling back, he could reach the station and lose them. He looked up. She had stopped, but they were talking. After a conversation that seemed to go on forever, they shook hands and the other woman moved off. The searing pains in his stomach subsided as she crossed the road. He waited behind the pillar. She mounted the steps, turned a key in the glass door's lock, and opened it. He moved out from the pillar and followed her in.

"I'm sorry about all of this," she said. "Wait over by the lift and press the top button." He did as he was told and watched her lock the door again, this time from the inside. She crossed the foyer and stood next to him. He did not move. The lift arrived and the doors opened. He entered the lift with her and the door closed, leaving them in total darkness. He sensed her hand reach out and press a button. The lift began to ascend. He laughed nervously. The lift stopped and the doors opened. They stepped out. Fifteenth floor. It had to be one of the last high rise buildings in the whole of London.

"You haven't been at work for three days," she said, taking off her coat.

"I felt a bit under the weather," he said. He watched her spreading out her coat on the floor. She kneeled down on it.

"Come and sit down," she said. He took off his coat and spread it out next to hers. He couldn't stop smiling. He really couldn't. Just to have gotten this far, to be sitting next to her, on her coat.

"You've grown a beard."

"They didn't have any razors where I was."

"Where was that?"

He moved across to her and stopped, his face about three inches from hers. Could that be skin on her face? In the moonlight that came in through the upper window it was like a soft glowing whiteness. He felt the strength ebb out of him, sucked out by the calmness of her expression. He wanted to say something, to phrase words, to describe himself, to describe her, but the need fell away.

She leaned closer, so their lips were touching. Her eyes closed. A kiss. She put her hands to his face and they kissed again, this time more slowly. She worked at the edge of his mouth with her tongue until it gave way. Her mouth was so soft; he could feel his rough skin scratching her, but it just seemed to make her pull in closer. Eventually, he closed his eyes too. His head was pounding; not the throb of panic or despair, but a rhythmic embracing of all the pleasures he had ever felt. This was all of them.

He lay with his head to her breast, his arms around her waist.

"I'm in the shit," he said.

"You certainly are." She kissed him on the forehead.

"What'll I get if I hand myself in?" She shook her head.

"You're a Classified Twenty, which means not only are you an activist, but you're a named wanted activist. Your chances aren't good, Morda."

He knew it, but to hear it said at that moment gave it the jarring quality of an established truth. He drew himself up over her, eyes level.

"Where are we?"

"Acorn House. It's a listed building; they're pulling it down at the end of the month. It's owned by *Palby's*. I was finishing the clearing out operation last week and they gave me the keys."

"Why are they destroying all these buildings? It's such a waste."

She laughed and held an index finger to her lips.

"You ask too many questions. The answers will only make you ask me more. Suffice it to say that I am the answer to all of those kind of questions. Will you let that suffice for the time being?"

He kissed her again, and then they turned over and she was kissing him; her voice was so calm and her words so unrushed, but she kissed him with a fervour. She was working at him, pulling the dark jumper over his head, pushing her fingers into his skin.

The last time he had felt such strength forced upon him had been outside Leeds in 1917 when he had been attacked by an unarmed man and leapt upon. He had fought back then as he did now, worming his fingers up to the upper part of her dress from his supine position. She slowed as she took his shirt off, rubbing her face into his chest, running fingers across the side of his ribs. She lifted herself up, popping open the line of dress buttons down to her waist, throwing herself out of the top part of her dress. Released, her breasts fell freely over him, his eyes fixing on their shape. He had never seen anything like this before, and his hands fell paralysed at his side. She took them and pushed them into her chest, holding them there against her for maybe half a minute, before his fingers came alive.

He was arrested for a moment with the feeling that he would have to return to Hammersmith soon, to beat the Curfew, so Provlyn did not suspect, but then he remembered, and relaxed.

"What's wrong?"

"This is, I suppose," he said, impulsively. She sat up and looked out at the night sky. She took a cigarette out of her coat pocket and lit up.

"Take the rest of your clothes off," she said.

All he had left on were his slacks and underpants. The foldings of the upper part of her dress trailed at her waist. Obeying, he stood up and took off the rest of his clothes, the elastic of his underpants catching momentarily on what felt like an unreal extension of himself, raised out in an arc in front of him. They both watched it as if it might say something.

"You, er, going to do the same?" he said. She stood up and pulled at the waist of her dress; it fell into a pool of material about her feet. Perhaps it was the darkness, but he could not really see anything there, where he was looking. It was just a fine growth of wispy hair. He tried to look without making it obvious, but it was a bit difficult with both of them standing there in front of the window.

"The moon's bright," he said. She looked round, but not long enough for his desperate visual search to come up with anything more tangible than it had done previously. She looked round at him. They walked back to the coats and lay down. As he joined her, she moved back over him and took hold of him between her fingers, allowing each a journey across the swollen skin.

The first thing he felt was the wetness, and then, across the folds of skin, he found entry into her. Even at this stage, his earlier fear of failure returned; such a sophisticated instrument; how would he work it? She didn't seem to be having any problems with his. She stopped to pull his wet fingers up above her opening. So that was how it worked.

A few minutes later she drew him up to her again, and guided him to the edge of entry; he could feel a welling of sensitivity poised at the meeting wall of her thighs, but he stopped.

"We can't do this," he said. "You'll have a child."

"Don't you think I've had two already?" She sighed. "Because I haven't. I wouldn't fertilise at thirteen. They tried me for two years, but nothing happened. I was the only girl in the school who could not conceive. The Headmistress said the last girl like that was in 1965. I felt so ashamed. No-one made fun of me or anything, but I could always tell what they were thinking. *There goes Rocassa Milo, the barren bitch.* So, anyway, there is nothing to worry about."

Morda looked up at her, pushing her hair back so he could see her face. The wetness of her eyes caught the light. She wiped them.

"I know women aren't supposed to cry," she said. He went to sit up, but she lay back over him and stroked his face. "Don't stop on account of a few tears. I want this."

He found the place himself this time, but once in the warmth he was a little shocked to discover how poor he was at holding back, the whole process completed in just over a minute. She held on to him, nevertheless, pushing herself into him, holding him there with her hand, until she slowed and her head gradually lowered to his neck.

He slowly became aware of the carpet and protruding coat buttons from under him and moved round slightly, drawing her hair over his face. Even though he was naked, her body heat drew up against him like a cosy wedge of night-warmed blanket.

Her breathing had slowed to a pace that gave him a feeling of immeasurable calm. The warmth of her hair and smell of her body made him feel complete; he would not even begin to consider how temporary it might all be. For all the shortcomings, impulsive mistakes and instability of his life up to then, he could still lay back and wallow in the knowledge that he had made love to a woman, and he had enjoyed it.

He passed several police officers on his way into Block Three of Nuneaton House, but their expressions of concern were not directed at him. They looked beyond the complex, back in the direction of London.

The nurse recognised him immediately and sent him to the Waiting Room with a cup of coffee. He looked back out at her as the time passed; she made a few phone calls and looked nervous. When she called him back to reception almost an hour had passed.

"I haven't been able to contact the main distribution doctor, but I'm afraid I have instructions that preclude me from letting anyone take children from here unless they arrive with their partners. You both have to sign for it, you see." Provlyn looked at her in disbelief. He was ill prepared to suffer again because of misplaced trust.

"I was told that you knew I'd be arriving alone."

The nurse picked up the phone again and dialled. Since she had seen the paper on Wednesday, she had hoped she would not have to do the Friday duty, but the School was short-staffed due to the extra work it had taken on after the closure of the West London School at Shepherds Bush. To think she had taken an activist round the building, feeding him information about the siring process that would go straight back to one of those radical groups. It was almost as horrific as the thought that he might not have been discovered for another week and then she would have given away the baby to them. At least it was safe for the time being.

"Oh. I have Provlyn Ranshell here, doctor. I'm just phoning to check that... I see. You're sure? In that case, I'll see you there in a moment." She looked across at Provlyn. "You'd better follow me."

There had been no phone calls or letters in the last three days, though Provlyn had only left the house twice since his release. He had almost made himself late that morning in the hope that there would be a last minute phone call, but there had been nothing. He had tried not to think about it, but had been unable to get a recurring picture out of his mind of the bodies being carried out from the house in Whitechapel. He realised he knew nothing about the activists, nothing that might ever help him find Morda again, if he had gone into hiding. He had been eleven when the war broke out; old enough to know it was happening, but too young to make any sense of it. By the time it had finished he had accepted it as an everyday process, and the fact that it was over had made him believe, somehow, that all the trouble in the country was in the past. His father had been shot on a training exercise on the edge of Manchester. They had been practising an ambush strategy planned for a central republican group reportedly on their way to London; the police had found the group eventually, and they had all been put to death under the common civil war charge of treason. The Manchester fifteen year old that he was had concluded that all the hate and fear was over. Even those who had only intended to kill had been punished. He had met Morda, left Manchester for London. Things had looked to be safe for him.

He followed the nurse to Block Four and climbed the stairs to the familiar ward. The only child in the pen was number 107, dressed not only in a new crimson jumpsuit, but wearing a cap and carrying a little multi-coloured bag labelled *'My Medical Records'*. The boy looked lost, but smiled when he saw Provlyn. The final signing sheets were presented, and Provlyn signed, interested to see the black stamp *C20* against Morda's name. He looked at the child; in all the furore of the last three days, he had forgotten about the name.

"I'm sorry about the earlier confusion," the nurse said. Provlyn grimaced at the euphemism. She opened the pen gate, and the boy waddled out. It was a terrible moment for Provlyn; the boy gurgled and dribbled. Provlyn took his hand and they left the building. It was another oddly warm day, but Provlyn felt uncomfortably cold, pacing slowly to the tram terminus. He had willed this day on from a fifteen year old's fanciful hopes through determination to his signing a few weeks ago. His son giggled at the bus stop, looking round at the people in the queue. He was a lot happier than he had been on their last visit to Nuneaton House, holding on tightly to his father's hand. His father, though, looked away, his expression solemnly dark.

The newly-named *Government House,* a collection of yellow brick four-storey office buildings behind the Houses of Parliament was a success as far as the architect's brief was concerned, completing a Westminster island of central administration. The new brick had even been discoloured with a chemical dye after it was found to be a little bright, and the match was now near perfect. The decision to centralise the Populite's administrative house, previously located in York, had been made towards the end of the war, but the move had, not surprisingly, taken nearly ten years to complete. The governments had taken on the majority of tasks demanded by the postwar 'resettlement' programme, but there were difficulties. The amount of money and speed it had been pumped into the Treasury by the administrative house had led to an over-ambitious programme of reforms. The current government, fired by the successful implementation of the Clearance Act had already drawn up several clauses of the first Reform Bill, not planned for another forty-two years, and had brought forward the introduction of the Toll Tax by nine years.

Government House had finally opened its doors after the last of the administrative house had moved down from York, in April. The meetings conducted during the first six weeks had raised an agenda for action. It was generally accepted that the power of the Populite Bureau had, if not wrested, been used by the government for a little too long. Keeping the government as the administrative force of the Populite was to be desired, but it would be necessary to slow down the wind of change, or there would be a democratic swing away from anything that was currently on offer to the people. They were good enough judges of history to realise that. Also on the agenda was the need for a tightening up on the activists. They were an agreed necessary punchbag for the media and politicians, but there were rumours of established communities, and plans to kidnap women in key administrative positions in London. Security for the Populite had always been high priority, and, even in the war, no woman had been taken prisoner; however, the Populite's control over procreation and everything stemming from that control would be seriously threatened by any activist-organised programme of kidnapping. Meetings were already taking place between newspaper proprietors, government department heads and high-ranking members of the Populite Bureau. Their first job would be to unite in London to round up all the known activists at large, through an organised programme of searches and checks on offices and homes, borough by borough. It was a pleasant irony that the swift implementation of Toll Tax cards and information provided on completed Tax forms would facilitate this process considerably. The Bureau had set themselves the target of returning themselves to overall power behind the scenes by the end of the year, in an atmosphere of healthy democratic debate, but devoid of any serious social threat to their long term programme.

Morda looked out of the window down at the toy carriages and people fighting their way through the day. She had left just before midnight, a journey back that most women living in the area had to make, to *clock in* to their residential blocks. All this entailed was engaging a phone catch fixed behind the front door to her flat. The higher social position a woman had, the more care and security she was afforded, though at twenty to twelve at the door to the lift it had seemed something of a disadvantage.

They had woken up just after eleven, so there had been virtually no time to set any plan in motion, but she had opened up the whole of the fifteenth floor to him and had promised to return with some food after work the next day. There had been no suggestion of his leaving, but he was interested to find that the lift did not work when he tried it.

The office he sat in was a lot more comfortable than the room in Burnt Oak. It was not by accident that she had sent them up to the fifteenth floor. The office was semi-residential, with a small shower, living room and kitchenette. There was no electricity or food, but the water was hot, and the shower he had that morning after four days in the rough was as close as he had ever known washing to get to sexual intercourse. It was still difficult to enter the shower at first, though. He had the smell of her all about him. It was probably a lot of his smell, too, but it was proof to his tired senses that last night had really happened. He thought about it as he looked out of the window. *'Smoked glass,'* she had said. *'They won't see you.'*

The view from Acorn House was a panacea to his weariness; Hyde Park stretched out East, uniformed men playing under the bandstand to a small gathering. Beyond it he could see the Serpentine stretching out in a thin green line. The view out of the window to his left was no less impressive; Green Park, and beyond it, the oatmeal building behind black gates where Queen Edwina sat, waiting for old age to finally claim her. Beyond that, the grey of Westminster and the Thames; such a splendid view from one small room in London. Few people would see London this way in the years to come. The old republican slogan *'Detechnology Means Less'* (in the War many people had been shot daubing it on walls) applied to high-rise buildings, too. He could have sat at the window for hours, but he remembered something he had seen earlier. Something that was still bothering him. He lifted it up and a tone sounded. He held it for a few moments, deliberating, until the tone died. He restored it with a tap on the base of the one piece holder and dialled. Two rings and someone spoke.

"Provlyn."

"Morda... ?"

"I'm alright. I haven't been able to phone."

"Where are you?"

"Whitechapel. Listen, I can't stay long. I just wanted to tell you..."

"I've just got back from Nuneaton House..."

"...I'm alright. I've found somewhere to stay..."

"...with the boy. It's nearly time for me to feed him."

"... what?"

"I've decided he'll sleep in your bed."

"You went back..."

"If you come back now... I've been trying to arrange things with Lady Challis. There's a chance things might not be too bad. You'd only have to..."

"You went and collected the child? How could you do that? I was ringing to make sure you didn't... I might not..."

"...come back for a while. I could meet you somewhere."

He squeezed the base of the receiver and the tone resumed. Another lunatic impulse. He should have left it. A romanticising fool and now a fucking sireling to worry about! He went into the next room and picked up the glass ashtray on the long mahogany table. He lifted up his arms in frustration, looking for somewhere to throw it, something he could hit with it. In the end he put it back on the table. The idiot was probably mouthing off to everyone in Wimbledon about *rehabilitation* or some such other shit. And for the Queen's arse, what was he doing with the kid? Lorkoz had too many of his own problems to worry about a dribbling eighteen monther.

He picked up the phone again. The tone reassured him. It was just a voice from the other side of London. It meant nothing.

The instruction complete, *Files Found* came up on the screen. The operator punched in a few more commands and a breakdown of names, borough by borough emerged, page by page, from the printer.

"Thirty-one? Is that all? I would have thought since the war we might have compiled a more impressive list than that." The operator keyed in a few more instructions.

"One hundred and fifty-seven," she said. "But that includes the ones who have been caught. Forty-two in prison and eighty-four dead."

It looked as though the government had achieved some success with its police force, if the figures could be trusted. It only remained to be seen whether the number of activist incidents declined after the thirty-one were apprehended. With the mobilising of special units working exclusively on the search programme, many new short-term posts were being drawn up for people with proven records of senior efficiency. Even government officials were being considered; the police force could not possibly provide enough candidates for the positions at short notice. The Senior Operations Secretary at the Bureau watched the information cross the screen, picking up the printed sheets.

"I think we'll have fifty booklets made up to hand out to the team this evening."

The sound of the computer operator's fingers on the keyboard created the inspiring impression of hoards of tiny people hurrying down an unending staircase. Looking out from the window of the Government Building office, there were plenty of people to provide a visual realisation of this, moving swiftly in small bunches across the street.

Morda lay in the corridor on the floor, next to the lift. He pressed his face into the carpet, warmed by the afternoon sun, hoping he might find something in it of yesterday, but it was odourless. He turned over on his back and stretched out. It was an improvement on Hammersmith. He might consider putting in a bid to the developers before they knocked it down.

He jumped up with a start as sounds of movement groaned from the lift shaft. He stepped back defensively to the floor entrance, his eyes fixed on the lift. When the doors opened he breathed relief. In the half darkness, a figure emerged, carrying several bags. She had on a dark brown coat, lapels buttoned across the neck, with a black beret. Even though the sun had almost set he could see more of her face than yesterday, he was watching her with different eyes. She didn't look concerned that there was no welcoming party to meet her, but moved, instead, towards the door behind which he was standing. She put the bags down.

"You're beautiful," she said as he came out.

"I've been waiting all day for this," he said. Their faces moved closer, but stopped short. A moment of inertia hung before them; Morda could still feel a wrongness in his desire, a sense of being misplaced, but it vaporised to nothing and their lips touched.

"You felt it too," she said. He tilted his head and pushed his tongue past her lips. The kiss was a lot better this time.

"It's not me; it's this fucking world," he said, as they sat down in the kitchenette. She took out a bag of crusty rolls that proved to be as hot as the flask of soup she had poured out for them. "But we're here, aren't we? It's happening."

"We have to talk," she said. Her tone was out of key with the kiss he was still tasting. "I can't keep you here for too long. The woman you saw me with yesterday was from my block; wondering where I was going. She knows I have the key to this place. If she sees me here again... She's on the *Walkway Watch,* unfortunately. I'm sure she spends most of her day wandering round looking for criminals, though we haven't had any crime in this area for nearly seven years. It's just lucky she saw me and not you." They ate the soup, but the subject matter seemed to have impaired the flavour.

"I'll take risks," he said. "Any risks."

She smiled. "You've become something of a cult hero at *Palby's.* I've heard that Pridge is boasting the two of you were good friends. Though he didn't say that to me of course."

"You interviewed him?"

"I have to. You were in my department. I have to go to a police meeting tomorrow. I think they want me to reassure them that the company isn't a hotbed of political activity."

She took the plates over to the sink and gestured towards the next room. He followed her. The sun had gone down and the room was now only lit by streetlights and the security lighting across the park from Buckingham Palace. He kneeled in front of her as she sat on the sofa.

"Do you think they'll kill me when they find me?"

"They may not find you," she said. "I know for a fact that there are many small communities of people who have escaped classification to reach off limit cities, and who run their own lives there."

"But I haven't escaped classification," he said. "I'm a Twenty."

"Perhaps we ought to just enjoy the time we have together," she said. "Nothing lasts forever." She sat back on the sofa and he moved alongside her, taking her hands. He had made a list earlier of all the things he wanted to tell her, but it was in the other room. Right now, he had no intention of moving from the sofa. He ran his fingers round the edge of her face. So soft. He could not remember an unadulterated joy like that he now felt in her company. His eyes glazed with the intensity of his feeling; Harvil had a saying about there only being one way to travel from the zenith of anything.

"Have you ever loved a man before?" he said.

She pouted her lips and nodded slowly. "Four years ago, in a place called Wood Green. We had a grand closing of one of our old shops; it was my first year working for the company. This man, he was there for most of the day; dark-skinned, handsome. He kept asking me about the closure; kept saying that we were sending another three hundred people into service. That we were helping the government destroy job choice. He must have picked me out, because he made sure he didn't talk to anyone else. He walked back to the bus station with me - I didn't have a lift that night. We must have both realised we were alone. We did it around the back of his flats." Morda looked at her curiously, trying to picture the event. "It was crazy, but there was no-one around. Afterwards I got on a bus and went home. I never saw him again, but I learned something new about myself that night."

A one night stand. Morda had experienced plenty of those when he was younger. But two men out together late at night was no crime. The worst they could have got was a Public Order offence fine. What she had done, though, contravened the Sexual Relations Act as well as breaking obscenity laws. Just a year in her first job; she could have thrown it all away for a single moment of madness. And how many more of those moments lay ahead?

She looked across at him. "I read a book at school about two lovers who stayed in an old house together. One of them had killed someone and was on the run from the police. I think the boy who was being chased was called Tess."

"What happened to them in the end?"

"It was only a book."

He moved up and kissed her, pressing himself close until he knew she could feel him. He could smell a scent of something under her blouse, and pressed his face into the material, the yield making it clear that it was the last item of clothing between his face and her breasts. She worked at it until it was free, and threw it aside. He kissed the orbs until they grew to little stones in his mouth. At the same time he was trying to relieve himself of his own clothes. He could see her this time, in the light from the street. Her feet worked at his trousers until he was free of them, and she drew her hands around his buttocks, teasing a fingered line between them. Gradually he felt her work two fingers in closer, and grabbed her hand before she could advance.

"Don't you like that?" He couldn't answer her. He had the sensation that he was suddenly above Provlyn in this cage of a building, their bodies matted together against the sofa. He was unsure about himself again. He smiled reassuringly and brought her hands up, kissing them.

"There's something I'd like to do," he said, and he stood up, taking the rest of her clothes off. She understood, moving round on the sofa, pushing her legs up towards him. She had shown him where she wanted his fingers, and now he put his mouth there, tasting her, providing her, it seemed, with a great deal more entertainment than he had managed the previous evening. Some moments after she had pulled him away, she moved back above and this time he let her move into him with her fingers, and in turn he moved into her until they locked together and he came.

"Do you think this has always been wrong?" Morda asked as they lay back on the sofa.

"It isn't wrong," she said, flippantly.

"The law says it's wrong."

"Laws change."

"Not these laws. But I want you to tell me, to speculate if you like. Do you think people were ever allowed to do this legally?"

"If they were allowed to, we'd have no control over the population. There would be too many people, countries without food, unwanted children, women would become prisoners of their own bodies."

Morda laughed. "Is that what they taught you at school?"

She looked up uncertainly. His smile waned.

"You do think it's wrong, don't you? Are you just doing this as some kind of revenge because you can't have children? Are you fulfilling some kind of personal fear that you aren't normal?"

She wasn't looking at him now. Her eyes were on the ground.

"The bad news is that you *are* normal - in fact you're the only fucking normal one in the whole of that sexless school you went to. To think of the superiority - half of them thinking they are doing the world some kind of favour by staying chaste. Human beings were made to have children together, in a unit; in a *family*." His stare drew her confused expression upwards. He wanted the icebag there and then to show her. However, she was not arguing back, assailing him with indoctrinated logic. She just looked at him dumbly.

"I wish I could have children," she said. "I'd have your child, I'd prove it to you. I don't want you because I'm different - I want you because *you're* different. The way you looked at me when I first met you, the way you talked to me that evening at the meal. There was no prejudice. No wound up misogyny. I knew that even if you didn't want me, you wouldn't be offended by me." She looked at him wistfully. He put his arm around her and kissed her forehead.

"I'm not offended," he said. But she was still distressed.

"I've got to make it safe for you here somehow, Morda."

"Making it safe for me is bound to make it dangerous for you. You mustn't take any risks for me," he said. "Promise me. No risks."

She looked past him at the dimming lights of London, filtering less and less into the room, their bodies grey against the darkness of the room.

Crackdown On Activists. New Government Body To Act.

'The first duty of the Government's new political criminal division will be to round up the seven main activists at large' the Home Secretary Serboth Challis said today, speaking from her home in Wimbledon. 'The right of the individual to safety on the streets of London is paramount,' she added. Our correspondent writes that top of the division's list will be Lorr Djvarich, Antol and Morda, seen photographed below. A reward will be offered for information...'

The Saturday morning *Informer* had given the four day old story a final kick with the criminal division angle, but it was the statement by Challis that had worried Provlyn, suggesting he might be aiding enquiries.

He had not slept the previous night due to the aborted phone call amongst other things. It was impossible to tell why they had been cut off, something that made Morda's comment that he was alright less than reassuring. The boy had slept soundly through the night and he was still sleeping, but Provlyn was unwilling to leave the house to buy food in case the phone rang. The contents of the larder amounted to one apple and a tin of celery soup. *The Guide To Siring* recommended a sophisticated diet of tinned and packet items only available from *SireWire*, its west London branch somewhere near Westbourne Park. It would have to wait.

He had spent the early part of the morning on a fruitless search through drawers and cupboards. He had hoped to find a collection of names, phone numbers or addresses, anything that might give him an idea where Morda might be staying. He had no intention of handing any find over to Challis, or the policewoman who had started to pay him regular morning visits, even though the phone call had fired him to sacrifice all his personal ethics about Morda's belongings. He knew he was in Whitechapel; he would research every avenue of information he could to keep alive the flickering image of his future with Morda.

He was on his last morsel of tobacco, creased out thinly in two papers to resemble a cigarette. Lighting it, he reflected how, throughout the protracted morning search, he had kept coming across the week's copies of *The Informer*, with that recurring picture. For someone wanted so badly, there didn't seem to be a single concrete accusation amongst the list of transgressions, and he could only think of the one. Either Morda didn't have any faith in the judicial system, or there had been other crimes he did not know about. Neither reason did much to make him feel Morda was likely to appear at the door again of his own free-will.

When she came out of the entrance to her block in Audley Street, Rocassa was surprised to see the limousine parked out in front of the building. There were few enough cars in the street during the week, let alone Saturday mornings. She switched the bag of food defensively to her left hand as she passed the car, but the rear electric window buzzed open and a voice called her back.

"Rocassa Milo?"

"Yes?" She moved slowly back towards the car. She fancied she could smell the warm broccoli pie.

"Would you get into the back of the car, please?"

Her heart stopped as she saw the identification wallet. *Head of Defence.* The woman who had spoken to her was thin and angular, with the poise of a high-ranking official; her voice sounded like it only ever spoke commands, and she was soon sitting in the back of the car alongside her.

"I hope we are not interrupting your work. I understand you run quite a tight ship at *Palby's.*"

Rocassa smiled at the compliment, but her thoughts were of Acorn House. The limousine moved slowly up the street and accelerated past the tall building. She kept her eyes fixed on her new guide.

"We have been, as you might understand, *interested* in your career so far since you joined the company. Up to now your progress has been more than satisfactory."

The Head of Defence took a small file from a cabinet in front of her and turned pages. The back of the car was like a small office: a drinks cabinet built into the frame in front of her, a small bookcase to the side, a telephone on a slide out glass tray under the cabinet, even a small fan above their heads in the corner, silently keeping the air cool. The page found, she was offered the file.

"You recognise this man?"

It was Morda. The file picture was the same one that had been appearing in the newspapers over the last week, but the page opposite was blank. She looked hard at the picture.

"That's Morda," she said. "He works for *Palby's* but he hasn't been into work since last Monday. But I'd have known who he was anyway. His face has been in the papers all week."

"Yes," the Head of Defence said. "We are particularly anxious to apprehend him, as you'll have realised by the way the story has run." She had an unpleasant mannerism of staring hard at people when she spoke to them. It was hard enough coping with this without the faint smell of the broccoli pie which the bag seemed unable to conceal.

"We think you can help us find this man," she said, with professional enthusiasm. She returned the file to the cabinet. "We'd like you to join a short meeting we're having in one of the conference rooms this morning."

She gave her a small sheet of tissue-thin yellow paper with *AGENDA* in brown print at the top. It was new government standard recyclable paper she had only ever seen previously on orders to the Management of *Palby's* from upper echelon sources of the Populite.

"I apologise for interrupting your routine this morning, but we tried to get in touch with you for most of yesterday evening. You weren't in, it seems. Where were you off to this morning?"

"It's work again," she said, patting the bag at her side. "We're looking at ways of contributing to the promotion of the government's *Revolution for Industry* programme."

"Oh, could I see that?" the Head of Defence asked, putting out a hand towards the bag.

"Er, well that's just my lunch in there," Rocassa said, with scarcely time to admire her own brand of mendacious invention. "The documents I'll be looking at are at work. It doesn't pay to take that kind of material home, as I'm sure you'll appreciate." She smiled knowingly and swallowed hard. At the bottom of the bag was Morda's cleaned shirt, socks and underpants, documents that would have taken rather more creative fiction than she felt capable of.

The square of buildings at Westminster was very quiet, but they pulled into a rear car park that was quite full.

They got out of the car and headed towards the rear Government Buildings, past a red notice, declaring *Bureau Conference.*

There were about thirty people in the conference room, gathering coffees from the table at the side, some smoking, all women. Rocassa felt immediately on her guard in the officious atmosphere. She did not recognise a single face from the table, but she had heard enough about the Bureau to know that it worked behind the scenes; the women who took these kind of decisions could not afford to have public faces. Even the woman who had accompanied her on the journey there had carried no name on her identification wallet. She was just *Head of Defence*.

Everyone at the meeting except her carried a copy of the same file she had been shown in the back of the car. She was able to gather that there were thirty-one other such activists that the Bureau were concentrating on, but her own role in the matter remained unclear until the Head of Defence addressed the meeting under Item Two on the Agenda: Operations.

"Members of the Bureau, under our agreed creation of special units to develop the search programme, I would like to introduce Rocassa Milo to you. She is the Chief Sales Accountant of *Palby's*, London, and she is probably the one member of the Populite who knows most about Morda. She employed him, she gave him details of his job, she has access to his work file. She is precisely the type of professional we need to join our search programme working in the unit dealing with this Morda man. She has proven organisational skills and anything she lacks, her police junior will provide. I've spoken to the Director of *Palby's* and we've arranged secretarial assistance to second Rocassa to the first unit to plan search strategies and co-head the operation with senior police." All eyes fixed on her and the women at the back began to applaud. The Head of Defence beckoned her to stand up, looking on at her proudly. "We want you to find him, Rocassa, and set a standard of success that all the other units will be anxious to follow. We'll make available whatever force you feel you need. We know you won't let us down."

The applause continued and then died, suddenly, as it became clear that she was expected to deliver some kind of spontaneous speech to welcome the appointment. The Head of Defence sat down. She looked round at the serious expressions in front of her. She was in front of thirty of the top members of the Populite Bureau. It was as surreal a moment as the task they expected her to undertake. She cleared her throat.

"It is unquestionably a great honour to have been appointed to the unit. The Head of Defence has said some very pleasant things about me. I would just like to say to you all that I will find this man," she looked slowly round the table, catching every eye. "...and I will do everything in my power to bring him to justice." She sat down and felt herself reddening at the applause. She felt the heat of her face and then moved her hand down surreptitiously to check her bag. When she looked in front of her, there was a small file, headed *'Known Activists'*. She nodded at the Head of Defence and sat up ready to glean anything she could from the rest of the meeting. Above all, she was interested to discover what the full extent of her power was likely to be.

The frustration of an enforced trip back to work after the meeting, was soon over. She sat in her office on the second floor of the Palby building and watched the limousine drive off. She could not ring Morda; she would have to watch her movements the way those above her would. She had been given an opportunity any of the other girls at her school, wherever they were now, would have died for. The chance to directly serve the Populite Bureau; future senior placement in the Bureau itself a probability. She looked through the file she had been given. A supplementary section at the end provided extended biographical details of all those in the file. They would expect her to read through them. Perhaps she ought to give him the chance to go through it for her.

Born: January 30th 1938. Boarding School. Army Record... The upper half of the details were routine, but darker printed details continued underneath on the photocopied sheet; once interested, they furthered their researching grasp.

Partners: Harvil [us] d.1/09 (Known activist: criminal record AG403L) 1919-1914

 Provlyn Ranshell (In service at Parkside - Challis - LIB) 1914-1909

Indictable Crimes: See latest G407c; Check unsolved incidents since 1912
 Crime before January 1909? (Employed Feb.: Palby's)

Two longstay partners, both of five years, the first over the course of the war. The work file carried a multitude of short term job references, the last at a brewery in Mortlake! The army record, though, was good. In fact, apart from his relationship with this Harvil, the criminal element seemed to be complete speculation. The expected damning evidence was not there. She didn't imagine she would have found anything more tangible even if she had been able to get hold of the G407c. She was now in a position to find out everything else they knew about him; she could demand access to it now she was working with the unit searching for him.

The first meeting was scheduled for Sunday evening, where she was to meet the senior policewoman appointed to set up the units, to be directed from Whitechapel Police Station. She would have to watch her movements.

"I'm flattered anyone should think I'm that important, especially this Bureau of top women." He drank from the can of beer she had brought him.

"Haven't you asked yourself why all of this is happening to you?"

"I used to live with an activist; it was an accident, but I killed a man when I went to see him just before he died in hospital. I'm spending time with you... If necessary, I'm sure they'll invent some more laws I'll have broken before the week is up." He took a bite of the broccoli pie. It was cold and a little runny, but it tasted as good as anything he had eaten for some time. He smiled at her. He had lost a lot of the fear that he had been carrying around with him when he'd waited outside the building behind the pillar two nights previously. She bent over him and kissed his forehead. Warmth.

The sky was darkening outside again. It was strange how she had not seen him in daylight since she had given him the ticket to the Ballet. She pulled up his hair into black folds as he ate.

"This will have to be your last evening here. They want me at a meeting with the police tomorrow night, and anything could happen next week. If I can't get back here, you could be stuck. Imagine watching the demolition people arrive from this window."

"It would probably be a more humane death than whatever's waiting for me when I get caught. You don't know what it's like, being part of the Populace and being on the run. You get to feeling like you're... well, like an animal."

"Like a *what?*"

He looked at her, trying to gauge whether it would be worth the effort of explaining.

"Before the Death Age, I found out that there used to be things on this planet called animals. Odd, furry things; they would run around a lot, a bit like humans, but they were smaller. Some humans liked them and kept them as pets, they looked after them and fed them; others, however, went round and killed them for people to eat. You, well, I've become like a kind of pet to you in the last few days. But there are people out there who have no intention of looking after me. I'm not suggesting they intend to serve me up at the next anniversary banquet, but I'm sure you understand the analogy I am trying to make. Incidentally, we've both been that second kind of human; remember the meat at the *Palby's* meal?"

"Oh, how horrible," she said, her face wrinkling up like a paper bag. "You mean that stuff was bits of something that used to be alive?" He nodded. "But how do you know all this?"

The rest of the evening was spent talking about the Other World, and Morda detailed his find at the Caricott Building on that Friday. She went through the misery of her school days and it was much as he had imagined, minds fostered with a combination of social responsibility and fear, children turned overnight into adults, their bodies used as machines to continue the rolling programme of formula humanity. She had managed to break the women's role in this by her infertility; her sexuality could also be related to this, although she still maintained it was his attitude that had interested her, not any genetic flaw.

When midnight came she went off, but this time she came back later as promised, in the early hours of the morning, to stay with him until dawn. Then, he would leave and make his way back to

Burnt Oak. She had cut his hair short and his beard was a lot more substantial now. She had even found an old pair of *pince-nez* spectacles to complete the deception, along with a plastic white Toll Tax card, with the printed name, *Pridge,* at the top.

Meeting again was something they had left to the last minute to discuss, but as the first lifting of light showed in the distance, Morda spoke.

"How are we going to meet?" The silence that followed described the weight of the problem.

"Let's plan two meetings. If things go well I'll meet you at the tramline terminus at Hendon on Tuesday night when it's dark. I'll only come if I can sort out the alarm on the flat and if things go well at the unit. If I'm not there by seven, go back. The second one can be the same as the first, but on Friday."

Tuesday. It seemed such a long time away; sixty hours. He turned to her and ran his face against hers. Her mouth was soft, her face wet. He did not know whether it was just with his tears; he closed his eyes.

"It's funny," he said. "Employing you to find me. Do you think you'll have any luck?"

"I'll find you," she said. "I just hope I can come alone."

He sat up and looked out of the window. The crown of the sun sat at the back of St. James' Park.

"Do you believe in God?" he said.

"What's that?"

"Something people used to believe in when things were going well in the Other World."

"I believe in you."

She leaned forward and kissed him.

Revolution for Industry

"You must tell them everything you know," Lorkoz was saying.

"I have told them everything I know. Do you think I would have stayed here all this time if I knew where he was?" Provlyn stubbed the newly-rolled cigarette out after just a few puffs. He poured himself another glass of whisky. It still cut the back of his throat even though the taste had become more familiar over the past week.

"I'm worried about you, Provlyn. Morda should have telephoned you back after that last call. Wherever he is, it can't be too much of a problem to find a phone."

Provlyn stood by the French windows.

"You have been very kind, Lorkoz. I appreciate your help; I'm very grateful that you have got my shopping done. Nevertheless, I will sort this problem out myself. Whatever they promised you for extracting information from me, I hope they still pay you for trying, but there's nothing to say."

"It's my freedom," Lorkoz said, defeated.

"Morda used to say that freedom never comes cheaply to anyone. I'm sorry." He followed Lorkoz out and kissed him at the door. He wondered, as he watched him cross the street holding Hadanna, could he be watching an older Provlyn, clinging to the living remnants of an old life partnership? Doubtless Lorkoz would be carted off again, promised another slice of freedom for more *favours*.

He looked to his right to see his morning house call on her way towards him, accompanied by a slightly shorter woman, dressed in a light green suit. News about Morda, perhaps? He ducked back into the house and responded calmly to the bell when it rang, though his head was still singing slightly from the early morning drink.

"Good morning, Mr Ranshell. This is Rocassa Milo, officer in charge of the unit that are looking for Morda. She wants to ask you a few questions."

He closed the door behind them and led them into the lounge. The policewoman then left to make tea. It seemed an odd thing to do, as if this woman might be about to do something the policewoman had to turn a blind eye to.

He noticed for the first time that she was quite short, her black hair pinned back in a knotted thread. She did not seem interested in him at first, wandering round the lounge, looking at the various photos and items on the different pieces of furniture.

"Have you any news for me?" he asked.

"We could have. If you have news for us."

"Do you know where he is?"

She was looking at the army photograph above the radiogram. He stood over her defensively as she studied it.

"It's not a good likeness," he said.

"Really?"

He was trying to remember where he had heard her name before. He did not enjoy the confidence she was showing; it was more than he would have expected from someone looking for Morda. She was of the unfortunate figure eight shape he had noticed one or two women carry. She looked as though she was stored nightly in two parts that screwed together in the middle. Eventually she sat down on the edge of the armchair, focusing hard on him.

"You've lived together for five years."

Provlyn nodded.

"You see, all I want to find out is what kind of person Morda was. Whether he went out a lot after work; whether the two of you socialised much, that kind of information, really." Her voice sounded terribly bored or tired. He recognised the approach, similar to the police sergeant who had interviewed him the previous week. He finished the whisky in one gulp. She crossed the room to the boy, who sat in the corner pen Lorkoz had loaned him that morning. The boy began banging his hand enthusiastically on the rail of the pen.

"What's he called?"

"We haven't decided yet," Provlyn said. "You see Morda and I haven't really been talking much during the past week. Strange, really. If things settle down next week I'll let you know what we decide." He looked at her coldly and began to read the newspaper. He thought he might have a better chance of finding Morda than her if he went round the streets on his hands and knees, but he said nothing.

"I used to be his boss," she said, writing something down on the memo pad she was carrying. Provlyn nodded. He had seen her name on Morda's employment contract, but he had never spoken of her. The policewoman brought in two cups of tea, but her superior looked on enquiringly at her, expecting something else.

"There's nothing there," she said, gesturing upwards with her eyes.

"Have you been looking upstairs?" Provlyn said, moving towards her in the doorway. The two card trick. They might have been two conmen at the house of an elderly man. The policewoman left the room.

"You could have asked me, but you didn't. That's illegal without my permission."

"Your co-operation has been paid for in full by your last employer," Milo said, "so unless you have anything to say that could be of use to me, I would prefer your mouth to remain in a closed position."

She now made no pretence of searching the room, and within a few minutes she found a small diary hidden underneath the radiogram. She flicked through it with undisguised alacrity. Provlyn wondered how he could have missed it earlier that weekend. It must have been hidden on a ledge underneath the radio; there could be no other reason for his missing it. Rocasso Milo took a sip of her tea and left the room.

"Sorry about that," the policewoman said, re-appearing in the doorway. "Orders from higher up." She gestured again upwardly with her eyes. Provlyn looked at her in disgust and returned to the newspaper.

She had not turned up. He had waited until eight, but all the trams except one had arrived and left devoid of passengers. The exception had delivered a man in his mid-thirties in a dark coat and hat, face hidden in the shadows, who had walked off in the direction of West Hendon, where the last estate of occupied houses lay. Morda watched his uncertain movements; he stopped twice as if following half-remembered directions, but even his faltering steps were soon gone.

She was probably in a meeting right at this moment, calculating strategies to find him. It was difficult not to consider the possibility that she might fail to turn up on Friday. He had no chance of contacting her again and very little chance of letting her know where he was without letting others in on the information as well.

He had found his way back to Hendon on Sunday afternoon, taking the tube to Golders Green and walking. He had decided not to take the tram in case they had been observing his movements earlier. The problem with approaching Hendon from a different direction was that he had been unable to find his way back to the house he had stayed at earlier. His resting-place for the previous evenings had been more like a tomb than a house, a windowless set of concrete rooms, but rooms that had four walls and a roof, and as it had begun to rain the past few evenings, there had been no choice. He had exhausted his food supply, not intending to move position until tonight, and now he was back at the tramline terminus, it might be a good idea to retrace his journey to the carpeted house.

It was pitch black and all possible extraneous sources of light were negligible. His disappointment had let his guard down somewhat, and he trudged off moodily in what he thought was the right direction.

It was as he approached the army base corner house that he heard something. It could have been a piece of stone falling off the edge of a pile of rubble, but it was a self-conscious noise. It had stopped only a split second after he had. It was behind him, so he turned and walked in the same direction, but backwards, facing the source of the noise. He threw a stone off into the distance. Crash. Nothing. But there was no point going on until he had sorted out what it was; he would not sleep, he could not, until it was investigated.

"You had better come out where I can see you," he said, slow steps to the rear. He became aware of an overwhelming tiredness. It was not unexpected as he had spent the best part of the last two days revisiting the weekend's experiences, courtesy of a now perpetually flaccid member. Silence again.

"I am unarmed and quite harmless," he said, his right hand cradling the handle of the cudgel. He was thrown suddenly to the floor by the weight of someone jumping out at him from behind. He was stifled by the smell and surrounding texture of a large coat as he tried to pull himself free. Strong arms were pulling his arms behind his back, a knee pushing into the small of his back to prohibit any retaliatory move. When he realised he was beaten, he stopped struggling and was unexpectedly released. He turned around to see the man in the grey coat he had seen at the tramline terminus.

"Harmless," the man repeated, picking up the cudgel that Morda had dropped. He threw it over the roof of the house in front of them before sitting down on a pile of broken paving stones. Morda sat up, but could currently do little more than that, due to the pain in his back. He picked up his pince-nez which had come off in the fall.

"I suppose you're going to tell me I'm trespassing," Morda said. He was still unable to see the man's face because of the shadow of his hat.

"What the fuck are you doing here, man?"

"I live here, sometimes," Morda said. The man kicked him rather hard on his right shin. He winced. "It's the truth." The man stood over him.

"What do they call you, Bonzo? You look like a woman-fucker to me."

"My name is Queen Edwina VII," Morda said.

"Pleased to meet you. I'm Gairn," said Gairn, looking at him closely. "I think I understand why you live here - *sometimes.*" He laughed wryly. He had a way of chuckling that did not sound quite right interspersed with the deepness of his voice. "I recognise your face from the paper last week, even under all that bum fluff." He pulled playfully at Morda's beard.

"*Fuck,*" Morda said and held his chin.

"You're taking a chance running wild round here, aren't you? They have patrols every few days. Shoot you before they ask you why you're here!" He chuckled the high-pitched chuckle again. Morda sat up carefully. His back was trying to tell him something about the end of his life. His intuition was telling him that Gairn was in some way at odds with reality; unpredictable in the more dangerous sense. He shuffled back, but he still could not get up.

"Which union are you in, anyway? East London? Northwest? Who you with?" He was standing over him again.

"I'm with East London, E44 Division, Whitechapel. Or I was. I'm on my own now."

"No kidding," Gairn said. "No kidding. I'm just a republican, though. Work for any of them. All brothers against the State. Break women's backs before they break ours."

"They've been breaking ours for four hundred years," Morda said, acerbically. He lay back and felt his neck on the cold concrete, swiftly followed by the large foot planted again in the middle of his chest.

"Now I'm going to break your back," he said. "What have you done?"

"What do you mean, what have I done? You've seen the papers."

"Papers don't always tell it how it is," he said. "You know. Now tell me." To emphasise the point he drove his foot down into Morda's chest again, painfully, across the ribs.

"I killed a guard in a hospital and resisted arrest." Gairn looked at him. Morda saw the heavy face under the hat for the first time. A frowning, heavily-bearded face.

"And?" A face that was not convinced. A hunted activist would have done more.

"I broke into a Siring School with a chain saw and cut up a few children."

"No kidding," said Gairn. "No kidding. Nobody would sire me either. I've always kind of wanted to do something like that. Your way was messy though. You want a hand gun, simple loading cartridge. Fast action, and a silencer. Straight in and one, two, three, four... right round the ward. Put the nurses away for good measure, too." He swivelled round in an arc, simulating the feat. Morda, though he was still winded, could feel his legs returning to him, and was raising himself very, very slowly, up on the balls of his feet. Gairn was still rotating round, emptying his handgun, one bullet per hospital bed.

Morda bent his head down as he stood up and ran at the pirouetting republican, driving his head into his midriff with all the strength he had. The giant man fell backwards, his gun suddenly empty, and struck the back of his head on an old iron lamppost, coming to rest on the pavement. He was still breathing, but only just.

His pockets were full of old junk; press cuttings, a dispenser of *Archid* Jelly, a *Republican* Handbook *(1945 - revised 1918)*, a tin of foul-smelling tobacco and a small bottle of a colourless liquid labelled *Vokka*. The press cuttings dated back to 1912, and covered activist incidents in London where there had been fatalities. Amongst them he found the Whitechapel Siege and the incident at Guy's Hospital. There was also a pencilled list of five names, his own amongst them, but the others were unknown. It was not a government wanted list - it was something else. He copied the names down in his notebook before returning the list and the other contents to the man's pockets. He stood there for a moment, staring at the man he had incapacitated. He must have been a survivor from the war, down but not defeated, linking himself to whatever anarchic anti-state cause he could find. He was enormous; six and a half feet and broad built. Seeing him on the ground made him feel the attack had been a mistake; if this man ever found him again he would have no problem at all in choking the life out of him without a weapon.

He crossed the street, breaking into a run. Perhaps he should have killed him. Wherever he went, there was always the possibility he might... He looked back. The figure, now just a large dark shape, was not moving. He began to run faster, but as he ran, he lost his way, crossing street after street, passing half houses, stump buildings and strips of wild green. His eyes pumped with adrenaline, saw more and more into the night, his running body bent as if to fall any moment. He slowed down. He was now in the centre of a well of darkness, circled distantly by clusters of light; which was Hendon? He no longer had his cudgel, his only weapon, and he was many streets from the house he had stayed in. If it were true about the patrols it would be important to be near public transport and not lost in this wilderness of decayed nothingness. It started raining. Hailing. He ran across the road, diving under the porch of the first house and sat in its windowless front room watching the emptying sky blister the street with water pebbles. The music of the driving slush, a hypnotic resonance, eventually forced his tired eyes to close, and lulled him to sleep in an unbroken rhythm of tireless sound.

The Head of Defence seemed pleased with the progress of the last two days. The unit had been fully staffed, many of its members hand-picked from policewomen and members of the Populite who had been involved in incidents with activists, from arrests and killings to crowd control at some of the early republican marches of 1920 and 1919. The latest meeting in the Board Room at *Palby's* was further evidence that they had appointed the right unit leader.

Rocassa Milo had interviewed Morda's partner and several employees who had worked with him as well as the policewomen whom he had overpowered to escape. Concern had been expressed by the police about his determination to take a particular work bag away with him, but the contents of the bag were still unknown. It was known that he had made one phone call to the Hammersmith home during which he had said he was staying in Whitechapel, but replays of the tape of the call had cast doubts on the truth of the statement. In any case, the unit was not staffed to field a full search in Whitechapel without aggravating the delicate situation there on the many housing estates.

Rocassa herself had organised the unit to merely collate and speculate on the information they had at that moment. This would buy some time to find a way of having it suggested that Morda might not be an activist, but she knew this would mean establishing as a fact that Morda was not involved with Harvil professionally. Establishing facts about men who were enigmas was difficult, but she knew very little about Harvil from any of the sources she could quote. However, she had the address book Morda had told her about, and the information in that could set up a hundred avenues for misdirected investigation.

"I've asked Rocassa to call this meeting in order that I can express the full objectives of our search programme to all of you." The Head of Defence sat up, tall and angular, looking hard round the room for lapsing attention. Finding none, she continued. "Some of you have dealt with the most evil aspects of this corruption we call activism, some just with those on the periphery of the movement. One thing you must all begin to understand is that you are functioning first and foremost for the Populite Bureau, the organisation that exists to maintain the administrative position of women in this country. Whenever this is threatened, as it often will be, we must rally round to identify the area of the Populace that requires cauterisation. Historically it has always been a dissatisfied minority, where efforts at raising their social status have failed to placate the situation. We have allowed the creation of unions, and a degree of democratic freedom where activism is concerned. After all, we are a democracy. Now, though, we must ensure that there is no further civil unrest. The century has suffered two crippling civil wars; we cannot afford another."

She began to look round her audience again, each wary of her lack of notes or prepared speech, each concerned that they should wear an expression of enthusiasm.

"Therefore we have drafted those of you with the most experience to this unit to work with Rocassa Milo and the Senior Police Officer from Whitechapel, to find and, if necessary, kill these activist leaders. We have, as you will all be witnessing, built up a comprehensive file on our first man, Morda. I only hope we can have him out of the way as soon as possible."

Again the applause. Rocassa Milo was the only one present who had also been at the Saturday Conference, so she was the only one to notice a slight change of emphasis in the delivery of the unit's brief. It was nevertheless a significant one, that chilled the blood around her throat. It was the first time there had been a mention of the word *kill*.

The burly figure struggled steadily along the street, his hand held to the sizeable bruise on the back of his head. His money was still there so the next course of action was almost reflex. He squeezed himself into the phone booth, his coat sodden with rain, and began dialling. It was early, but he had phoned earlier in the past. Someone would always be there to answer the phone. He waited for the ringing tone to end, watching drops of rain run off the end of his nose, breathing in the boxed atmosphere of cold dampness.

"Hello," a voice said.

"Good morning. I would like to speak to Chatwick."

"I think you have the wrong number," the voice continued. Then it gave out another, which Gairn scribbled down.

"Thank you," he said. "I'll try again in a few minutes."

He left the phone booth and wandered round. The pain in his head had slowed to a dull pulse, but he still felt groggy. The last time he had reported a sighting, they had given him twenty pounds as well as found him a small room in Poplar that he had stayed in until earlier that year when the police had become interested. He paid no taxes and carried no identification - they could lock him up for any number of reasons. But soon there would be another reprieve; he could almost feel the warmth of a new flat, gas heaters, warm carpets. A new newspaper every morning, some beer in the larder.

He moved back into the phone box, almost immune to his wetness. He dialled the new number and waited.

"Hello." It was the same voice.

"Good morning. I would like to speak to Chatwick."

"Who is speaking?"

"It's Gairn. N42. Ringing from Hendon. I met a Mr.Morda last night. I thought you might be interested, seeing as his name was on your list."

"It would seem that he is on everybody's list at the moment. Nevertheless, where is he?"

"Round here somewhere. He threw me against a lamppost last night after winding me, but I'll find him, don't worry. Do I ring this number?"

"Listen carefully, please. We want to question him, so we would like him alive and brought to the Hackney address you used earlier.

And so you don't run the risk of being damaged in the process, tell him that if he refuses to come with you, we will pay his friend in Hammersmith a visit. So we know where you are, ring Garvit at midday, seven o'clock and ten o'clock every day. If you haven't rung by a quarter of an hour after the allocated time, we'll be on our way to Hammersmith. That should be good enough for him."

"How important is this man?"

A single laugh was heard at the other end of the phone.

"About fifty pounds worth, I should think. No reason why we shouldn't find you a more secure place this time, either. In one of our *off limits* communities, perhaps." He put the receiver down.

It was a stroke of luck, the sighting. Since the newspaper interest of the previous week, Lorr Djvarich had phoned him several times to enquire about the man and what, if any, information they had about him.

Chatwick left the phone box and looked about him. It was four o'clock. Just a few gas lamps at the corner of Wimbledon Hill Road provided the light. He wore a black cloak and moved stealthily behind the trees into the High Street of the village. He had the numbers of each of the five telephone boxes around the house, rotating their use to minimise the chance of setting a traceable pattern. He hurried down one of the backstreets, his cane ready in his right hand, but the town was quiet.

Djvarich had already made the connection with Harvil, but had been impressed with the way they had facilitated the employment of Provlyn at the Parkside house. It was still a toehold they could exercise over Morda, even though Dorjess' excesses had almost brought them to Morda's attention. The strange sense of duty he had always felt to the monster of a man he had found a job and covered up gross acts for, was not unrelated to the fact that he was his twin brother. On the rare occasions when such a phenomenon occurred, the second twin was invariably terminated at birth. The fact that he himself was that second twin was a good enough reason to keep the matter quiet.

Several months had been spent waiting for Morda to make a move; it was known that he had visited Harvil before he died, and suspected that he had somehow set up the killing of a fellow unionist, Palapsis, to clear his path from the police. Djvarich was worried that Harvil might have, in a moment of weakness, provided Morda with information he could use to set himself up for life with. 'Deals' had been struck with activists in the past that had crippled the progress of the republican network. One of the things Morda could now put a price on was his freedom. Harvil had been one of the top undercover activists, with access to a mine of information, of particular use to the government in their current wave of head hunting.

As he locked the sidegate, Chatwick remembered the most significant part of Djvarich's concern, which was the whole set-up at 47 Parkside. It went without saying that if this cover was blown, they would lose their closest link with government activity. Chatwick was aware that, as far as he was concerned, the link was not all that would be lost. He moved swiftly downstairs in the darkness, unnoticed.

Rocassa Milo drew up the last of her plans, sitting at the desk in her flat. Using the graphics computer they had installed there, she was able to link up with the government's city file to co-ordinate her planning of search movements. She had suggested the first full search for Thursday to cover just the immediate square mile of land around Whitechapel. The next search would be further south to Shadwell for Saturday evening. Taking Friday as a rest day had been risky, but the Head of Defence had passed the plan. She would not be needed again until the early afternoon of Saturday.

She had dismantled her security alarm and discovered how the timer worked. On Friday morning it would just be a matter of making a link circuit to bypass the time switch, thereby rendering the alarm redundant. Working from home had allowed her more time than she usually had. Racing around from the main *Palby's* to other branches and on to new factory and warehouse installations often took her all hours from seven to nine-thirty, after which she could only sleep or listen to music on the residential muso-select.

Now, though, she had access to the computer. The directors at *Palby's* had always echoed the newspaper line about computers being unreliable, a waste of human resources with the need for so many operators and more *unfashionable technology.* Were there any left? Well here was one, on her desk and working. She had mastered it on the Monday morning at the first Government Building, and had found this one set up for her when she got back. Now she was ready to print out her Whitechapel streetplans she put in the command for fifty copies made up with the rest of the information into complete workfiles.

As it began printing, she accessed the menu. One of the choices, *Revolution for Industry,* interested her. *Palby's* were openly concerned with the project, but information about its history was a little vague. Morda had given her his own opinion of the project; she had good enough reason to investigate. Access RFI. She waited. A few seconds later, a page appeared, which she read.

'*The first histories of this country we have access to detail a surrendering of the basic resource gifts inherent here. Energy - through Oil and Coal, a loyal workforce, organised power, an elite regime behind the government - then the Church, now the Populite Bureau - and control of information to the Populace.*

'*We are in a position to correct the political flaws of the Other World, hence the Revolution for Industry. Laws are in progress to remove the wheels of four-hundred years of consumerism from our society by the end of this century. Redefining the Populace's role as a workforce by the wide introduction of implements of manufacture: factories and warehouses, will return us to self-sufficiency and help sever the remaining ties there are with other countries in Europe and the world.*

'*The Populite Bureau will provide the financial and administrative push for this industrial programme, and once intact a first Reform Bill will propose...*'

A small light was flashing on the top left hand of the screen. It turned out not to be a light, but an instruction in tiny print - *Access Denied - Recall Menu* - the picture was breaking up into what looked like a green snowstorm. In panic, she recalled the menu. The machine whirred noisily and settled, buzzing a red-lettered instruction to the screen.

'YOU HAVE REQUESTED ACCESS TO HIDDEN FILES. PLEASE TELEPHONE THE BUREAU FOR ACCESS PASSWORDS.'

The computer had given her some access, though. Mention of *Church,* something that Morda had made last weekend, though he had not known what it meant. It would not be wise to write any of it down. She would have to try to remember as much as she could. She returned to the plan of Saturday's Shadwell search. It would be wise to go on and finish the weekend file. If they had any way of tracing the content of her afternoon of work, it would hopefully be construed that she had made a simple access error. She called up a streetplan and began to divide the unit up into eight sections, again asterisking an instruction that they be armed.

Morda watched the distant activity from the roofless upstairs room he had found that morning. It gave him a reasonable view of what was happening in the place he was staying. He had kept away from the gargantuan Gairn in the last three days, moving each morning at the crack of dawn a few streets away, but near enough to keep track of where he was.

He was to the South-East of Burnt Oak, a mile or so from the garage where he had hidden the icebag, perhaps two miles from Hendon Central. It was not only a long walk, but a dangerous one, with Gairn and patrols to worry about. He looked out at the broken landscape; buildings stood virtually untouched in the city, but this area had become a sports stadium for the rival war factions, breaking up buildings with crude weapons, creating a refuse area for the city planners' waste. He watched a large section of lorries moving together along some broken road, preparing to dump tons of concrete rubble onto the lifeless estates.

From his vantage point he could also see the tower clock at Hendon, which read five minutes past six. He would have to move now, to find his way to the station on time. He had made a few greengrocer purchases on the Wednesday morning last him till now, but he felt weak and tired. His back ached; it was two weeks since he had slept properly. He took a final look across the greying skies. There was no movement in the streets around. He had been struck by the thought that Gairn might find the icebag; it was extremely unlikely, but in his possession the contents themselves could be abused, misunderstood, even destroyed. He had enough time to collect the bag and still get to Hendon by seven. If she wasn't there, he would leave the area, move across London to find somewhere else on the outskirts.

He moved across the street, across gardens, through alleyways, watching the streets from behind the houses. It was a windy evening, too, blowing leaves and dust all around, creating deceptive sounds that were sometimes footsteps, sometimes distant calling voices. He stood in an alleyway watching a sheet of polythene blow across the street, scratching at the concrete. He crossed the street, past the *Burnt Oak* sign. A few streets later, he was at the house, moving through the growth of weeds to the doorless garage. In the drawer, the towel, underneath, the icebag. Behind, a shuffling.

He looked round and a heavy hand threw itself round his mouth. He tried to bite it, but the grasp was almost mechanical, clamping his mouth shut. Attached to the hand, Gairn appeared, smiling malevolently. He released his hand and struck Morda a blow to the head with the other, a square-edged ringed finger, drawing blood from the side of his face. The icebag fell to the ground.

"There are quite a few people who would like a word with you," he said. Morda was looking round for a weapon, the time ticking away in his head.

"A few in particular that have asked me to bring you along tonight." Morda lifted the frame of an old tyre from the corner of the garage and threw himself at Gairn, pushing him back. Gairn sank his fingers into the centre of the frame and threw it effortlessly back over Morda's head, where it crashed noisily off the wall behind. He crouched over Morda and threw a hand at him eyewards, the fat fingers formed into a steel v-shape. Morda recoiled back into the wall, holding his face. He had the appalling sensation of blood or something else streaming out of his eye sockets. Blind and pained he moved backwards against the wall, curling himself up into a ball. Gairn, however, stayed where he was.

"The point is, woman-fucker, you and I are going on a trip across town to a little place called Hackney. And before you bother planning to attack me again, let me tell you I am supposed to ring these people later on, a number that is in my head only. If I fail to ring that number, a few of my friends will be popping round to a house in Hammersmith to pay a friend of yours a visit. So we'll wait for you to recover and then we'll make a move. I've been waiting nearly three days for this."

The pleasure in his voice was almost as pronounced as the pain in Morda's eyes. It felt like he had two fireballs turning in his eyesockets, even though the bleeding seemed to have stopped. Who the fuck was this great clown working for? He coiled back into a ball. If he went to Hackney he would miss Rocassa. If he managed to get away, Provlyn would be dealt with. At the moment he would have to go with him; he was powerless to do otherwise. He got up, head bowed, and moved towards the exit, stepping over the abandoned icebag. Gairn stood back and let him pass.

He straightened up once they got outside, but his vision was blurred in his right eye. Gairn walked a few feet behind him and stopped at the front of the house. Morda looked at him.

"I've left my icebag in the garage."

"What do you want ice for? It's freezing."

"I have to get that bag. They'll only send us back for it."

"It's a chance I'll take, now *get!*" He pushed at Morda, the weakness of his legs causing him to lose balance and fall over. He got up and struggled on.

"This isn't the way to Hendon."

"We're going to Golders Green. There's a tram that runs to Hackney direct from there."

They crossed the street and began to move away from Hendon. The dip of the sun in the sky was proof, if Morda wanted it, that it was nearly seven o'clock. They were soon within visual distance of the clock tower at the Golders Green bus station, and Morda slowed down.

"Let me rest for a while," he said, holding the base of his calves. Gairn moved towards him and kicked him in the thigh several times. Morda lay there, unable to move. Both legs had gone completely dead.

He closed his eyes. Now is the time to die, he thought. I've missed my last chance to see her. There is no point going on. They were in a sidestreet that led into the square and the bus station. From his prostrate position, Morda watched feet pass ahead of him before he rolled over and his eyes closed. Gairn saw the time and stopped.

"I had better make a phone call or your friend will be getting plugged." He lifted Morda up and carried him to one side of the street behind some bushes. He lay him out on the grass and looked at him. His eye was badly gauged, dried blood chalking up one side of his face. He would have to ensure that there was no recurrence. He looked around for some string so he could leave him tied up while he made the call. He had nothing on him, and there was nothing appropriate around either. He bent over Morda and pulled back his ear.

"If I were you I'd listen carefully. I am off to save your friend's life; I don't advise you to do anything stupid while I'm gone. Just sit still and rest. You've only got to get across the square to catch the tram." He got up and looked over the bushes. It would not do to have anyone witness this. Satisfied that the road was clear, he moved off. Watching a dim reflection of his face in the back of Gairn's left foot, Morda sprang from inertia towards it, pulling him over onto the grass. He turned at him, bringing his right foot high up into the mass of Gairn's testicles; his face went blue as he recoiled backwards, knocking over a dustbin whose contents spilled everywhere. With sickening suggestion, an empty soup can rolled across Morda's path, past his right hand. Gairn had seen the contents spread and scrambled backwards to find his feet, but Morda was on top of him, knees pinning his grotesque body to the ground.

"If you even scratch me, just a scratch," Gairn gasped, the edge of the open can a few unfocused inches from his face. Morda held his hands perfectly still, clenched around the tin, only the *v* of *vegetable soup* visible. Gairn's eyes were so large, so bulgingly large. Close up they looked like white marbles with blue centres. He lowered the can until its edge touched Gairn, his own right eye still failing to directly focus on the face of his predator. But he was not a killer, not like this; no matter how tightly he held his hands round that can, how determinedly he drew up his expression of hatred, he was unable to strike the smiling face of fear beneath him. It relaxed and took his arms, this gross man, all sweat and body odour, he took his arms and held him, smiling. He pulled his arms towards him, but not viciously; the strength symbolised something else, other feelings. His face continued to smile, but the fear left it, like dust blown from a pile of house rubble. Then his hand moved, slowly at first, down his arm, across his waist; it moved as if it were coated with a thin layer of jelly, deftness that such a bulk of a man should have been incapable of. The deftness terminated with an ecstatic lunge at his lower half, and Morda groaned as he realised Gairn held his fully developed erection in his hands. Disgusted by the fullness of his own reaction, he shook his head to clear it and found, instead, Rocassa Milo photographed glossily at the Kensington Store, but this time the red tape she was fastening around its doors was a growing winding line issuing out from under the ends of his fingers. His hands were not clammy this time with sticky sweat; this time the stickiness was a deepening red, it was growing underneath the push of his hands. The hand that clutched out at him now held nothing but space; it was as empty as the open-mouthed stare above it. Morda wiped his hands on his handkerchief and looked down in horror at the dawning of his deed. All that could be seen of the twisted can was its end, the sides driven up, into and around the fullness of the man's throat.

He eased out the press clippings and name list from the man's inside pocket, keeping his fingers inches from the congealing mess before them. As he backed away, Morda observed how the eyes of the face were still smiling slightly. He took a last look before turning back into the sidestreet and crossing the road towards the bus station. There were no sounds behind him. All was silent.

In the square his heart began off beats as he stared at the clock. It was now half past seven. If he ran all the way he could get back to Hendon before eight, but by the time he got there, possibly sooner, the visitors would have paid their visit to Provlyn. He looked up. Another two minutes gone. He sighted a tram parked in one of the furthest bays, its destination on a painted wooden board: Hammersmith. He wandered towards it vacantly, looking back every so often at the minute hand of the clock.

A little rain in May

The tram moved off noisily across the street, turning round in a movement that almost dislodged the passenger halfway up the stairs. Steadying himself, he reached the open top and moved to the front. A few minutes later, as the tram conductor had promised, they pulled into the Hendon Central terminus area. Lit up brilliantly like the front of Buckingham Palace, the forecourt was nevertheless devoid of waiting passengers. A few hundred yards across the street, in the shadow of a newsagent's shop, someone watched the tram arrive. At the furious beckoning signals from the top of the tram, the figure emerged, breaking into a run across the central aisle.

Morda looked towards the figure; he was still bent nervously across the seat, biting his thumbnail, but the androgynous long coat had not fooled him. The tidal sensation of relief was so great that he almost embraced the stomach pain that grabbed at him. He stood up weakly as she reached the top of the stairs. She looked at him from the opposite end of the deck before the tram moved off and she was thrown into the back seat. He balanced his way towards her, hands clipping the edge of each seat on his way to the back. They sat together and held hands, moving them under the seat as the conductor's face came into view in the mirror at the top of the stairs.

"Are you alright? How has the week been?"

"Awful," Morda said, stealing a kiss after a long look at the mirror. "I've been chased around Burnt Oak for three days by some ex-army lunatic. He's a kind of self-appointed activist bounty hunter. He was going to take me to some people who must have thought I knew something they didn't."

"Where are we going?"

"Hammersmith. You see I ended up getting rid of this bloke. I had to. The people he was working for know about Provlyn, and they were obviously prepared to use him to get at me. Now because this lunatic can't phone them back, they may well send someone round to kill Provlyn."

Rocassa stared at him.

"You mean *you're* going there? What can you do?"

"I've got to try. It's me they want, not him. I can't ring him because he'll panic; if you wanted to send the police in, you'd have to explain how you knew the activists were coming. And this way if they don't come, there's no harm done. I can't let them just kill him."

"You'll be caught. There's a continual two officer vigil around that house, in constant contact with the unit section at Hammersmith. And if they find out I'm involved at this end..."

"They won't. It's just that I couldn't leave you there."

She looked at him in disbelief. "Your coat is stained. Was that...?"

"Never mind. Look, fuck it. *What am I going to do?*" He looked out at the moving pavement below them, watching the cracks turn intermittently into dark cream concrete paste.

"Don't be a fool, for a start. I've been reading about these activists all week, I've been investigating some of those people in that address book of yours and I can tell you that you are not one of them. They're ruthless. These are people who are convinced that the power of this country should be in their hands. They are convinced that the Populite have used their intelligence about the end of our world for political ends. They are convinced that detechnologising the country was in the interests of breaking down communication, not conserving energy. And to communicate their ideas to other people they are prepared to do anything, including killing anyone who gets in their way."

"You haven't left the class of women, yet," Morda said.

"I don't really care if you believe that. I am just not prepared to let you put yourself at the mercy of those lunatics. I love you, you fool, even if I am a woman. Go to the house, by all means, but I'm coming with you."

Travelling under the night sky alone together was poor preparation for the rest of the hour ahead. Even if he was not a genuine activist in her eyes, Morda had killed another man, and could not hope to run around London for much longer without being caught by somebody.

It was a despairing conclusion that they were both eventually forced to reach. His encounter with Gairn had shown him what months spent on the run would be all about. He was no longer able to find any hope from the thought of that kind of life.

Rocassa had come without anything other than a small handgun in her bag; members of the Populite had been always recommended to carry them if travelling alone late at night to Outer London boroughs. Morda's only form of defence in the last few days had been his wit; he had little time to give it the mental oiling it so obviously required.

"Can you alert the police outside?"

"We'll stop at the station and radio them. If I have you with me, that can explain how we know about the threat of an attack. I'll keep a gun on you and tell them to let me go alone. At least to say you've helped will mean they won't expect me to..." She made a firing gesture with her fingers.

"If I could just get out of this alive, if I could just have the chance to see you again after it's all over," Morda was saying, now crying quite shamelessly. "This has all got to lead to something good in the end - it must."

They stayed together upstairs, even though a gentle rain began to fall; Morda felt a sob sticking in his throat. His lover was to become his jailer.

The night grew dark and her arm curled itself round him. He pressed his head into her shoulder, thinking about a world with families and children, a world with no Sexual Relations Act, where it was not a crime anymore to want to love somebody. He felt the closest he had ever been to her in the short time they had been together. It was not possible to declare this love; he had been forced to declare his love for Provlyn, like a Capital Gain, on the Toll Tax return form. This love could only be written on a sheet out of a time-capsule from the Other World.

The lights of Paddington and the Great Western Railway bathed the upper deck of the tram in a great pool of light, and they separated in a jolt from their embrace. She laughed at the forced movement. There were more people out in the street below them now; innocent, laughing faces in crowds, unaware of the gathering of events a few miles away, even as they watched, where someone was travelling from another direction, to the same venue, on a mission of death.

"Don't look so down," Rocassa said. "Remember faith."

"What's that?"

"Something you have to find fairly quickly if we're going to be able to achieve anything in the next hour." She ran her hand up along the inside of his thigh.

"Faith," he repeated, mechanically.

She walked behind him as they approached the doors of the police station. Morda looked up at the red brick roof across the entrance. Another dwelling for the agents of the law, it was not unlike the Whitechapel building, though it seemed a long time since he had decided to pay a visit there.

As they crossed the threshold, he raised his hands at the elbows, pushing open the door with his foot. The counter was unstaffed, but an officer soon appeared from the next room, a gun in her hand.

"It's alright," Rocassa said. "He's no problem. Just tell me how things are at the Mews house."

"They aren't due to call in for another twenty-five minutes." She was watching Morda with interest; a real person squeezed out of the front page of the newspaper. He had already noticed two examples of his current notoriety either side of the counter, covered in small print.

"I thought we were in constant contact with them."

"There is only one officer there until half past nine. Sergeant's orders. They've called the other three who were available out to help out on an emergency street search round Golders Green."

"So they've left half cover on a unit priority. Just try and locate some officers from another station to stand by on my call. And don't try to contact us there unless we contact you." She pushed Morda out through the doors forcefully enough so that he fell down the stairs. As he got up he felt a shooting pain in his right foot.

"I've done my foot in. There was no need to do that."

"There's every need. Move!" She pushed him forward. He tried to keep his full weight on his left side, limping uncomfortably across the road. She did not take on her role with anything less than full commitment, even though there was no-one else around.

They were soon in Hammersmith Grove, cutting through a back garden in order to approach the house from the rear. The gas lamps were on, but the gardens were only lit in patches, and these were areas to avoid, as they signalled life in the rooms beyond. They got over the wall into the garden of a house further down the Mews; the only sounds were of coughing and distant voices from the houses in the Grove. They scaled garden walls and cut through hedges, but in the darkness it was proving difficult to establish just where they were in the street.

"That should be it," Morda whispered. "But it isn't. I don't think we are as far down as I had thought." They both looked across the alleyway into the next garden. It was only when Morda saw the shed at the back that he realised.

"That is the house. Someone must have put a set of French windows in there. Why the fuck would they do that?" They both froze as the fingers of a hand gripped the wall above their crouching position. Rocassa fixed her gun on the target, but after a long minute the strength drained from the hand and the grip failed. There was a rustling sound behind the wall.

"Stay there and listen." Rocassa moved to the rear of the wall and climbed into the alleyway; ahead, in front of her, the climber lay slumped. She advanced before the figure, the gun held taut, and kicked at it. It folded open like a halved tomato. It was the officer who had been watching the house, a red notch under her cheek from a recent bullet. They had just been watching the final minute of her life. She drew back and looked up at the window. Everything inside was dark. She leaned across the wall to find Morda's staring face opposite hers. He went to kiss her and saw the body. She directed him behind and over the wall. They sat at the back of the alleyway, watching for movement inside.

"Can't we just break in? You have a gun."

"Shut up. Just follow me." They crossed into the rear of the garden, their movements camouflaged in the darkness by the tree. They turned as the screech of a message crackled out of the dead officer's radio. Muffled sounds followed from the upstairs of the house. Rocassa stood up and taking Morda's hand moved round the far side of the garden, past the bushes, bent-kneed, calves taut. Morda winced with pain at the throbbing in his foot; he felt like he had been shot again.

They worked their way agonisingly slowly round to the side of the french windows, Rocassa the eyes for their feet, Morda watching the windows for movement as best he could. Out there in the darkness they shared a second of oneness as they looked at each other; Morda thought, even in the deepest moment of his fear, that he would never love anyone as much again.

Moving back from the windows, it was now obvious that they were slightly open. Perhaps the officer had left earlier from the lounge to investigate sounds that had sent her to her death. Rocassa reached out and took the door handle furthest from them, pulling gently at it. The door eased open, pulling the edge of curtain with it. Morda felt like he had been holding his breath for ten minutes, his heart pounding noisily in his chest.

They entered the room together, but Rocassa moved on to the foot of the stairs. She pointed back at the gas lamp, and Morda understood. He watched her crouch at the base of the stairs and struck a match, lighting up the lamp. There were no sounds at the sudden light except for Morda's own gasp at what he saw in front of him. On the sofa before him, the smiling, lifeless face of a stuffed dummy child, one red jewelled hole between his eyes. A curdling of bile gurgled at the base of Morda's throat as he crouched, head between his knees. More death. They were too late. The visitor had been and gone. Runny eyes looked up to see Rocassa moving up the stairs, almost out of sight. He staggered on towards her, watching her advance. He followed silently. At the top of the stairs they looked round. The bedroom door was the only one closed. He was going to be sick again, he held his stomach; she kicked at the door and finding something behind it threw herself at it twice more until the force dislodged the obstacle and it gave way. Morda watched her lower her gun to her waist. She took him by the arm and threw him into the room in front of her.

Morda swallowed the bile at the back of his throat. A thin man, his skin almost white in the half-light, sat back on the bed, holding one arm round Provlyn's neck, while the other pressed the nozzle of a small gun into the side of his head. His face carried a half-smile, but he was shaking his head, looking at Rocassa's gun.

"You can take him," Rocassa was saying, pushing Morda further into the room with her foot. "Go on. I'll stay here. Just leave the boy."

All Morda could see of Provlyn was the fullness of his eyes which stared at her with a hatred he had never seen. The gunman kept his position, watching both of them. He didn't seem too keen on her idea.

"It's your only chance," she said, watching him. "You can get away now, but the police will be here soon. Just let the boy go."

It was an appalling impasse, death hanging in the room like a cloud of dust. They watched each other for a while before the gunman waved her towards the door with the gun. She nodded silently and moved back, but as he got up from the bed and pulled Provlyn towards him, the bed moved on its castors away from him and he lost balance. Provlyn immediately brought his elbow up into the man's groin, and the gun dropped to the floor. It seemed an eternity before the shot sounded from Rocassa's handgun. The gunman, half back on his feet staggered across the room for a moment as if he was finally going to speak, but dropped clumsily against the wall and slid to the floor. Morda threw himself out of the way of the falling man in horror, crouching in the far corner of the room. He looked up to see Provlyn holding both the guns, grinning wildly. He held one to Rocassa's head and, twisting her arm behind her back, forced her to the floor.

"You can stay there, bitch," he said. "Looking through your things, she was," he said. "Nosing around till she found that address book." He seemed pleased with himself. "That's how she found you. Through that book. I would have put it away, but I couldn't find it. I knew there'd be something somewhere, but I couldn't find it." Rocassa looked across at Morda but could not catch his eye. He was studying

Provlyn, following him as he moved across the room.

"They only want to ask you questions," he said. "That's all." He pushed Rocassa's gun at her forehead, pushed her head against the wall. "Then they'll kill you." He took the gun away and her head dropped. He laughed. She might now understand what it was like to be at the mercy of the roll of someone's finger. He crossed the room to Morda and lifted his dropped head, kissing it, embracing his still figure.

"It's over," he said. "It's over, now." He pushed something at his hand as he stood there, dumb. It was the gun.

"You do it," he said. "She would have done it to you." Morda took the gun. Even in his moist palm it was cold. He couched it in his hand, felt its weight. Provlyn watched him. Rocassa watched him.

"You don't understand," he said. "I don't think you ever will." He held Provlyn close to him, his left hand pushing back the short dark hair, pulling the face towards him, the right cradling the handgun. He fired, once, into his chest, watching the dark spray touch the wall behind him like the wave of an artist's brush. He dropped the gun and held Provlyn, kissing his forehead.

Rocassa watched, alien, joined in the other half of the room by the dead gunman. Morda wiped the sweat from Provlyn's brow as he lowered him down under the window. He sat with him, holding his hand, until the tension eased to nothing. A single tear wound a path to the edge of the still cheek and hung there for a moment until it splashed against the face of his watch. It was the first sound in the room since the shot. Morda wiped Provlyn's face with his bloodstained handkerchief and stood up. Out of the window he watched the policewomen scaling the wall and turned back towards Rocassa. He picked up the handgun and threw it across the room to her.

"You had better go outside and tell your friends what has happened," he said.

Search Policy A Success - Top Republican Activist Held After Shoot Out.

'Within a week of setting up a programme of security operations, the government-run search scheme claimed its first major victory last night after a siege at a house in west London.'

Chatwick turned the paper over and ironed the reverse side before putting it on top of the pile he had already ironed. The initial comments he had made about Morda after the observation in January should have been heeded. Gairn was no dramatic loss, but Thorp had been a rare find - a professional killer who was both discreet and swift; it sounded, from the report, as though he had been unlucky. Without the chance to question Morda, it would be difficult to discover whether any of the other so-called groups existed or were just inventions of the press. On the eve of the next century, and the political reforms that would greet it, it was going to be essential to harness an allegiance of all the anti-Populite activists, to mass a force that would be a serious challenge to the powers lying behind the government front.

He bowed as Lady Challis took the tray of newspapers. She did not seem exactly overwhelmed by the first cover story; it was clear that the genuine administration was flexing its muscles. She had set up three meetings that week at the house, all with central government ministers. It was not just the republicans who were likely to be affected by the paranoid spate of anti-activism.

"I heard that Provlyn was killed last night," she said, as Chatwick reached for the handle of the door. He turned back to face her.

"You were very kind to him, madam, though I read that he had got himself into some rather bad company."

"I don't think he was nearly as much involved with that company as this paper is suggesting. I always found him quite a credible individual in the time he spent here; didn't you?"

"He did his job well enough," Chatwick said.

"Thank you Chatwick," she said.

He left.

"It makes me sound like I organised it," Morda was saying.

"How do we know you weren't intending to have our operations manager killed?"

"Look, my partner was fucking killed! Would I risk his life on the off chance that I might be given some kind of amnesty afterwards? I lived with him for five years... that was our child that lunatic shot last night!"

The Head of Defence watched Morda with interest from behind her desk. Other than his underwear he had only been allowed one item of clothing: a thin cotton pair of white trousers, cut off below the knee. It showed the rush of blood to his chest as well as his face, emphasising the projection of anger.   There were, indeed, aspects of his behaviour that contradicted the picture of an anti-activist male, faithful to the status quo approach of his political party. He had not been sired; it had often been seen as an initiation test qualification for some of the more radical organisations.

"It was the story they decided to run. If anything it detracts from the image of a killer that those main features displayed last week. Let's say we're satisfied that you are not a killer, but there is a long way to go until you convince us that you are not an activist. You have been identified by the Whitechapel Branch as a man we've been looking for for some time. You made enquiries about a terrorist after he was shot in January. A man named Harvil."

"He was my lover. I lived with him for five years!"

"He was a ruthless killer. You must have known that."

"He never talked to me about his work."

"Why did you give a false name?"

"I knew what he was doing was dangerous."

"Why that name, and how do you account for the fact that the same man was murdered several weeks later?"

"Only that policewoman heard the name I used. I had no reason to kill him; you ought to investigate leaks at your end."

Morda broke off into a fit of coughing. There was dust gathering at every corner of the room, blown in through the vent from the air outside, collecting inside in small piles that crunched underneath his feet. Morda leaned back in his chair. He would hold on for just a little longer; his only chance was to make sure his timing was perfect. Though Gairn's stare gathered in the folds of stationary objects, he was not a murderer. He was *not* a murderer. *He was not a murderer.* As if she had heard his thoughts, she moved out from behind her desk and left the room.

The questioning had been run for three days in his new home, the constantly lit white room. The sessions were only ever taken by this tall thin imperious-looking woman with the gravelly voice and the hard staring eyes; she was more than just a policewoman, but that was all he could conclude about her. He had seen no-one else except the officer who brought him soup and bread, twice daily. It was a transient lifestyle, but currently preferable to living out amongst the rubble.

The exponents of demolition would be sealing off the area around Acorn House, taping off the dark carpeted corridors, the smoked glass front, the weekend of memories. But he had beaten away sentiment, out of necessity. Whenever he had felt moments of weakness crawling about him (they had been mainly at night), a longing to confess his love for a woman, his joy at the differences in him, he would harden his expression and construct a mental image of ineffable pain; his testicles torn from him whilst conscious, held in the clasp of a pair of pliers; a thin rotating pole with razored pins sent, furiously winding, into his dry backside; the dead Gairn and his tin can throat taking him from behind, the can knocking in rhythm against the back of his neck. No erection could survive such thoughts, no wilful longing for feminine flesh ride out such a picture of pain.

An hour later, she came back. He was ready. So ready, in fact, that he was smiling. His chest had lost its swelling redness; the veins were just faded lines under his skin. The change in attitude was marked.

"You look ridiculous," she said.

"Give me some proper clothes, then."

"You're wearing those for security reasons. If you let me know why you ran from the police, what you did when you were away, I'll get you a proper pair of trousers."

Morda continued to smile. His mind was strikingly steady, concentrating, confident. He was more in control of his thoughts and his actions than he had ever felt allowed to be. Even this tall woman and all the authority she carried could not shake the history buffering him from behind; he was now ready to release it. Cocooned in the knowledge eked out from the blue denim satchel, he could feel the rising strength within him, a confidence and self-esteem that he had always feared in women. This was how the history he had discovered might help him; he had been wrong about wanting to throw away the icebag; every sheet that folder contained gave out the same message - as a man he was every bit an equal of woman. The fact that they had managed, somehow, to cauterise man's active role in the process of creation, the fact that man's sexuality in this New World was contained in three or four sperm banks throughout the country made no difference. He made the substance every time he came, and therefore, he could be a father, he could be the first New World father if he wanted to. So he smiled.

"Are you a member of *CYNID?*"

"Are you a member of the church?" he said. The simple question had an unexpected effect; the Head of Defence was unable to conceal her surprise. He continued to smile. He felt strangely like a visitor from the Other World, ready to highlight the cracks in the architecture of this particular version of civilisation. If it had been someone else out in the street, a man in a pub, a friend at work, his knowledge was useless. To use the currency of one particular country, you would have to travel there, you would have to enter its system. It only remained to be seen whether or not he would be offered a substantially rewarding exchange rate.

"Just who are you? Where do you come from?" The hard stare continued, and got up from its seat, crossing the room.

"I'm not an activist," Morda said. "I can promise you that. But I have discovered certain things in the last year that have frightened me." He paused, ready to be questioned, but his interviewer was silent. "You might tell me what you intend doing with me before I discuss them."

"Do you presume to be in the position to barter for your life then, Morda?" His interviewer had evidently not lost her confidence. He leant back on his chair.

"Do you think what you are doing is right?" he asked.

"What kind of a question is that? I'm interviewing you, that's what I'm doing."

"You know what I mean. I want to know why you are running things this way in our country. Why men are subjugated in everything they are and everything they do; why you've detechnologised in the name of economy and yet you've kept computers for members of the Populite; why there is that artificial division in the first place between men and women. What made you change it? People will want to know one day."

She laughed at him, laughed with something of the chuckle he remembered from Gairn. It was just laughter, but it possessed the quality of justified disparagement; as it sounded in his ears his smile vanished, his eyes ran along the bridge of his nose to the carpet like a small scuttling creature.

"Yes, one day," she said. "You were born sixty years too late, Morda. You could have joined the equality movement, you could even have died for the cause if you had wanted to. But I don't think you want to die. With your knowledge you have something to live for - the hope that you can use it to change things... But they didn't want to change things in this country even with thousands of open years ahead of them. They could have changed it then, but they didn't. We're looking down the barrel of a time-gun; nineteen-hundred and nine years left before we finally spin out of orbit and burn up. Each new diary, each new journal means one less year. So why should anyone be interested in change? They're not, Morda. Little groups of bored activists, maybe, but the Populace, the Populite, whatever label you stick on them, they're satisfied. They can raise their voices from their own little corners every so often."

She was sitting on her desk now. Morda began to think about the pliers again. He had overestimated the power of knowledge. If they had held the reins of power for four hundred years, they were unlikely to feel threatened by the arrival of one clued up historian. She moved off the desk and looked at him, speculatively.

"Perhaps you aren't an activist, Morda, but you're unquestionably an idealist. It would be interesting to see how you might fare in the

Other World if there was some way of getting you there. I have no doubt that you would find plenty to complain about. The church, for example."

Morda watched her leave the room; he searched for some cutting rejoinder, but there was smoke in his mind, fogging out free thought.

The moment he noticed the green and gold cufflinks, he moved to the bar. The wearer was about five and a half feet tall with short blond hair and thin ginger sideburns; he stood casually, one foot balanced on the bar rail, waiting for his change. Chatwick stood beside him at the bar, the cigar in his left hand.

"Does wonders for the garden, a little rain in May," he said. The wearer took his change from the barman and moved to the far corner of the room. Chatwick followed him.

"Soul of discretion, aren't you, Chatwick?" the wearer said.

"I'm not so worried now I've seen you," he answered. "That photograph is a very poor likeness."

"I couldn't risk talking about it on the phone; I'm a little concerned about our lack of success with this Morda. You were right about him; that scraping probably sold out the first chance he got. They've already rubbished the organisation in the press; makes us look a right set of clowns, losing three all at once."

"But we only lost Thorp."

"That's what I would have printed if I owned a newspaper. But I don't. So the way the story's gone, we lost three."

"Well, what can be done about it?"

Chatwick sat with his back to the door, leaning forwards when he spoke. He was still uncomfortable in a Wimbledon pub just a few hundred yards from the Parkside house. Even on a quiet Monday evening it was awkward. Djvarich, however, seemed masterfully calm. It was difficult to imagine that this man was one of the leaders of the English Republican Activists.

"I'd obviously prefer the chance to organise a surprise jump and take him alive, but even if he'll be heavily guarded, I'll be able to set up something. When will you see your contact?"

"I'm in town on Wednesday morning; I can make a detour on the way back. It should be straightforward enough; I spoke to her yesterday. She seems to think she can give me some account of his movements by the end of the week." Chatwick finished his half pint and leaned forward.

"The moment I know anything, I'll ring Hackney." He pushed two sovereigns across the table. "The Brothers in the North," he said, and left.

The limousine drew slowly up in front of the yellow building, past the red *Bureau Conference* notice. Two young women walked out to meet the car, greeting Rocassa Milo as she stepped out. It was a bitterly cold Tuesday morning, but there was a cheer of success in the air. The smiles of professional empathy and congratulations communicated it to her as she straightened the collar of her blouse. They made their way together through to the rear buildings.

In the entrance hall, a small group, identified as Populite Bureau members by the yellow triangular brooches on their lapels, waved her over. She recognised the Head of Defence immediately.

"Ladies, this is Rocassa Milo who co-ordinated the activities of the unit. She is also a top accountant with *Palby's*." Admiring nods and glances were everywhere.

"Thank you very much," she said. The Head of Defence steered her away back outside the building.

"We haven't had much success with your young man."

Rocassa looked down at the floor.

"What do you mean 'my young man'?"

"Just a phrase. Had quite an outburst yesterday, putting the world to rights. Studied his history, though." They walked round the side of the new lawns.

"He knows when he's beaten," Rocassa said.

"You beat him, did you?"

"Just a phrase."

"We're thinking of letting him go."

"What?" She tried to make her response sound casual.

"We'd like you to find something for him to do. Set him up at *Palby's* again, perhaps. Whatever you can come up with. Then we can keep an eye on him. See what he gets up to. I've cleared it with the senior officers." She crossed the lawn towards an elderly official who was waving hand signals at her. "Ring me to-morrow morning," she called back.

Rocassa completed the walk round the edge of the lawn, turning the words of the conversation back over in her mind. She was more on edge now, even than she had been turning the keys to the door of Acorn House. She had been thrown into the Bureau's spotlight, she was about to host the search programme's next unit meeting. She felt terrible cramps clutching at her stomach. It was impossible to know what they had forced out of Morda to precipitate his release. The other unaccountable event was that the newspapers had dropped the story, though that could have been part of the Bureau's strategy. *Putting the world to rights.* They had agreed that the contents of the time-capsule would be a last resort. Perhaps the interviews had driven him to use it.

She returned to the entrance hall and went in to take her seat in the conference room. At the top of the table, alongside her, three businesswomen sat, with nervous expressions; they were not wearing the triangle. Three more, like herself, drafted in to complete the final stitching up on the lives of activists that by some quirk of fate their lives had crossed paths with. They were smiling in a way that told everyone - this was the greatest day of their lives.

The white room had remained unvisited since the announcement that morning. The officer had arrived with a roll, some soup and even a cup of tea this time. She had told him he was to be let out on Friday morning, and that he was going to be found employment in the meantime. He would be escorted from Hammersmith Police Station to Palby House at ten o'clock. Everything would be sorted out then. She had refused to discuss anything with him; anything he had asked her subsequently was met with the same monotone: *You'll find out on Friday.*

No further visits from the gravel voice. No more interviews. No more white room. And no charges. Keeping on your toes, running from your enemies, that was one thing, you were prepared for the worst. It was quite another thing to be shown an open door just at the point when you were certain you had lost the fight to keep yourself alive.

June

Morda stood in the doorway of the police station looking up at the sky. His view was blocked by one of the officers who had kept him company over the past week with meaningless stares and humourless conversation. From what he could see it was mostly dark, but he was wearing his own clothes again, pressed and clean. He looked across the street in the direction of the house. He was wearing Provlyn's watch. In his hand he carried a letter written to him on a piece of tissue thin yellow paper.

'Having accepted your word that you are not an activist, and with no-one prepared to submit any direct evidence against you for criminal activity, you are to be released this morning. I hope this will do a little to alleviate some of your cynicism about the New World, and that you will settle down in the job that Rocassa Milo will be offering you later. To this hope, I must add my most sincere regrets at the death of your partner, Provlyn Ranshell, and your sireling, who, I have been informed, were both buried at Mortlake Cemetery on Wednesday, plot 422. If you have any further enquiries, please contact the Citizen Administrator at the Town Hall. I have sent your file details on to her.'

He looked around the building. There was a great deal of activity in the surrounding streets. The builders were in town. Perhaps finally putting down the foundations for that factory on the park side.

The officer indicated a readiness to leave, and they moved round to the rear of the building, where a battery carriage waited. Morda looked up at the rooftops of the nearby buildings, at the chimney tops. They shot out in rows at the left edge of most of the commercial buildings beyond the police station, active and inactive, cigarette stubs against the skyline. It was taking some time to prepare the carriage, but the officer eventually stood back to allow him in.

"Are you talking today?" Morda asked. There was no response.

The carriage moved slowly round and out into the street, following some geographical anomaly; a route into the city passing Altrop Mews. The curtains of the house were drawn; it had all the external appearance of a domestic home whose owners were at work, fighting through the last working hours before the weekend. The reality sat uncomfortably in the back of the carriage, eyes hunting each new street corner. On his left he saw Lorkoz taking in the day's milk; still wearing his pyjamas, a lost old man.

The journey to the city was slow, but uneventful. They had not only drawn the line at providing him with a conversational companion, but had not even had the decency to provide him with a newspaper.

The carriage stopped directly outside the doors of Palby House behind a florist's van. The officer stepped out and Morda followed. There was the little café, the proprietor watching the police arrival over a counter of ready-made sandwiches. Morda raised a finger to him in greeting; he disappeared.

A small group of people could be seen inside the building, one of whom finally appeared on the pavement. It was Rocassa, elegant, no face paint, but hair down. She was wearing exactly what she had worn on that Thursday in Down Street. He tried to hide a smile as he saw her; strange that a particular combination of clothes could so publicly communicate what was, in effect, quite a private sentiment. Morda raised his hands in mock surrender as she approached.

"I'm not armed," she said. The police officer handed her a sheet of paper which she signed. Morda felt like a consignment of office equipment. Others emerging from the inside of the building included Pridge, nodding his way towards them. Even the green-suited elderly clerk had decided to form part of the welcoming party. He looked across the road and back up the street. A few passers-by had stopped to watch the spectacle.

"Come inside, Morda," Rocassa said, looking out beyond him, past the police carriage. He moved with the party onto the familiar crimson carpet, shaking hands with the suited clerks, clearly pleased either by his arrival or the morning off work it had given them. Inside the chairs had been moved round into a corner, the glass tables laden with bowls of crisps and slices of cooked food.

"It could only happen to you," Pridge said. "Still, I was sorry to hear about your friend. What's it been like?"

"He died quickly," Morda said. "Let's hope we all go that way." He took hold of a glass of wine a hand from the crowd was offering him and sat down.

"The whole thing must have been a nightmare. Where were you?"

"I was kidnapped by a bunch of lunatics. They seemed to think I really was this activist leader the newspapers had run the story about. They took me back to the house and tried to make me tell them who I was. That was when Provlyn was killed; thank the Queen the police arrived or.... Well, I wouldn't be here!" He looked up to see Rocassa watching him, listening to this first *public* account of events. She did not look particularly impressed.

"I didn't believe any of what they wrote in the paper," Pridge said. "Well, you can't can you? Still, you haven't missed much. Apart from my Toll Tax card being stolen. Someone *handed it in* on Tuesday. Shows how dangerous it is giving everybody one. You could do anything and then produce it and claim to be someone else." He took the card out of his pocket and ran its edge across the table.

"Excuse me," Rocassa said, "but I must speak with Morda about his job, if you don't mind." Pridge moved from his chair and made a cut-throat sign to Morda before disappearing into the throng of people, drinks and food.

"I've suggested you return to the clerk's position for the time being, until we can think of something else we might be able to offer you."

"I'll be happy here," Morda said, "for the time being." He watched Rocassa take a cherry from her drink and pop it into her mouth. It seemed an unnecessarily sensual act. He leaned back against the wall, uncomfortable.

"Am I going to be able to..." he started. She held up her hand like a policewoman directing traffic.

"We'll discuss the terms of your employment this afternoon," she said, bluntly. One of the younger clerks had joined them, obviously looking for a way into the conversation.

"Excuse me, but there's a messenger at the door with something for you," he said. "I would have collected it, but he wanted to deliver it in person." Morda looked at the clerk and then at Rocassa. She nodded and got up with him. He walked through to the edge of the crowd and the open doorway. A short dark-haired man in a brown uniform waited just outside the entrance. The street was otherwise empty. He recognised the design on the man's jacket from the florist's van, which he noticed again, parked a little further up the street. The man caught his eye and moved towards him.

"I'm looking for a Mr.Morda," he said. "I have some flowers and a telegram of congratulations for him." Before he could even identify himself, Morda heard a sharp cracking in the air that seemed to come from behind them, and the messenger dropped to the floor like a destringed puppet, a thin dribble of blood at the edge of his temple. A gun dropped out gently onto the pavement from underneath the bunch of flowers. Rocassa took the telegram from him. Behind them people were screaming. Hurrying footsteps came across the street, belonging to two young policewomen. In amongst all the noise and confusion, Morda noticed that the florist's van had driven off.

"*Goodbye.* That's all that's on it," Rocassa said.

"Are you alright?" the first officer said.

"Yes. Was that you that...?"

"There are women in two of the buildings opposite. Though we didn't expect it so soon."

"Expect it?" Morda said. "Just what is all this about?" He looked around him into the emerging crowd of clerks, and others who had left their work areas at the sound of the shot. Rocassa was amongst them, staring at the dead messenger.

"Can you get back inside," the first officer was saying. "Please return to your offices. This is a police matter. It is an offence to obstruct the police in the execution of their duties...."

"You *know* about this," Morda said.

"I wasn't sure it was wise of them to let you out, but I didn't know about this," Rocassa said. Held out of sight of the others, she waved an index finger at him. Behind her still placid expression the eyes were screaming at him to shut up. He turned away from her. The crowd had begun to disperse. An ambulance had arrived.

"He must have been working alone," he heard one of the officers say as he re-entered Palby House. The crowded foyer of a few minutes ago was now empty, half-finished drinks on tables, crisps and broken pastry fragments on red serviette ends. Two of the younger clerks emerged from the washroom in conversation, passing him hurriedly. He sat down at one of the tables and lit a cigarette. After a while he looked up, aware that someone was sitting behind him.

"I sent everyone home. They are going to close the building in a few minutes."

"What about all this?"

"It'll be cleared away in the morning. You had better go home and get some sleep or something. You must be exhausted." She handed him a toiletries bag inside which were the keys to his house, some money and his Toll Tax card. He looked at her in disbelief.

"Someone has just tried to kill me. You want me to go home and try to *sleep it off*? What the fuck is wrong with you?"

The censorious stare she gave him made him look past her, up the stairs, back at the entrance, into the hallway. He could see no-one. But she was still staring at him.

"I can't go home," he said, weakly. "Provlyn's dead." He rubbed at his eyes. He found he had no desire to move or to speak. He pressed his head into his hands and made his vision a sea of blackness. She left him and went up into her office.

As she climbed the steps, the face of the messenger returned. He had called at the building earlier that morning, but she had told him to wait. She had chosen not to inform anyone. She picked up the phone in her office, tapped out a number and spoke quickly, detailing events and offering her own ideas for resolutions. The reply she got to her request was unexpectedly prompt and decisive.

"...as a matter of fact I've just been talking to the senior officer. I am prepared to take your advice, but it'll be your risk. I'll inform the janitor and organise some extra security. And, Rocassa... just make sure you're armed at all times. I'll send a car for you first thing to-morrow."

Rocassa put the phone down slowly, holding on to the receiver for a few seconds before releasing her hand. She looked at herself in the mirror she had brought into the office that morning from home. She thought she looked a little harsh; she pouted at herself, almost provocatively. Was it possible, she wondered, to contravene the obscenity laws with a facial gesture? She took her coat off its hook and picked up her bag.

"If anything happened to you..." Pridge said.

"It's a few stops on the tube for fuck's sake, man, I'm not asking you to risk your life or anything."

"Aren't you? If it hadn't been for that rooftop gunner you'd be another part of the mosaic out there on the pavement. Look, I'm really pleased you're innocent; I'm delighted they've let you out; I'm on your side! But I think I'll go home by tram all the same."

He got up and took his lunch box; in the event Morda had not queried its fullness, but it suggested that the Palby House welcome had been organised without the prior knowledge of the staff. He watched Pridge make his way across the street towards the tram stop. He did not bother to walk over to the other side of the entrance, he knew he would double back over the road further up, to reach the tube station entrance. Whether or not his gesture was engineered as a compliment or an insult, it was a deception. He leant back in the seat's false comfort to see Rocassa coming down the stairs. Even in the hour he had been there that morning, he had begun to be irritated by her determination not to break the facade of professionalism she conducted herself with in the building. It seemed exaggerated and pompous, haughty and derisive. Perhaps it was only the fact that he thought he had seen the real Rocassa. This act was just as real to the others.

"We'd better leave," she said.

"You're giving me a lift?"

"I've been thinking," she said, as they passed the administration counter. "You ought not to go home after this morning's incident. I've suggested to my superiors that you take alternative accommodation this evening. I have made some arrangements to that effect."

They left the building and headed towards the tube entrance. Morda followed her with interest. She had access to a fleet of business cars, so it was intriguing that they should be using the tube. He followed her onto the escalator, looking down past her at the two men the up escalator was ferrying towards them. Faceless anyones.

"Can you tell me what the fuck is going on?" he said. She looked round as they got down onto the platform and then accelerated slightly, disappearing ahead under one of the corner arches. He slowed as he approached it. He looked back down the platform. Nobody. Distant rumblings of trains, but no voices. Was she behind him, holding a gun directly to his head? Not yet. He eased his head slowly round the corner. She was there, but smiling, with arms folded. He looked back out at the platform; it was clear.

"You're staying with me tonight," she said, in a whisper. "I just arranged it." He looked beyond her at an advertisement on the wall of the platform opposite. Two young men, one in a green cardigan, the other in a shirt, walking arm in arm; the slogan underneath declaring *'I have our future sorted out, Anton. I've secured it with Lastkey Insurance!'* She followed his eyes to the poster. The society norm. Two healthy young men in a loving relationship planning carefully for a secure future together. Perfect faces and plastic, mocking expressions. Rocassa looked at Morda and they moved towards each other, the other images fading, both focusing on what was before them. They joined hands and held each other, eyes meeting, lips touching.

"I've missed you," she said. Her hands were cold round his face, but her lips were soft, like the skin of an overripe peach, yielding when he pressed his mouth into them. He placed his hands over hers round his own head to warm them and shut out the distant tunnel noises. He could feel the shape of her chest against his, and he closed his eyes, remembering that first release of her breasts in the shadowy darkness, how she had pulled off her dress like a layer of unwanted skin. Now he could feel himself growing against her; a feeling of pleasurable warmth that made him forget. She put her arms round him and dropped her head on his shoulder

"Every night since they took you," she said. "Every single night.

Sometimes in the day, too. I close my eyes and pretend it's you." He felt her warm breath against the side of his face, her lips brushing against his ear. They both straightened as one of the distant echoes gathered in volume.

"I think it's our side," he said.

Down Street station was even more ornate in the daytime, the dark-pillared front impressively set against the gold-painted station lettering above the doorway. It was still difficult to escape the routines he had developed in days spent wandering around London, perhaps it would be unwise to attempt to shake them off. Walking close in on the least open side of the street, glances behind, always conscious of a full picture of the immediate area around him. He walked behind her, eyes trained on her symmetrical strides. He had made a pact with himself that morning that from now on he would live every hour as if it were his last; an attitude that, whilst likely to bring that hour a lot closer, would help him enjoy more intensely any successes he might record on the way.

It was nearly two o'clock when they arrived at Audley Court. Drawing out a black card riddled with tiny holes, Rocassa stood at the entrance and tapped out a number on the silver grated intercom. At the sound of a high-pitched note she inserted the card and the door opened. They both went in.

"They're obviously expecting you," said Rocassa. "Or you would have triggered the alarm." He stood well back from her, fascinated. It was presumably commonplace for members of the Populite to enjoy such security measures, but quite a comment on their own view of society that they should think they needed it. They waited for the lift which, apart from a fire door, seemed the only possible access to the upper floors. The rest of the cream-walled ground floor was a collection of other doors: *Janitor, Laundry Room, Garages, Cleaning Equipment;* he stepped into the lift and looked back out. A building with only three floors, yet with a lift, the contents of which amounted to a carpet and a panel of buttons. She pressed one. He looked at her but her eyes were fixed straight ahead, expressionless. He was about to comment when he saw the tiny camera above them, its lens angled out of the corner for maximum vision. The sense of so much for so little that Morda had gained from the building was further compounded when they arrived on the Third Floor. There were just two flats, numbers three and four, either side of them as they left the lift. He looked quizzically at his guide as she moved to number three, the door of which opened on production of her card. As he crossed the threshold, a buzzer sounded, quelled immediately by the press of a button inside the door. She pushed her weight against the door as it closed.

"Sorry about all that," she said. "This is what you get when you have a job like mine." She gestured down the hall. "It's too big for me, really."

"Are we really safe here?" he said, looking across the hallway. There were eight or nine different rooms as far as he could see, and a stillness broken only by their breathing and a somewhere clock.

"To think," she said. "A situation where you can be with me in my own flat." He looked back at her.

"You haven't answered my question."

"You want safety?" She opened a hatch by the door, inside which were four colour screens surveying the lift, the downstairs foyer, the doorway by the entrance and a longshot camera running across two or three hundred yards of the street outside. She pressed a sequence of buttons below the screen which added sound to each picture; the final push closed the hatch automatically. He was surprised to see how pleased she looked at the display.

"What about the windows?"

"We're on the *third floor!*"

He listened again to the stillness from the rooms ahead, expecting it to be disturbed at any second by a loud peal of breaking glass. The stillness, however, continued, unabated.

"Where do we go?"

"To the lounge. Up ahead, third on the left."

After a few yards of carpet he turned into a large room, with an enormous brown corduroy sofa parked at the end of a fawn carpet. Under the far window was a small wooden table and chair, and stretching out from the centre of the room, a fluffy white rug. Two black boxes were set at the end of the room either side of a black cabinet. He took his jacket off and loosened his tie. The room was too large; he felt small in it. He moved across to the window. The street below was empty of traffic and people. The police had released him at nine o'clock that morning and within five hours he was in her flat, having survived an assassination attempt.

He went to the door of the room and looked back out into the hallway. Again, he could hear nothing. He instinctively moved back into the room and took off his shoes. He crept into the hallway and further on to the door at the end of the hall; it was ajar and swung open on silent hinges when he pushed at it. Inside the windowless room was a desk, a cupboard and a filing cabinet. On the desk, a blank screen, in front of which lay a book of scribbled notes. He pushed the power button and the screen lit up after a few seconds with the words *'Choose From Menu: OPTION MORDA UNIT'*. He felt a cold hand clutch at his stomach as he looked at the different letters on the keyboard pad. Any given sequence of instructions and he might call up the time, place and method of his death. He switched the machine off and left the room.

"I thought you might like a hot drink," Rocassa said, as she entered the lounge. Morda sat facing the wall on the edge of the sofa, his back to her. She put the tray of drinks down before them.

"Are you hungry?" she said. He sat up and looked at her. She had taken off her clothes.

"How much longer do you think I will live? I mean, *seriously,*" he said, looking away from her. "Because if you know, *I* want to know. I don't mind if you know, I'd just like you to tell me."

"What do you fear?" she whispered, crouching in front of him. He leant forward and cradled her face in his hands. She looked genuinely concerned, and he kissed her; it was the first time he had given her the reassuring kiss he thought his life had singled out for Provlyn.

"My fear?" he said, his hands resting at the top of her hips. "That all of this will, in the end, count for nothing." As he spoke, he could feel her warmth below him and she was soon on her knees, caressing free his shirt buttons and trouser clip. She drew back from him to the centre of the room, beckoning him forward. As he reached her she stopped, and, crouching, she began her most intimate exploration yet. Her mouth was cool, gentle, her tongue weaving. He felt the edge of her teeth massage the knotted veins under the faltering release valve at the top of his thighs; he sighed as her tongue etched alternating half-circles on him. He closed his eyes, still standing, in perfect surrender to her interest, and gasped as he finished. He waited, but she did not release herself straight away; she pushed her face forward to meet the dying muscular pulse, and swallowed what she had taken from him.

A few minutes later they lay on the sofa, drinking the tea she had made earlier. He watched her mulling over a question that had clearly been in her head for some time. He looked expectantly at her to draw out the comment.

"What is it like when you make love to other men?"

"Much the same as it is for you, I should imagine. It's making love to a woman that's different. But I don't suppose you'd know what that's like."

"I was interested in other girls when I was growing up at school. Before I went for my first fertilisation tests; afterwards, though, none of them seemed interested. Not even in the mild way they had been before."

"Does something happen to women after they have had children?"

"I only know from what I've seen, but they all change, I know that."

"Does the sexuality of a woman die when she has children? Maybe it is there before; it just seems impossible to me, since I've known you, that women can live on this earth for seventy years and never have or want sexual intercourse with anyone."

"Didn't it ever occur to you that it might be me who is different?"

"You are different. I'm glad of that." He ran his hand down the side of her body. "I only wish there had been something about sex in that time capsule; something to show just how different things really are today. I mean, how do I know whether or not women ever felt sexual? It might have been exactly the same in the Other World, just that women tolerated sex so they could have babies. Nowadays they don't have to tolerate it at all - they have sperm banks."

Though the knowledge would have been quite useless, he still wanted it. The only real knowledge he had been able to gain in the last few weeks was just how powerless he was to change the society around him, for himself or for anyone else. Rocassa leaned over above him and eased down his eyelids gently with her thumbs.

His eyes closed; his thoughts drifted to the calm businesslike expression of the messenger earlier in the day; he might have been an ordinary postman. There had been nothing in his expression or demeanour to even remotely suggest that fifteen seconds later a shot out of the sky would reveal him to be someone on a mission of premeditated killing.

"How long am I going to stay here?" he said, after a while.

"Anything longer than one night would look suspicious."

"Aren't you prepared to take the risk? Wouldn't you want a situation where we could make love freely; or do you only prefer me in short bursts?" She sat up and, leaning over to the pile of discarded clothes, took his shirt, which she pulled up over her shoulders. She took out one of his cigarettes and lit it. He watched her smoke badly, becoming increasingly fascinated by the shape and differences between their bodies.

"I don't know how you can say that," she said, eventually.

"Say what?"

"About short bursts. Do you know I have been physically sick with longing for you over the last two weeks. Physically sick. You don't know what it's like to have everything and nothing. Look at this flat, it's twice as big as that house of yours in Hammersmith. I earn over ten pounds a week - I can't spend the money - I have to have it put in a bank. I get promotion without doing anything particularly inspirational, but the point is, the thing that would make all of this worthwhile, the thing I really want is, well, you. But it's not enough that you're a man; no, you're seen as a criminal, even if they might not have any charges to bring against you. There are enough people after you, Morda." She looked at him in despair, all the more wistful wrapped in his shirt.

"This thing is so fucking exasperating," Morda said.

"I'm supposed to find a new job for you by to-morrow. I can let you look at a *Palby's* catalogue; you can pick what you like."

"What would happen if you told them?"

"What do you mean?"

"If you told them - *Well, you know this activist guy I helped you catch. Well, you see at the moment I'm fucking the arse off him and I'd kind of like it to continue. How's that?* - what would they say? What could they do to you?" He looked up at her, testily. But she looked away, and there was something in her look that told him these were not thoughts she was prepared to entertain. He sat up and began to put his clothes on. She threw off his shirt and went out of the room.

The telephone woke him. He checked his watch; it was two in the morning. He sat up in bed and looked out of the window. The street was empty, but a quarter moon was in the sky, bathing the gas lamp dimness in an extra fine haze of light; a light that he had watched from the rooftops of abandoned buildings; from the window at Grove Mews many times, looking back at Provlyn's sleeping innocence. It was in that light that he had first seen a woman's body, first touched and known that discovery. In nearly two thousand years that light would finally shine for the last time.

He had lain on that bed for the last six hours, alone, after a painfully silent meal, but the silence had come and remained with the feeling that he was right. He had taken the life of his best friend for her; he had, in effect, *chosen* her at that moment, but because of her position, of what was at stake, she was not prepared to make such a choice her own.

He heard a muted ring outside in the hall consistent with the sound of a telephone receiver being replaced. He got up and went out into the hallway. Everywhere was in darkness and yet despite having no idea which room her bedroom was, he set off, feeling his way along the wall towards the other end of the flat. He could hear breathing as he approached the first door.

"Morda?"

"I'm sorry," he said, peering round the door. She was sitting up in bed wearing a small silver-framed pair of spectacles, seven or eight files spread across her bed, a notebook in her lap.

"I'm, er, just finding something for you for to-morrow."

"Would you mind leaving that for a bit?" he said. "Only I can feel one of my short bursts coming." She entered a fit of half-laughing and half-coughing as she stretched out to clear the papers from her bed. He stood in the doorway for a few moments and then crossed the room to the bed and got under the covers with her. She turned the light out.

"Who was that on the phone?" he said. His hands felt cold against her body.

"The Head of Defence from the Bureau. She wants to see you to-morrow. All this," she pointed to the files, "has been a bit of a waste of time." She pulled her nightdress up over her head. The grey light in the room lit up her silhouette in a remembered moment. This time, he was thinking, it will be slower; it will be perfect. It will be as though it is the last time. He moved across to her and drew her into him, losing himself in the folds, the smell, in the warmth of her body.

"I have to accept that the decision was wrong. You're probably only here this morning because of the determination of Rocassa Milo that you should not represent another victory for the activists."

The Head of Defence stirred her coffee and sat back in the armchair. Morda stood beyond her desk with his hands behind his back, looking around the room. Books, books, everywhere books. He had never seen so many. He wondered how many of them she had read. "Perhaps you might like to tell me why they should want to kill you?"

"If I could," he said, "I might have resolved it with them by now, because it's certainly a mistake." He studied her expression. Despite her voice and her superior manner, there was something intrinsically different about her; all the other women he had met seemed to be halfway through some social climbing mission, unable to stop, to reflect about their lives or the world. This woman had whatever it was the others were still trying to reach. She thought. She understood things. There was a kind of inner calm about her, a self-assurance, an enviable oneness with the content of her life.

"Have you ever held meetings with the activists? Discussed their aims with them?" he asked.

"Part of their problem, though you might not call it that, is to do with their conception of sexual class. In the Old World it was called misogyny. As far as they are concerned, to meet with us on level terms would be to concede victory from the start. I would have thought you would have understood that."

"Let's say that I understand it, then. From both sides. Because as long as there is no dialogue between the Government and the activists, I will remain a prisoner. Your ability to guarantee my safety will always be under threat. If they break it, they score a moral victory over you and I'm dead." She made no attempt to refute his words. Indeed, she nodded slightly at the conclusion.

He had woken up that morning before Rocassa; he had watched her sleeping. He had been with many different lovers, but he had never slept in a full size bed with anyone before. To find her there in the morning and to hold her covered warmth had made him feel unspeakably happy. He had fought so hard and so bitterly for that happiness that, even as he stood here now, he thought his life was worth very little without it.

"How much power do you have in the Government?" he asked her.

"I am not part of the Government," she said. "I am part of the Populite Bureau; we are really the heart of the British Constitution. The Government are our public face."

"You have two faces, then?"

"More, sometimes; but if they continue to be democratically elected, they are not so different. If they continue to be part of the same system, they somehow advocate it by their very existence. Real radical change requires a change of society, not a change of political party." She followed the statement with what he considered to be her most significant gesture yet. Her arm was outstretched to the other side of the room, clearly offering him a seat. He drew it up to behind her desk, like a student at the front of a classroom looking for extra help.

"How much power do you have, then?" he said.

"Is that all you are interested in - power?"

"It's all the activists are interested in."

"You're probably right. But I am not prepared to flex muscle; I am first and foremost an administrator; most of my muscle is made out of paper. You can kill people with it - the newspapers prove that - but I am genuinely here to work for a safe future for as long as we have. There are programmes. We are working to them."

"Why are you answering these questions, though? You didn't bring me to trial. You even let me go free."

"You were nearly killed."

"You had me covered. By six police officers - and they were only the ones I saw."

"You are right about one thing, and that is that we do have an interest in keeping you alive. That is why you're here now. On your own admission, unless the political situation changes, particularly in London, your life expectancy is limited. If you're to be any use to us now, we need you alive. You see the activists want you - my belief is because they think you might pose a security risk to them in our hands. If we can get you to them, without an accident, you represent a bargaining position. We have no intention of destroying the activists, just tempering some of their anti-Populite activities, the killings. We want to offer them help; give them a newspaper of their own, give them a chance to strengthen their organisation, even offer them political candidates at the next election, provided they are prepared to forgo the violence."

"You expect me to be able to convince them that you are prepared to do all that? You've got to be bananas!"

Morda thought of Harvil, of Raptel and the many other dedicated activists. If the promises of armistice in 1914 had been truly realised they

202

would have been alive; the republican unrest would have crumbled like the abandoned towns. But there was something heterogeneous about the sexes, some insurmountable obstacle of difference.

"Give them this." She reached under her desk and pulled out a light blue bag. Morda inspected it in disbelief. It was the icebag.

"Where did you get this?"

"Where you left it. It was abandoned by someone in a terrific hurry. Not far away from a rather unpleasant murder at Golders Green." Morda's expression hardened.

"Murder?"

"With evidence to link this bag to the last movements of the murdered man and the recorded statements you made about the Other World... it might be necessary for us to change our minds about your innocence."

"You think I can use this to persuade them to meet with you?"

"We know you can try. It isn't as though you have much choice.

He opened the bag up and took out the folder. The sheets had been treated with some kind of spray; they felt stronger, they did not flake when he ran his fingers over them. The photographs had a greater depth of colour. He held the folder up and looked at the gravel-voiced woman. He had both in the same room, the past and the future.

"When they see this, they'll want a revolution."

"Not if you tell them what it was really like. Not if you tell them about drugs, about religion, about rape, about families. You can tell them how you found this, how it changed your outlook, and how you've convinced us to let you try and change theirs. I know enough about the Republicans from the last war to understand that the majority of their grievances are historical." She was imploring now, tapping the side of her hand on her table with each new point. Morda shook his head.

"But I don't know about drugs, rape, religion, all that stuff. I've only read about them in the folder. I don't know what it was really like. How can I convince them if I don't have a complete picture? They've still got a world with Curfew, the Toll Tax, Unsired Children,

Obscenity Laws, Detechnology..."

"Things are better here, Morda. I can prove it to you. In the high-security vaults of these buildings we have millions of video discs stored with information about the Other Age, about its cruelty, about its greed, about its lack of trust, about its intolerance. You can show them that these are the qualities their organisations currently espouse. We can make those discs available to you; we can give you time to watch them. All you will have to do is deliver the bag to a contact address - meet whoever is there - and communicate our offer with your living testimony."

"But a dead testimony is worth nothing. How do you propose to get me to them without an accident? And how do you know they are a group others will listen to?"

"We don't - yet. But we'll get the answers to those questions. We won't send you out until we're sure you'll at least have a safe passage to one part of their set-up. From then on it will have to be up to you. Your own life is at stake, too. Hopefully that is the sort of factor which will improve your performance considerably."

Amongst his dread, Morda saw a shaping of the visions he had often experienced when he was running. He was always looking behind; looking down the platforms of tube stations, across rows of derelict houses, behind him as he stepped out of police stations. It was the only direction in his life he had been able to focus on. He could speculate about what was ahead, but he had never been able to affect it. Pointed forwards, armed with a sense of purpose, he could channel this striving into a worthy goal. It was easy to fuel a mental picture of himself as a missionary for the New World. If he could actually talk face to face with these people, it might be different. He would be dead soon, anyway, he had accepted that. Now they were trusting him, prepared to give him access to some notion of history.

"I will only go back out there if there is a chance, no matter how slight, of coming back alive. With that, these discs will have to convince me that the New World is a better option than a return to the values of the past."

"You'll be convinced."

"I doubt it. You see, you can't do that because right now the only reason I have for staying alive is to continue breaking your laws. Things have changed a lot for me lately, and I don't just mean all of this, but..." He watched his floundering gestures in the glass of one of the cabinet doors opposite. His eyes wandered anaesthetically back to the floor. He had accepted the imminent death his actions had been preparing for him, but even in the gore of his death, the hope Rocassa had given him was a force; latent, lurking, like a withheld sexual urge. He knew its strength would prolong surrender to his final breath. But if he was not to surrender his life, he would need to surrender his position.

"I can't tell you all of this without implicating someone very close to me. You see I'm having a heterosexual affair. It's not a case for regret, either. I have been having it for sometime now."

The Head of Defence did not flinch. She did not ring for him to be taken away. She just sat there watching him, a thumb on the collar of her white blouse, a finger on the edge of her lips. He stood up and walked to the window, just as he often had done when wondering how to say things to Provlyn. "She has no intention of allowing it to come into the open for obvious reasons. The point is that, were I to come back alive from this mission you want me to undertake, it would be on the understanding that we would be allowed to conduct our relationship without any interference from the police or your security forces. Similarly, if I were to be killed by these people, in whatever circumstances, you give me your word that she would never know I told you."

The Head of Defence smiled wryly behind the hand she held to her mouth. It was not the response Morda had expected from a senior member of the Populite Bureau, but he had seen the smile before. It was not entirely without danger.

"Very well," she said. "Let us say we will tolerate it, if you return. Whoever it is, it will be for you to ensure that it is discreet; if that is the case, then you will not be bothered. I would however," she smiled again, "add one proviso to my agreement. That is that you return this evening to my flat and give me absolutely everything you have given her so far."

He looked at her curiously. Had he heard her correctly?

"I mean *everything*. Fucking. That's what you do, isn't it? You can make your way there after you have spent this afternoon at one of the videoscreens." She handed him two cards, one with her address and entry code, the other a black hole-punched entrance key. He pushed his hand across the front of his mouth to hide his own surprise; Rocassa would not have to know - it was a small investment for the promised dividend.

"Where do I go?" he said.

"Next door. My secretary will take you downstairs and set the machine up for you." He took the folder from her table and nodded deferentially at her on his way out.

He spent each day of the next three weeks in front of a videoscreen, freeze-framing and note-taking each occasion when he felt he had observed another feature about the past on which the current society could be said to have improved. Despite the persuasion of his intimacy with the Head of Defence, he soon realised how ignorant he was about the Other World. Drawn to it in the first disc, he had pondered the picture of Britain he saw in the twentieth century. In most of the historical commentary it was generally referred to as being part of the *free world,* but it seemed a misplaced notion of freedom. Appalling acts of crime committed by people in the name of armies, religions, leaders, countries or under the influence of stronger personalities, drugs or insanity. The victims were more often than not committed to lifestyles that embraced similar values, but it was astounding how the crime seemed to proliferate rather than offer itself up as something to be shunned.

As he worked his way through to the present, it was clear that the society he was now a member of had made a positive attempt to destroy or prevent as much of the evil existent in the Other World as they could. They had, in the end, identified man as the greatest cause of wrong, and had turned one of his newest weapons, a sophisticated Neutronic warhead, against him in a single determined act of apocalypse.

Through the Death Age, after coming to terms with the scientific consequences of their act, the surviving communities had organised a programme of controlled population growth and moved towards what he could only describe as aping history. Scientists had, in the first two hundred years of the New Age, noticed astral behaviour that ran parallel with documented observations from the Other Age, except that it ran in reverse; it was noticed well after the first Populite World Convention had decided to table the years backwards to the earth's last days. There were, he noticed, several modern theories about how the Death Age signalled the reversal of Einstein's expanding universe theory, but Morda could only listen to these; he was unable to go much beyond the words that described them. In any case, what had happened in the past was more significant; he could offer some kind of answer to most of the questions he might be asked, if he was able to convince anyone to take the whole idea seriously. He possessed a unique chance to be an agent of history, to show those who wanted to kill their way towards change that it had already happened, and that the only evil worth challenging was their own ideology about how to effect political reform. The violence of men towards women in the Other World had been even more institutionalised than the autocracy of the Populite's hold over men now. If he chose to believe even a quarter of what he had seen over the last few weeks, he would be forced to accept that the system was immeasurably fairer, more effective and more likely to enable Britain to survive the couple of thousand years it had left rather than a return to any of the values of the Other World.

By the end of his last week, Morda was gravely committed to the task; he combed through all the files there were at the Government Buildings on the Republicans and subsequent activist movements; he schooled himself in channelling the militance of their activities and philosophies. He had read about many historical envoys who had no reasons to undertake their missions other than the strength of their own commitment to the various causes for which they fought. Most had died for their causes, but they had almost all been on missions to affect the world in ways that history had later judged to be correct.

For his mission, Morda could see the judgement of history behind him, even though it had never been a guarantee of success to have right on your side. He had demanded other items to build up the folder in the icebag, the documentation of moments of history that might tip the balance in an appeal to reason. He would now only have to make that appeal; to give them reassurances, to arrange a meeting for them with the Populite. With that first step towards detente, he could return to Rocassa, they could live out their lives untroubled, they could finally love each other without fear.

As far as Rocassa was concerned, the Head of Defence had explained the project they had organised for Morda, and asked as a personal favour to her if she would look after him at weekends so they did not always keep him in the same place. Rocassa was sufficiently convinced of the security of her own block not to question the reasoning of her superior; in any case, her defensive guard had been substantially lowered by the chance offering to exercise her sexual proclivities unchallenged. Morda was never sure just how much intelligence had been behind the arrangement, but he had padded the space between what he thought he was doing and reality with so much blind faith that he had stopped worrying about the ground.

It was arranged that he would travel by tube on the morning of the mission to the address he had been given in east London from the flat in Audley Court. Being driven anywhere in a car made you a sitting target as well as attracting unwanted attention from whoever you happened to pass on the way. On this night before, he lay in bed, thinking about his death, as he had been doing for most of the night. Rocassa had seemed less edgy about the relationship intruding into her working life in the last few weeks; she had even rung him at the Bureau on Friday to tell him she was going to be late back to the flat. As it might prove to be the last time he ever saw her, he continued to wonder whether he ought to tell her that the Head of Defence knew he was heterosexual.

"How long have you been awake?" she said, stirring at his side.

"Not long," he said. "Listen...," he moved back under the sheets into the warmth and put his arms around her. It was like his temperature had been controlled by a thermostat which had just broken and was pumping waves of heat up to the surface of his body. "I want you to know something." He fixed his eyes at the centre of her gaze.

"I don't want any last minute confessions," she said. "I love you, Morda. If you've got anything to tell me, save it until you get back." She smiled at him and kissed him softly. If anything was going to fire him in the days ahead, it would be the warm trusting expression she wore at that moment.

July

The address on the printout card Morda had been given was located at the back of Victoria Park in Hackney on Rockmead Road, which ran beyond the outer boundary wall of the park. One of the more recent Second Unit searches in Limehouse had uncovered a suspected list of contact addresses. On the advice of the Bureau, none had yet been raided; he would be the first to visit the address since the list had been found the previous Thursday.

The journey involved catching a tram outside Liverpool Street station with directions on foot from a bus stop next to the park entrance. He carried Provlyn's work bag, with a change of clothes and the icebag inside. It had been agreed that he had a better chance if he arrived at the house in daylight, but from then on, his strategies would have to be formulated as the situation demanded. His notebook was in his side pocket, littered with ideas from the three week videoscreen feast. There were additional jottings from Rocassa on the inside back page, private euphemisms for activities which would take place on the day of his return. He also had his old diary which Rocassa had given him; even though the majority of the names there were still unknown to him, they were certain to impress any genuine activists and possibly further his cause.

It was quite warm for July, and he carried his jacket over his shoulder as he got off the train at Liverpool Street. He stopped to do up his shoelace at the edge of the platform to let those in his carriage get ahead of him. He had trimmed his beard that morning. It looked cultivated, as though it might have sat around his face for some years. He watched many black shoes pass him before he got up and began to move with them towards the exit. So many young men dressed in the black and grey suits of the service trade, travelling in from the suburbs to wait on Populite dignitaries. A trade created to cut the leisure time of the Populace, but it was well paid. Provlyn had been earning almost twice as much working at *Parkside*.

He stopped outside the station to catch his breath. Everyone was rushing. He looked at his watch and saw the tear splash across its face, saw again the expression of slight surprise. It was an expression that had replaced the darkness of Harvil's back as the dominant image of darkness in his mind.

He crossed the road to the tram station where two trams were waiting, and although they were both bound for Hackney, he moved for the one that was empty, passing only the conductor, who sat on the first seat, filling in his checking in times for the morning.

"We're not going for another twenty minutes," he said. "You'd best get the other one."

"I'm not in a rush, actually," Morda said, pleasantly. As he looked up, he saw a man in a trilby hat watching him from the platform of the bus. The conductor saw him, too.

"I was just saying, the other one's going first," he said. Morda was already getting out of his seat as the shot pumped gently out from behind the hatted man's newspaper. The conductor, halfway to his feet, fell backwards with the impact of the shot into Morda's arms. Morda pushed the man back with grotesque reflex into the path of the advancing intruder, who dropped the gun and fell back onto the platform. Morda leapt over both of them, nimble movements carrying him safely towards the other Hackney-bound tram as it began pulling away. As it reached the corner to turn onto the main street, he could just see the gunman jumping off the other tram, but they were soon gathering speed and out of sight of the tram station.

"Victoria Park," Morda said, looking up suddenly at the conductor who stood directly in front of him. He wondered idly whether he had known the other man.

"Which end?"

"Er... Rockmead Road."

"Fourpence." Morda reached into his pocket and noticed the blood smear across the edge of his right cuff. Manoeuvring his hand behind his back, he eventually produced a sixpenny piece, delivering it with his left hand.

"What are you, some kind of money magician?" the conductor said. It was not quite the way he should have been talking to someone who had just avoided being shot for the second time in three weeks, but Morda grinned and turned to take the stairs to the upper deck. After he had pushed his cuff inside his sweater he found a seat. *Fuck and bitch;* you did not expect to get shot at in a tram station in full daylight.

He got off at the first *Victoria Park* sign, and followed the road round on foot until he found one of the streets into which Rockmead Road ran. All of the houses in the road were three-storey terraced, not particularly different to any of the others in the adjoining streets. He passed a small boy who sat on the steps of one of the houses, eyeing him suspiciously.

The fifth house his side was the one he was after. It was less well kept than those either side of it, green paint flaking off the dull wood of the surrounding door panel. Morda stopped outside the door and looked up. A pair of black-gloved hands rested on the edge of the tiny balcony above him, attached to the white shirt of a young dark-haired Eurasian man.

"Is this number twenty-three?" Morda said.

"Who are you looking for?"

"Anyone who'll talk to me," Morda said cheerfully. His stomach lurched as he watched the change in expression. He had obviously been recognised. Less than twenty seconds after the gloves had vanished from the balcony, the door in front of him opened slightly.

"Come in," a voice said from inside. Morda pushed gently at the door and went in. The door was shut behind him and in the darkness he felt something cold and metallic being pressed into the back of his neck. The force remained constant, guiding him in the darkness up a set of stairs towards a landing light he was beginning to see reflected in the eyes of his assailant. It was not the man who had spoken to him from the balcony.

"Have I got the right house?" Morda said. He was bundled through a door onto the floor of a room, lit only by a dim red light, its effect accentuated by heavy sheeting across the windows. His bag, which had been taken from him at the door, was thrown in after him like a disconnected false leg. His new host stood behind the light with his back to him.

"Morda," he said, smugly. "There are quite a few people who have been looking for you. Three of whom are dead."

It was not quite the start the Populite's envoy had been hoping for. If he took the folder out of his bag now he would be behaving like a travelling salesman.

"There were some photographs of some friends of mine placed alongside yours on the front page of the odd national newspaper just over a month ago. I suppose it would be unreasonable for me to expect you to explain how your picture came to be there."

He was surprisingly handsome, and quite young; though he wore an expression of mild irritation.

"It was a mistake," Morda said, weakly. "I lived with a man named Harvil about five years ago. He was involved with the republicans after the war. I went to try and see him after he was shot by the police in January; they must have thought I was involved with him because my picture was put in the paper with all those others. They ended up raiding my house on one of their searches. I escaped, but only for a while."

"Lucky you," the man said. "So what do you want here? I'd quite like to find out before I kill you." He spoke in a tired voice; it didn't seem as though killing anyone would particularly bother him. Morda looked up towards the door; the man who had brought him there had left. He had voluntarily taken on all of this; a bored man in a dark room, probably with a gun, possibly with an Other World predilection for blowing people away. He composed himself, weighing the dancing words in his head.

"You know every time your organisation sends someone out to kill me you are showing your hand. You are ready to kill one of your own kind because you don't know who he is, or why he is up there sharing the headlines with you. It's gang warfare and it has nothing to do with the activist principles Harvil used to tell me about. Do you still operate a set of principles, or did those days disappear after a few unsuccessful sieges?"

He listened to his words as they reverberated around the room, but he had the impression he was holding the half empty chamber of a gun towards his own head. The man looked at him with interest.

"What are your principles, Morda? Did you fight?"

"I was conscripted. We all were."

"Did you kill any of your own kind?"

Morda looked at him, struck dumb. This was not the ill-reasoned violence of an activist. He looked back at the floor.

"I killed four men, I admit that. But they were desperate times."

"No less desperate than these. The war never finished, Morda. Harvil must have told you that."

"He never spoke to me about what he did. It was an unwritten pact between us. We only ever worked together when we had sex, if you really want to know. What happened in the war limited the chances of us ever making a go of things as a couple. I understand him more, though, now I know more about it."

He offered a cigarette to the man, who declined. It was becoming stifling in the room with its closed windows, the sheets and the two of them round that dim light.

"Give me a reason why I shouldn't have you shot and leave you here for the police to find."

"Do you need a reason? Only, if you would give it to me, I'd like the chance to speak with one of the other men on those front covers, or whoever is in charge of this organisation."

Morda looked earnestly at the man. He did not seem quite sure what to do.

"I've got some stuff in the bag your boss might like to see," Morda continued. You can look at it if you like." He pushed the bag across the room. The blond man picked it up slowly, feeling round it before unzipping the top.

"Where did you get it?"

"It's genuine. I found it in Hammersmith, but I need to see one of the top people. Someone who can make things happen. He could use this!"

"Fuck me," the man said, flicking through the folder. "Girls and boys together." He sat at the table, turning the pages slowly in wonderment, his eyes locked in rifling movements across each page. The expression of bored malevolence left his face, replaced by disbelief at the substance and power of what he held. It was the effect Morda had begun to doubt the folder was capable of producing.

"I've been in the vaults at the Houses of Parliament," Morda said, watching the enthusiasm grow, prepared to build and build on it. "If I could just begin to tell you what I've seen." The man put the folder back in the bag and took his hand.

"Chiffett," he said, offering his hand. Morda shook it firmly, noticing for the first time the youthful fullness of the face of his captor, worn in an apparent change of mind. A nodding expression of business partnership, and a hand dropping over his shoulder.

"This bag of tricks might well save your life," he said. "But there's still a few problems to overcome. You see there's a contract out on you across the three main groups in London since your star appearances in the national dailies. I don't have the authority to interfere with it in any way, but if we can get to someone who I think would want to see it, we might be able to change all that. You're crazy to come here, though. There are nutters out there who'll kill each other to get a shot at you. You must have passed through hundreds of places where those gun psychos go round in fives."

"*Gun psychos,*" Morda repeated, drawing back the cuff of his right shirt sleeve. Chiffett raised his eyebrows.

The knocking made them both jump. Chiffett pointed to the corner of the room and moved towards the door. He took out a handgun from his side pocket before opening it.

"What are you doing in there?"

"Come in," Chiffett said. "What do you think I'm doing - knocking him?"

"I was wondering. I thought it'd be all over by now."

"Like I said to you earlier. Not before I ask him a few questions. Now pop down the shop and get me a beer. And not that warm stuff off the counter, get it from the refrigerator."

He handed over a ten shilling note and stood, covering the doorway until the door slammed below, He turned furtively towards

Morda and picked up the bag. Morda understood and followed him down the stairs. He moved ahead into the parlour and returned with what looked like a cold tin of beer.

"Dozy cunt. If he'd bothered looking, he could have screwed things up."

He pulled the front door back, looking slowly out before beckoning Morda to follow. They crossed the street and headed in the opposite direction to the one Morda had come from half an hour earlier. They cut across Victoria Park, past a few old men in white coats on a bowling green; Morda noticed the boy he had seen earlier on the steps of the house, waddling in a few inches of thin grey water at the edge of the Lido.

"You won't do this without me - remember that," Chiffett said. He looked across towards the distant green of the railings. "We can cut back to Mile End this way and cut out anywhere they're likely to be hanging out."

"Where are we going?" Morda said.

"You'll find out when we get there. I've already left him behind, so if I lose you they'll be after me. Just follow me and walk quickly. We can do it in half an hour if we're lucky." He moved off ahead, still carrying the bag, Morda followed behind, looking left, right and behind him as he went. His leg was beginning to ache, but if anything it made him move faster, the looking behind becoming less frequent as they got nearer and nearer to the park gate.

"Rocassa Milo. It's good to see you." The tall red-haired woman shook hands with her at the entrance to Audrey Court.

"Thanks for coming, Landa. I wouldn't have bothered you ordinarily..."

"Just a little tonsilitis in ten years is an impressive medical record, and it's my call-out morning, anyway."

They stepped into the lift and Rocassa smiled a little shyly. Landa Verdis had first entered her life as a spiteful eleven year old, mocking her height and her hair, which she had worn long even then. Landa had always been the most intelligent in the group, quick to analyse problems and provide answers; irritatingly perceptive when anyone tried to keep things from her. Even so, she had been one of the few girls who had sympathised when Rocassa had undergone the fertility tests; after her own births she had lost her spiteful nature altogether. A deep friendship might have been allowed to develop if she had not been called off to study medicine at sixteen. Nevertheless, when she qualified, Rocassa had no doubts who she should have as her doctor.

"This is lavish. Does this come with the job?"

"My company own fifteen of these blocks; once you cross over into Senior Management they give you one of the flats. It's too big, but I'm not exactly complaining."

They made their way into the lounge, and she poured out two coffees from the waiting percolator.

"I've seen you in the paper four or five times recently. All that work you've been doing for the police. It doesn't seem very much like Rocassa."

"Sometimes I think it's all happened a little too quickly," she said, surprised at the interest. "Things have gone well for me, I suppose. Perhaps I'm just a late developer." She looked past Landa at the sofa and saw herself there the previous evening, knees either side of her face, Morda's looming expression hanging above her. Thank goodness there were some limitations to perceptiveness.

"What about you?"

"The practice is fine; when you're private you only ever see women, so it's just routine stuff like hormone balancing, stitching up cuts, treating accidents. Nothing like the problems I might be encountering if I were a school doctor. I did train in gynaecology, but they work much harder and it can be messy; especially the surgery after the second pregnancy."

She fell silent, aware of her *faux pas*. Rocassa, though, was thinking about a girl in their group who had died after her post pregnancy operation had gone horribly wrong. Landa had been with her in the group of five that had stayed in the outpatients' ward over the three days it had taken the girl to die.

"Where are you living now?" Rocassa said, eventually.

"Not so near the practice, though I'm only there two days a week. I've just bought one of the new flats in a block they've built on the site of the old *John Lewis* store in Oxford Street. It's not as big as this one, but it's got all the security I need."

"Do you have many friends?"

"What do you mean, *friends?*"

"From work... old school friends?"

"A few. I don't really see many people, if that's what you mean. But no-one does, really. This is a small city, you know."

"There are five hundred thousand people here."

"Yes, well... four hundred and seventy-five thousand of them are male," Landa said, embarrassed. "I didn't really come here to talk about them. Your line of work may bring you into contact with men, but as far as I'm concerned, it's bad enough having to travel on public transport with them, let alone having them raised as a serious topic of conversation." She opened her bag and took out some instruments and a small notebook. Rocassa watched the professional manner, reminded of the serious note-taking style she had often noticed in lectures.

"Tell me what you told me on the phone."

Rocassa looked thoughtfully at her friend. She had decided against chronicling the breast pains, as the unusual amount of attention they had been receiving lately provided a reasonably secure diagnosis of the problem.

"I've been getting up a lot in the night to go to the lavatory, even when I haven't been drinking much. I collected this about half an hour ago, like you said." She pushed the small jar towards her. "I've also been quite violently sick again, this morning. That was just before I rang the surgery. I thought at first it might be the different hours I've been working recently, and then I was worried it was the food they've been subjecting me to at these police stations..." Her voice tailed off as she watched Landa assembling various instruments in front of her on the table.

"Is there anything to clear it up pretty quickly? - only there are two very important conferences they want me for on Wednesday and Thursday."

"I think it may well be food poisoning," she said, dipping what looked like a thin splint of wood into the jar.

Rocassa watched the whole process in profound ignorance.

"What kind of diet do you follow?"

"Ordinary, really. Most vegetables, fruit, potato products. We have some foreign produce at some of the Bureau dinners, but as it's imported specially I can't imagine there's a hygiene risk. It's usually delicious."

Landa had been nodding until she looked back at the splint. She studied it curiously, fascinated by the glowing hue it had assumed. She took a deep breath and stood up, her surprise turning to an expression of distaste. Rocassa stood up with her, blocking the path she seemed to want to take.

"What's the matter? Am I sick?"

"You must be," she said, pushing past her. Rocassa hurried down the corridor after her.

"Where's your phone?"

"Who are you phoning, Landa? What's happened?"

"You're pregnant, that's what happened. I don't even want to think about it."

She pushed open the door to each room until she reached the bedroom. She walked around the bed as if it were teeming with bacteria, and grabbed the phone. Rocassa threw herself at it, pulling it free from her grasp and out of the wall socket.

"I'm infertile, you crazy bitch," she said. "You were there when they used to taunt me, don't you remember? You even helped me once when I got into a fight over it."

"You didn't have the operation," Landa said. "They didn't think you needed it. But you were right; you are obviously a late developer. If they had known what was going to develop, you would probably not have been allowed to develop at all. Now are you going to let me use that phone?"

"Who are you going to ring?"

Rocassa's eyes were wide; her face wet.

"A friend. Someone I know who might be able to save your career."

"Are you so sure? It's only a little stick, after all."

"This *little stick* as you put it, is the most accurate medical phenomenon there has ever been. Your urine can show everything about the workings of your body at all times, and this implement will show up, quite quickly, almost anything that is wrong with you. From the depth of colour here I would say the pregnancy must be about eight weeks. No wonder your bladder has been affected. Have you told anyone else about the symptoms?"

"No, well... only Morda."

"*Morda?* You've been having sexual intercourse *with an activist?* Someone who has cold-bloodedly *killed women?*"

"He has never killed a woman. Look, I can't expect you to understand, Landa. You've been very kind to come round, but perhaps you'd better go now."

Landa looked in disbelief at her friend's drawn features. She had always been bodily different, but the sexual act, and *with an activist.* It was the most perverse and corrupt act she could imagine; allowing the genitals of a man to come into contact with her. From the fading curiosity in her teenage years, she had viewed the whole sensual enterprise with disgust. It was the profound disgust she felt now, wearily hardened by five years of medical training and seven years of practice; of hormone programmes, stitching and prescriptions for creams and tablets. It was the first time one of those sticks had diagnosed a betrayal of their sex.

"You must get rid of it," Landa said, as she stood at the door.

"I never had the chance to have a child."

"But you are a woman of twenty-eight, not a child. There may be complications, not least with your work. In a few weeks it's going to show. Not only that, but this child would have a living father. I suggest you get rid of it before he finds out, if you are likely to see him again." Rocassa took her friend's arm and held it.

"Not a word of this to anyone, Landa. I can trust you?"

"For now, yes. But it's a heavy thing to keep quiet. Just try and phone me at home before the end of the week; my number's on the card. Remember, as every day passes it will become more and more difficult to hide."

Rocassa released the catch and let her out; she waved as she passed the security camera at the front of the block. Rocassa turned and went back to the bedroom, her face pale, her eyes wet.

They stood rigidly still in the cemetery alleyway, until the police carriage had trundled past.

"I don't know what they think they're going to catch in that," Chiffett said.

"Where the hell are we?" Morda said. "We've been wandering round here for nearly an hour."

"That's Tower Hamlets Cemetery. Do you want to pay a visit?"

"I'm not keen to go there this afternoon, even as a visitor."

"We've got no choice. We're only a few streets away, but they're everywhere once you get to Mile End."

"Do you enjoy running from your own people?" Morda asked.

"I'm not running from them," he said. "What the fuck's it to you, anyway? I'm sure if you ever had a conception of what loyalty meant, you threw it out of the window years ago." He turned round, reaching up on tiptoe to push the bag over the wall before climbing over after it.

"Come on," he called back. "We can't take the risk of going in by the main gate. Get over." Morda lifted his leg up gingerly and pulled the top of his right thigh up between two railing spikes. Who on earth needed to be deterred from entering a cemetery? He pulled himself up and over by the wall corner post and moved to catch up with Chiffett. They cut through a row of tall thin tombstones, one of which had fallen with its own weight at sometime and cracked exactly in half. *We Remember Him To This Day. 16th July 1994.* He wondered what was on Provlyn's stone.

Betrayed. 8th May 1909.

They crossed the second wall, joining a curve of the street.

"The red house in that side road," Chiffett said, breathlessly. "We made it!"

Morda leaned back against the rails of the cemetery and lifted his head. He was exhausted. He let Chiffett cross the road ahead of him, while he stood, watching his progress. The squeaky sound of a window opposite being forced open was followed swiftly by an explosion of sound tearing through the air. He instinctively broke into a sideways run for cover across the street before he began to realise the shot had not been intended for him. Chiffett staggered towards him, his eyes dancing out of sync over hands clutching at the lower part of his splaying face. As he edged towards him, Morda saw further movements from the window, and dived backwards, pulling the work bag away out of the dying man's grasp. Robbed of his meal ticket, Chiffett crawled a few wayward paces to the edge of the kerb before slumping across a drain cover, some expanding horror of dark reddish-green seepage at his temple. Watching the window carefully, Morda moved back towards the body and took the handgun from the side pocket. He felt the ruthlessness he had learned in every one of his hunted movements.

Morda took a few backwards steps before turning to run. He took the road Chiffett had been pointing at, slowing his run to an express walk as an old man came out of one of the entrances ahead of him. When he was out of sight, Morda moved slowly towards the red door and climbed the steps. After he rang the bell he waited a good few minutes, his back to the door, looking around him. Chiffett's life had, no doubt, been as shabby and miserable as his death; even from where he stood, he could still see the excited desperation of the curved corpse. And there was probably another one behind this door, ready to take him somewhere else, to the last place, perhaps. Any minute now, he was thinking, any minute now; waiting for the pain to his chest, his shoulders or his head. A chance to evolve an unpredictable strategy for death, he thought, his heart pumping noisily in his chest. The door opened behind him and he turned round.

"Can I help you sir?"

A butler stood in the doorway; a well-groomed man of about fifty, balding; a cardboard cut-out of deference. Morda stood for some time on the steps before he could frame a response.

"I would like to see the head of the house, please." The butler nodded briefly and disappeared. Morda stood in the downstairs hallway of a house whose rooms reached out several yards either side of the front door. The parquet flooring underfoot felt slippery under his plastic soles, so he put down his work bag. The palms of his hands were uncomfortably wet; he tried drying them on the upper part of his trousers, but the alien shape of the pocketed handgun made him stop.

A tinny sound came from up the stairs, a shrill musical noise, repeating phrases every so often for a few minutes until it faded away. The lighting was bright in the hall, its sources reflected on the varnished floor. Morda pushed at the door to the front room and it yielded gently, opening to reveal a heavy patterned rug over the flooring and an enormous padded chair, empty, turned towards some past heat the fireplace must have given out. The feeling the room gave was what he might have expected from a room at *Parkside*. It was very different from the bare boards and makeshift curtains of an hour ago. He walked to the window. There were people standing over Chiffett's body at the end of the street.

"He's dead," a voice said behind him. "Sometimes it's just not safe to go out for a walk. I don't know what this country's coming to."

The voice belonged to a tall and thin velvet-jacketed man with a high forehead. He wore a cravat under an open-necked white shirt, his voice gentle, but assertive.

"I was wondering if I might have a few moments of your time," Morda said. He was surprised at the calm resonance of his voice.

"Certainly," the man said. "I am *N*. You needn't bother introducing yourself - we take three national newspapers, here."

His gestures, words and unnervingly polite manner were strangely threatening, but Morda felt secure. If this was a leader of the activists, he was most likely an administrator, not a killer.

"Please follow me upstairs," he said. "You must excuse me for not joining you sooner only I was listening to the gramophone when you came in."

Morda followed him up and along the landing to an even bigger room that covered the whole first floor front of the house. He was directed to a seat, without any threat of a gun or a fist.

"The Supremes. Have you heard of them?"

"I don't think so," Morda said.

"A vocal group. Nineteen-sixties. Old World of course. Wouldn't have anything else. A friend of mine found some of these in the attic of a house he owns - I think they were called forty-fives, though I can't think why. He very kindly provided me with this machine to play them on, powered by my own generator, of course. I don't want to be accused of running down the country's power reserves, do I?"

He pushed a switch on the machine which began spinning the black disc around and around, until a mechanised lever lowered itself onto it. It was easily recognisable as a clearer version of the tinny sound he had heard downstairs.

"I like this one," he said, leaning back in the chair and closing his eyes.

"Could I...?" Morda said, when the music had finished. He opened his bag. The man watched with apparent interest, taking the folder when it was offered to him. He put on a pair of reading glasses and flicked through it.

"Do you like these pictures?" he said. "I mean, are you here to sell them to me? It's not quite my idea of photographic art, you know. A little old-fashioned, really." He handed the folder back.

"What do you know of the Other World?"

"What do you want to know?"

"I want to know what part it plays in your overall scheme of things. If you have a scheme, that is."

"I have a scheme," the man said. "I would like to find some more of these records." He turned the machine off and returned the black disc to its holder. He swivelled slowly round in his chair.

"Things should always be better in the years that lie ahead," he said. "The past dates quickly. There should always be better brains in the future to improve and develop the achievements of the people who lived before them. As people improve their lives, they should make less mistakes, learn more about themselves and be ready to pass on all that they learn." Morda nodded. "The trouble starts when the better brains decide they don't want to have anything to do with those who lived before them. They want to improve people's lives from a *modus operandi* that is entirely their own."

Morda picked up the folder and opened it.

"Is that what you think happened in the Other World?" he said.

"No. That is what is happening now." For the first time he looked directly at Morda, expectantly, as if daring a contradiction to his statement.

"Was it progress to kill the man who brought me here?"

"He has put me at a considerable risk. You now know where I live."

"He thought you would listen to me."

"He was right. I am listening."

"You killed him for being right? That sounds like the Other World to me."

"And what do you know of the Other World?"

Morda told him. Everything. What he believed, what he felt to be wrong, what he felt to be right. About Harvil. About Provlyn. About Rocassa. How he had found the time capsule. What he had seen on that screen in the vaults. How he wanted the killing to stop. The man studied him throughout the whole of his delivery, he absorbed him visually; the words did not seem to matter. But Morda still spoke them, his sentences weaving together, the purpose of his life pulsing out of every breath. He took his coat off; he took his shoes off; he sat on the carpet; he moved nearer; he moved further away.

When he had finally finished, he watched *N*'s benign expression. He did not know this man, but he had told him all he thought, all he felt.

The sun had gone down behind him; there were three empty glasses by his side. He had reached one of the men he had been looking for; he had done all he could.

"You have taken enormous risks with your life, Morda," *N* said, switching on a light by the fireplace. "The greatest one, perhaps now, sitting here with me. Have you done all of this for your beliefs, or have you done it for a chance to return to that woman and live in relative comfort."

"She is part of what I believe to be right and true, so I suppose they are the same thing."

"And you seriously believe they will allow you to live in their midst even though your sexual preferences, shall we say, are a contradiction of everything they have fought to establish?"

"Why else would they have let me come here?"

"They've bought you, Morda. You have character, but you are a romantic. It isn't enough for you to live in a world dominated by women; you have to surrender your sexuality to them, too. That's one of the few things that men still have left."

Morda looked at him gravely.

"I have my life left, and it still might be worth something. But men will have nothing left if they follow you."

N laughed.

"You know, Morda, you remind me of a man I admired very much many years ago; he was prepared to die for what he believed in, only for him it was the republican cause. He was older than you, but he had the anarchic spirit of youth, ready to burn powerfully and argue strongly for the cause, as if he had been born with its principles at the root of the workings of his mind. There have been others since. They will always be around to be won over. Those are the people you should tell your story to. My man died for the cause; there are many others like him that I cannot sacrifice simply because you tell me a pretty story."

"You'll sacrifice them anyway if you don't try to put down the weapons. That man who brought me here, the conductor this morning, that lunatic in my house, the guy who wanted to turn me in... they're all dead because of this *cause*. You have the influence to change it; don't you feel any responsibility towards those who have died? Don't you see that there is no shame at all in saying *this cause is not worth dying for - let's see if we can't live together to work round our differences;* at least meet with some of the women from the Bureau."

N looked up, gently fingering his lapels, surveying his audience. The clock chimed eight and he yawned. He got up to open a window.

A cool breeze came in from outside with the noise of children's voices from the street.

"I knew Harvil," he said. "He was a handsome, dark-skinned man. Worked with him when I was younger, round about the same time you were living with him. He was very fond of you; I suppose he had to be to live with someone who was out fighting the republicans."

"And you call me a romantic? Remember, he ended up dead like the rest of them."

Morda did not feel any better for having surrendered his knowledge. He felt suddenly naked. He had burned himself out fighting his way towards some distant glow of hope, only to find, now he had reached it, that it was another glossy fiction, another fantasy.

The butler arrived with a tray of coffee and biscuits.

"You'll stay for coffee?" N said.

"I came here to ask you to stop the killing. You know full well that I have no chance of getting to the end of this street without getting shot unless you call these gunmen off."

"I'll be sad to see you go, Morda," he said. "You've been quite scintillating company; I mean that." He poured himself a coffee. "You got to be front page news, which was more than Harvil did. Even when his name was mentioned it was only in conjunction with your standing as a top activist. Would you like a coffee?"

"Why all of this? The house? The butler? The genteel lifestyle? I thought someone like you would object to all of this. Doesn't it further demean the male - waiting on people?"

"Do you feel demeaned, Jenver?" The butler shook his head, simpering radiantly. The host smiled, biting a tiny corner off the biscuit he was holding.

"You might not know it, but Service is vital to us; it's an excellent way of filling all the important households with our people. The Populite think they've lured the Populace into a state of existence as the permanent underdog, buying them off with state money, but all that happens is that they have fissured all their own institutions with our men. So why should we meet with them? We know what they'll say."

"There are no men in the Government Buildings. You can't know what the Populite Bureau is saying; not even the politicians know that. I've met with these women; I know that they want peace. I believe them."

"They may well want something, but it isn't peace." *N* walked across to the window. "It looks like the night squad are out in force. You had better stay here for the time being. Jenver, show Morda to one of the rooms upstairs, would you?"

So that was it. Time to think about what they were going to do with him, no doubt. Perhaps tomorrow, perhaps tonight. But he still had the gun. Chiffett hadn't used it; it had to be loaded.

He followed Jenver up the stairs, the tinny sound starting again behind them. He was directed to a room at the back of the house with a single bed, a light, a window.

"I take it you'll be comfortable, sir."

Morda did not reply. He went into the room and closed the door. Laying back on the bed, he sighed. The whole enterprise, the videos, the hours of study, the icebag, several chapters of his life spurned like soya milk that had passed its consumption date. And even in his overtiredness, even with eyes that lay in their sockets like marbles, he could not relinquish his mental picture of Rocassa. He closed his hands around his face and rubbed it across his palms, embracing the wet surface, willing it to be her.

"Sorry to ring you this late, Landa, but I wanted to say sorry if I was rude to you this morning. You came over especially, and I hadn't seen you for so long. It was very ungrateful of me."

"Is this just an apology?" Landa said.

"Well, not quite. I've kept in mind what you said, and I'd like you to get in contact with your friend as soon as you can. My friend is, as I'm sure you realise, involved in something that he might not come back from. Ever since we met, the whole thing has been miserably frustrating; it's something we always accepted, but I've decided that if anything happens to him then there won't be any point going through with this. It couldn't have the life he would want it to have, if he died."

She gurgled the last words, as she reflected on the chances of seeing him again.

"But if he comes back...?"

"I'll have it. He wanted me to come out and tell the people in the Bureau about us. I wouldn't do it. If he came back, I'd want it. I want him now, you know, though I don't suppose you understand that."

There was a long silence at the other end of the phone.

"Look, don't worry," Rocassa said. "Just tell your friend. I'll be in touch."

She put down the receiver. It was nine o'clock. Just one more call to make, though this one was more harrowing. She got out of bed and poured a small measure of liquid into the glass. It came from a bottle that had only ever been a part of the flat before as a symbol of her opulence, positioned high up behind the glass door of an unopened cupboard. She tapped out the next number slowly, swallowing as she co-ordinated the order of her words.

"It's Rocassa. I just wanted to apologise again for not getting in today. I had the doctor round and she thinks it might be something I ate at the weekend. Incidentally," she made the jump, "have you any news on Morda?.... No? I just wondered, that's all. You know, you get to spend time with someone, even a man; you sometimes wonder how they are." She ran her finger round the swollen tips of her breasts as the Head of Defence voiced her farewell down the phone.

'*What is it you fear?*' she heard herself say. The answer was cut off by the thud of the receiver on the wall. She turned her thoughts instead to the fifteenth floor.

She was in the lift now, watching the illuminated numbers climbing up from one onwards. She was looking up, checking the hair of the woman above her in the mirrored ceiling of the lift.

Apocalypse

N looked out on the empty street. It was four hours into Curfew, and even the local drunks had moved on in search of an empty yard or an alleyway. His fingers rapped restlessly at the handset of the phone. There were others who had vired members off to other causes, formed splinter groups, steered themselves away from the struggle. They were rarely seen alive again, destined to a life of hiding, of plotting against both the State and their own past. Lost political lives, floating in between the prevalent ideologies. His own position of relative comfort looked under threat; the location could, by now, have been identified. He picked up the receiver.

"Djvarich? *N.* I have Morda here. He's quite safe. In fact, he comes with an invitation."

"How did he find you?"

"An ambitious member of my department, who was subsequently given a lift back for his troubles."

"You shouldn't employ ambitious people."

"The Populite seem to want a meeting. The usual demands for a ceasefire, only this man has been given access to some interesting political memorabilia from the Old World. There's talk about control of one of the national dailies and government concessions. I thought you might be interested." *N* watched Jenver pass across the hall in his dressing-gown. There was a long silence at the other end of the line.

"It could be beneficial if it gets us a stake in this Revolution for Industry."

"There is only one Revolution," Djvarich said. "Nevertheless, we could set up somewhere to invite them. If they came on our terms there would be little harm in it; they write what they like in the papers as it is. It would be interesting if they really were prepared to surrender their hold on general information, even to the extent of just one national daily. We will have to kill Morda, though," he added.

"Why is that?"

"I've lost three men because of him - he's made the whole set-up here look a bit thin; he's got government connections, he knows the location of your organisation... do you need any more reasons?"

"We can't kill him until we know how important he is to the Populite. He has a story about having an affair with one of them, though it sounds a bit unlikely."

"This Morda must be some kind of a pervert, or a lunatic, wanting you to believe him."

"I do believe him," *N* said. "He's quite convincing. The woman concerned is apparently quite high up in their Bureau, so I imagine they're tolerating it for the sake of security."

"Just keep him there," Djvarich said. "Ring their Bureau from one of the neutral terminals and say we're interested and that we'll get back to them. Make sure they know we've got Morda. We'll soon know how keen they really are."

After a few moments reflection, *N* put down the receiver. He could be playing a major role in establishing the first significant communication between the Populite and the Populace in Britain since the Death Age. He had, however, said nothing to Djvarich of the revelation to Morda about the domestic service situation; it would have to be covered up one way or another at a later stage. He climbed the stairs to Morda's room, planning the phrasing of his apparent change of heart. Turning off the downstairs light from the landing, he knocked at Morda's door. He opened the door slowly to a darkened room, the cold air from the open window blowing gently into his face. Being three flights up had evidently failed to deter their guest from departing. N sat on the bed, wondering at the ramifications of his mistake.

Morda listened at the door until he was sure that Jenver had gone. He was astounded by the abject failure of his efforts to even remotely interest his host. Now he was left with the probability that he would never see Rocassa again. He would never know whether or not the Head of Defence would use the information he had volunteered against her. He looked round the room again. Stark. Bare. Useless. Outside was a blanket of darkness. The window was clamped at the catch by a tiny padlock. He worked uselessly at it for a few moments with thin, nailbitten fingers. All the hope and psychological certainty he had carried with him when he had set out that morning, were now spent like old tea capsules, and, digging deeper, all he could find was the primeval desire to escape. Even facing the contradiction of streets littered with gun psychos and faces of hate, the desire ate into his bulging eyes as they tugged at tired sockets for a short term idea.

He felt at his pockets. The compact weight of the handgun against his thigh provided the necessary stimulus. Emptying it of the three bullets it possessed, he worked the muzzle against one end of the padlock clamp and twisted it until the metal tore from its holding, shooting the padlock loose. Catching it as it dropped, he sighed and listened. He could hear distant urgent words coming from downstairs. Releasing the clamp he eased the lower half of the window up, sickened by the unwelcoming cold darkness beyond.

He sat back on the bed, momentarily, wondering what they planned to do with him. Further tones caught from the downstairs voice returned him to the window. He returned the gun to his pocket and turned the light out. After a few minutes he became accustomed to the dark and surveyed his escape route. All he had outside to save a direct fall to the concrete back-yard was a single flimsy-looking drainpipe. Even such flimsiness pushed his own destiny a little further towards his grasp than remaining in the room. He lowered his legs out of the window, and holding onto the ledge with his right hand, edged himself towards the pipe. It felt as comforting as the arm of a corpse. Closing his eyes, he burrowed the fingers of his left hand into the wall behind it, and eased the weight of his body off the ledge. The bricks were old and crumbly but they chewed hungrily into the top of the fingers of his right hand as he thrust them behind the pipe. He hung there for a few seconds, paralysed with fear, fifty feet from the ground. Eventually he found the courage to release his left hand from the pipe and engage hurried movements that sent him sliding slowly, painfully, towards the ground.

Ten feet from the ground, he released himself from the pipe and landed steadily. He sucked at his fingers as he looked about him, spitting out the warm mixture of blood and brick. He could still see light in the house behind closed curtains, struck by a dread that his host would enter the yard from the back door and call him back like a departing guest who had forgotten his coat.

It was already past midnight, the new day a few hours old, Curfew with a half stranglehold on the quiet city. Through the back garden of the house opposite, Morda soon found himself back on one of the Hackney main streets. The road dipped slightly beyond him revealing a descending column of Mews residences not unlike his own. Behind him, a closed grocery store; everywhere the empty streets, no police, no gun psychos. He began walking quickly down the hill, trying to gather his bearings, looking for a telephone.

"Jenver!"

A door slammed on the first landing.

"Check the yard!"

The butler hurried down the stairs, wiping the sleep from his eye as he undid the back door latch. He took out a torch from under the sink and a gun he kept in the pantry. After several furtive waves of the torch outside, he found a few dark wet patches at the foot of the drainpipe. Once N had the details of the escape he ran up to his office, returning swiftly to the telephone. For the first time in several weeks, grooves of concern began to appear about the normally unruffled man's countenance. He dialled the number for the second time that morning.

"N here. Rather bad news, I'm afraid. He's got out."

"What do you mean, got out? I thought you had told him we were interested. Why should he want to leave after taking all that trouble?"

"He drew a gun on me," N said. He opened a grey booklet on the table in front of him. "I didn't exactly have much choice. He was upstairs in the office. He'd found a filing cabinet which he forced me to open. He has a copy of the last domestic service locations."

"Where can we find him?"

"I've alerted the department, but he could be anywhere."

"I want him caught. If he gets that list to the Populite... I don't have to tell you that it's taken nearly five years to set up those service positions. I want you back on this line within the hour telling me how he died."

"I'm doing everything I can right now," *N* said, and put down the receiver. He leaned against the banisters. Jenver stood waiting in the hall. They were both looking at the service locations list on the table.

"He knew," *N* said, irritably. "We had to cover ourselves. If it had got out that I had told him about the service set-up..."

"They'll kill him," Jenver said.

"He should have died months ago. I kept wondering when I was talking to him last night what it was that had kept him alive for so long. The continuation of that life seems to threaten the whole activist movement."

Jenver continued to watch him censoriously.

"They'll kill him this time," he said.

A circle of women stood around her, each clutching a long kitchen knife, each staring below her chest. They moved towards her slowly, one step at a time, eyes fixed, arms outstretched. For each step they took, each woman raised her arm a few inches higher. Rocassa begun to slowly rotate, watching the circle of knives as the light from the room bounced off each one in turn. They rose up and began to close around her in a fork of serrated steel. She opened her mouth to scream, but her emotion was soundless. The only noise that came was an intermittent high-pitched whine from the mouths of the linking abortionists. As it grew higher and clearer, the arms begun to descend on her and as she raised her hand up in defence, she knocked the ringing phone from its wall perch.

"Hello? Rocassa?" a voice said. She looked up at the familiar sights of her darkened bedroom.

"Hello?" A coffee-stained cup fell from the bedside table as she lunged towards it in search of the alarm clock. It was three o'clock.

"Rocassa? I haven't much time. This is my last penny."

"Morda! Where are you ringing from?" She felt herself raised to the very peak of consciousness.

"Can you get a car now?"

"What's happened to you?"

"I'm alright. Look, can you get a car? The Bureau are bound to give you one. Tell them it's vital. Meet me at *Palby's* at four o'clock."

"Morda..." Rocassa began. She was clutching at her stomach with her right hand. Was it her imagination... Something seemed to be stirring there.

"Four o'clock," he said. "I'll wait in the doorway of the café."

"Morda..."

"Yes?"

"I just wanted to tell you..." She lay back on the bed. He would be coming back. Count for something. She sat up again, listening for his voice. The pips sounded. "I love you, Morda," she said, but the dialling tone invaded the line before he could respond. He had been gone for less than twenty-four hours, but the nervous adjustments she had made had cordoned off the time span from the past to make it seem like two or three months.

She stood up and crossed the room to the full length mirror. Sweeping aside her night dress she stared at her stomach. Was she pushing it out? She stood up straight, sideways on. A curve. The childless schoolgirl, who would now do something no woman had done for nearly four-hundred years. A mysterious feeling of warmth and personal fulfilment came upon her as she stood by the mirror, a feeling probably deserving of the word pride. She lay back on the bed and picked up the phone.

"Hello."

"Good morning. I would like to speak to Chatwick."

"I think you have the wrong number. Try Wimbledon 4749."

"I can't fuck about," the voice said. "Morda's been at one of the departments in Hackney and has got hold of a copy of the service locations. He's somewhere in London, but he's on foot. We can cover Hammersmith, but you're one of the few with access to a car. We want someone in the city, quickly, before he can get across to the

West. Dorjess can drive, can't he?"

"I'm sorry, I really can't help you caller," Chatwick said, replacing the receiver. It was a quarter past three. The morning bell sounded at six am. It would leave Dorjess just two and a half hours to cover the whole of the city. He went up to his room to wake him.

They pushed the car out of the drive, wincing at the crunching sound of the gravel under the wheels. A few businesslike pushes, however, took it to the road, and just beyond the *Parkside* house. Chatwick looked about at each of the front lit houses where the prosperous Populite residents of Wimbledon slept. The success of their enterprise was threatened for the first time in his memory. Dorjess had been instructed. Chatwick watched his brother's expression at the wheel. His eyes were set; he rarely smiled and then only with irony. A few beads of sweat gleamed on his forehead; raised from sleep he had shown little sign of displeasure at the task handed him. The fact that Morda had been Provlyn's lover was not unconnected with the armed man's expression of sour determination. He still blamed much of the staff's changing attitudes towards him on the letter Provlyn had written to Serboth Challis.

Chatwick was pleased to have someone on whom to focus Dorjess' psychological need for grudges. It prevented any return to the bitter feuding they had taken to as men in their twenties, feuding that would have eventually shed light on their being brothers, or precipitated some other crisis at the house. Now, of course, was another occasion to be grateful. He would happily shoot Morda down in cold blood without a second thought, because he was like that. My poor brother Dorjess, Chatwick thought, as he pushed the main door to.

Morda found himself in the city again. He had the keys to the Mews house, but had no intention of returning there. It was easy to picture a sizeable welcoming party, preparing to give the hall wallpaper a dash of crimson.

He crossed the road in front of St.Paul's Cathedral, wondering at the size of the grey dome that cut into the darkness of the sky. Drawn for a moment, he began to climb up the steps. He was one of the few people in the country who knew the real reason why it had been built, its abandoned religious significance, its role as a place of worship in the Old World. And if he had stood on those steps six hundred years ago, what strange ritual would he have performed? Hands clasped, eyes closed in silent prayer? Body bowed towards his god? Blood drawn in sacrifice at the shrine? He looked up at the towering pillars, at its arches and towering doors. What if all those who had been worshipped really did exist? Where were they now?

He moved down the steps and crossed the street, heading towards his office. He began to plan an approach of guaranteed safety for his passage back to Rocassa's flat. He realised any car she got at this hour would be driven by a man; if his host really had an organised network of activists, he may have been able to brief them in great numbers. It would be a prestigious act to be the one who caught an escapee; it could be lucrative, too, with a price on his head. She would be in as much danger as he was; he would not be able to take any risks.

He darted into a shop doorway as a car came roaring past. The man at the wheel had a glazed, demented look as if he was searching for something solid into which to crash at significant speed. The roaring of his car could be heard for sometime afterwards.

Morda moved out onto the street again. It was ten minutes to four. He had timed his journey so he would arrive outside *Palby's* at one minute to four, for minimum risk. He would approach from behind the building in order to survey the surrounding streets before committing his presence to anyone's attention. There was something ironic about the watch whose accuracy continued to help preserve his life, but it was best ignored if he was to remain alert.

"Park over there," Rocassa said, indicating a narrow side street between two theatres. They were still several hundred yards from *Palby's*, but the requisitioned limousine parked in full view on an empty street seemed a risk worth avoiding. Her chauffeur, who had not volunteered a line of conversation since the beginning of the journey, crossed the main street with an easy twist of the steering-wheel, and reversed into the street between the two buildings. He got out of the car and opened the door for his passenger. His eagerness to return to the car, however, had not gone unnoticed.

"I think you ought to come with me," Rocassa said. She waited by the rear door of the limousine. "You can lead the way."

"I'm a driver," he said. "No-one said anything about being a bodyguard."

"Don't be ridiculous," Rocassa said. "I'm the bodyguard. I'm not leaving you in the car to be shot at. You'll be much safer with me. Now lead off. You know where it is."

Morda entered the main street in full view of the *Palby's* building at three minutes to four, but there was no sign of a waiting car. He stopped and looked around. He felt a growth of tiredness lurking within him, his eyelids heavy; he was close now. She would have found a way round the problem; he knew she would be there, even if she had to come on foot. After he had established that there was no-one anywhere in the street, he crossed on the *Palby's* side, slowing his pace, watching for movements in the shop doorways.

The building was dark, the doors locked. The windows, designed for departmental store displays, carried a model size layout of factories and warehouses planned for the outskirts of London in the coming years. What if the activists could monitor a force of men within a warehouse? If there was a sufficient number of them and they were strong enough, it would be like a stockpile of troops, scattered around the country, ready to be mobilised when the time came. If the domestic service situation was to be believed, this would be a feasible next step. Unless the Bureau were made aware of the situation, they could well be conscripting an army to manufacture their own defeat. Rocassa had been right about the activists; he would have to warn the Bureau at the first opportunity.

He moved to within one doorway from the café entrance; he sensed company. He took the gun from his pocket and couched the cold metal in his palm.

"Rocassa," he said, his voice steady. There was no response. Someone was there, though. He could still sense it. He eased out from the doorway and along towards the café entrance.

"Rocassa," he repeated.

"She's here," a voice said.

"Who's that?"

"She's here."

Morda moved into the café doorway, the gun held tightly behind his back, ready to use. He was greeted by the sight of a grey-suited chauffeur, his arm twisted behind him, and the silhouette of Rocassa in the darkened depths of the doorway.

"Rocassa."

"You're alone," she said. She released the grimacing chauffeur who began nursing his elbow as if it were broken. He looked at her, frustrated by the other presence. She looked relieved, but unlikely to surrender her guard of professionalism. "We must move," she said. "The car is a little further up the street."

"No," Morda said. "The driver stays here."

"He's here to drive us back," Rocassa said, a barely perceptible tone of chiding in her voice.

"We can't trust him," Morda said, adding authority to his words with a wave of the gun. He took the car keys from the chauffeur's pocket. "He can stay here and we'll send a car for him later. He's got nothing to fear. Everyone went to bed a long time ago." Morda smiled and took Rocassa's arm, directing the chauffeur back into the doorway with another gun wave. "I'll be watching you until I reach the car," he said, "...so please don't move."

"What are you doing?" Rocassa said when they had backed away a sufficient distance from the café.

"You once told me you could drive."

"I can drive, but why leave him here? If anything happens to him, they'll want to know why. He normally drives for the government."

"You were right about the activists, Rocassa. They've infiltrated the greater part of domestic service in this country and, well, it's impossible to know what else. If your chauffeur is on their books..."

"You didn't need to leave him there. You're armed, aren't you?"

"Where's the car?"

They were level with the theatre side street and moved into the front of the car. Morda watched his hired driver with admiration as she started up the low growling engine and drew the car slowly out of the side street. Behind the lowered tierage of the office buildings lay the hinting glow of morning sun. Morda lay back into the accommodating folds of the passenger seat, his eyelids fluttering, the tiredness returning. Only one item of revelation remained, the fact that the Head of Defence knew of their relationship. He could not hope to keep that from Rocassa for much longer.

"What will we do now?" Rocassa said.

"Will it be safe to go to your flat?"

"As safe as anywhere else. But there's one thing you haven't explained to me." She slowed for a red traffic light; they were approaching the Strand.

"Oh yes?"

"You're armed. You said that the Bureau wouldn't be giving you any weapons. Have you had to use that in the last twenty-four hours?"

"Only once. Though it was only to open a catch on a window." He turned the heater grill on. Warm air blew in from the floor of the car and Morda stretched further out. His revelation could wait. He eased across the automatic gearbox and took Rocassa's left hand, kissing the cold fingers, massaging them to a comfortable warmth.

"I met an old school friend yesterday that I hadn't seen for nearly ten years," Rocassa said, dropping his hand discreetly as she reached for the gear stick. Morda looked up at her, momentarily distracted.

"What's that rumbling?" He turned round to find himself facing a crazed expression, all bulging eyes and teeth under a combing of thin greased black hair. The glass partition between them was opened before he could turn to look for the gun. The man in the back seat already had one, the chamber of which he had used to open the partition. Morda looked in further disbelief as he saw a copy of his newspaper picture abandoned on the back seat.

"You're Morda," the man said. Rocassa jumped at the sound of his voice, steering the car wildly to the left.

"I have a message for you," the man continued, unaffected, and drew the nozzle of the gun level with Morda's eyes. "It's goodbye." He pulled the trigger, splattering the left hand side of the windscreen with a mess of blood and bone. As Morda slumped forward off the seat, Rocassa swerved the car round, letting go of the wheel as she caught sight of the man's face and what the gun he held had done. The car came to a halt up the kerb in front of a side street that ran down to the Embankment.

"Don't worry about him; just drive."

Rocassa closed her left eye to the crimson haze before her and swung the car down the side street into the Embankment. If I can find some way of crashing this car, she was thinking, or lurching it violently enough to give me time to get to the gun in my bag. She was thinking only of killing. Of emptying every bullet she had in that gun into this psychopath's face, of grinding her foot into his face until he had no face; her dishevelled thoughts, her child's father dead, unknowing of his child; her chance of sexual freedom dead; her own hate linked with the killing hate of the back seat driver behind her. As her rambling panic ran in ripples into tubes of logical thought, she heard the chuckling behind her and tugged one final time at the wheel, sending the car up and over the rickety parapet beyond the pavement, hurtling off the low tide beach filth into the cold darkness of the river water.

Surprised by the speed of events, the man whose face had inspired terror in so many others at Parkside, now wore itself the expression of a man who had seen the ingredients of his own undoing. He pushed uselessly at the tiny partition, panicking as the dim light of near dawn faded above the cloudy water. The newspaper photograph of the man he had just shot was lifted up from the seat by the force of water entering the car. It was beginning to rise above him now as the car leaned over, tipped by the combined weight of the assassin and his corpse. The last thing Dorjess saw as he turned from a frantic spate of ineffectual tugging at the car door was Morda's sightless head floating confidently in the water, the expression of fear quite gone from his face.

Rocassa struggled to pull herself up in the water, weighted as she was by her clothes. Throwing off her coat, she felt a heavy bubbling of release about her waist, the act helping gather the necessary inertia to carry her upwards towards the surface. Choking and spluttering, she pushed her way to the water's edge, collapsing wearily across a set of steps leading up to street level. Coughing up more water, she sat up and let her head drop between her knees, breathing in deeply. After a few minutes, she raised the strength to stand up on the steps and look behind her. The river was calm once more. There was no sign of the car, just a few dying ripples at the very edge of the water. She clutched at her waist, suddenly feeling the cold of the morning. The pain in the pit of her stomach told her, as she leaned weakly on the wooden balcony, that she would not have the chance to reconsider her decision. It had been taken for her. All the complications were to be removed from her life in a few unpleasant minutes. No-one in her future would mention his name; there would be nothing to link her with him again, or with any other man. She found as she stood on the Embankment that she could not even cry. All she could hear as she moved towards the telephone box were the words of a desperate woman, crying out to have the chance to be free. *'Don't stop on account of a few tears,'* she heard herself say. *'I want this.'*

The Head of Defence stirred at the dregs of coffee in front of her.

"Who knows what he could have told us that we don't know already?" she said, walking across to the window. "Still, the crackdown on domestic service will guarantee the Liberals another term of office."

"He was quite daring, for a man," Herben Asquith said, looking up at a painting of the Queen. "You know his lover was once employed at Lady Challis' house. Though I suppose that's just an unfortunate coincidence."

"I shan't keep you, Lady Asquith," the Head of Defence said, standing at the door of her office. The Prime Minister moved towards the door.

"Thank you for informing me of events. We will, of course, carry out an immediate full check on all of our domestic staff."

"Thank you, Lady Asquith."

The Head of Defence closed the door behind her. The service crisis was just what the Bureau needed as an excuse to slow down the government reforms to accurately meet the demands of the originally agreed timetable. It was the kind of inner crisis political historians had often fabricated to stabilise the economy or political unrest. She moved back towards the window. Groups of young men fresh out from work were gathering on the street corners, gossiping about friends in service they had seen lose their jobs. It was the healthy patter of the Populace, free to question the world around them; to question but not to change.

She reached for her satchel and took out the purple foil sheet of hormone tablets. She had prescribed them herself to counteract the strange pains she had been having the previous week; pains associated with that most unnatural of acts that no-one ever discussed.

And how unnatural it had been to find him waiting there, that evening. Waiting for her at a place where she had only ever slept before; waiting to operate on her body in a manner she had often been curious about. It had not been unpleasant, though it was obviously unnecessary. It had just been a simple no-risk situation which she had been quick enough to take advantage of. She had since discovered moniliasis and the historical reason why women were given labiotomies at birth and sterilised at sixteen. Hers was a labiotomy that had been only partially successful, but it was a secret deformity that she had proved she could live with. The operation she had ordered for Rocasso Milo to be carried out under sedation during her routine check-up was just to be on the safe side. The inter-sexual corruption of the Other World was a force that the new methods of pro-creation had yet to cauterise. It was the one aspect of the New World that the Bureau sought ruthlessly to control. But as she had closed her eyes when he came, when she felt the warm seed in her, as she pulled herself around him, as she said yes, so it remained. The memory was truly a physical one.

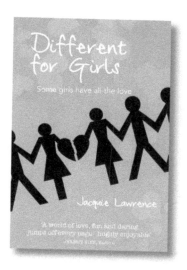

Different for friends

Fran and Cam, ecstatically reunited after a short break, but Cam faces the consequences of a random act she committed during their split.

Different for lovers

Gemma and Jude, new lovers torn apart by Gemma's fake fiancé. Just what is it about him that Jude has made it her life's mission to reveal?

Different for wives

Brooke and Nicola, married for seven years, are threatened by something and someone. But what and who is it?

Different for Girls

Enter a world where love, sex, and suspense meet betrayal, cruelty and heartbreak.
A world where the survival of love is all that matters.
A world where being different is the new normal.

OUT NOW IN HARD COPY AND EBOOK FROM ZITEBOOKS

www.zitebooks.com